Sweet Cornbread and Hot Green Tea

Sweet Cornbread and Hot Green Tea

Scribes and Vibes

Sundiata Alaye

A Moyo Press Book
Copyright © 2017 Sundiata Alaye
All Rights Reserved. Printed in the United States of America. No part of this book may be used or reproduced in any manner whatsoever without written permission except in the case of brief quotations embodied in critical articles or reviews.
Poems by Sundiata Najja Alaye*
*© 2016 Moyo Press * All Rights Reserved
Publisher's Cataloging-in Production
Alaye, Sundiata
Sweet Cornbread and Hot Green Tea/by Sundiata Alaye –1st Edition
ISBN-13: 9780692944608
ISBN-10: 0692944605

Edited by Sir William (Kiddo) Cooper
Book Design by Linda Cooper-Martin
Cover photography by Jeremy Mines
PRINTED IN THE UNITED STATES OF AMERICA
MOYO PRESS, INC. EDITION: January 2017

Sweet Cornbread and Hot Green Tea

Sundiata Alaye is the author of several books including *Empty Promises Private Pain— A Light out of Darkness*, winner of the James Baldwin Award for Outstanding Accomplishments in the Arts and The Audrey Lorde-Joseph Bean Award for Literary Excellence, and his most recent release, The *Power That Shapes My Way*.

Also by Sundiata Alaye

Love is Always Enough
Dear AIDS – Dear World
Pain or Peace
Sacred
Rejuvenation
Forgiveness
Conversations with Sundiata Volume 1
The Spirit Reminds Us Volumes 1 and 2

DEDICATED WITH LOVE AND GRATITUDE
TO

God
My Mother
Ashley
Bobby Cash
Paxton
Ivan Daniel
Anan
Gene
Joyce "Shine" King
Jamius
Justine
The House of Love - Bobby Edwards and Meechie Bowie
Queen Mary
My Entire Martha's Vineyard Family

And

All of the many people in this great big/small world who I have met, loved, lost, celebrated, laughed and cried with — those of all races, creeds, backgrounds, understanding and consciousness who have contributed and counseled in ways known and unknown to the loved, lovable, loveless and thoughtless still always with loving kindness and hope in their hearts and peace on their tongues.

Acknowledgements

Most especially my mom for her loving heart and for always being behind me in every single solitary thing I have ever possibly thought of doing.

Linda F. Martin, Colored Girl Art, for artful inspiration.

Sir William (Kiddo) Cooper, my editor, for amazing insight, quite heroism, wholesome heart, and an eagle eye.

And to Love. Always Love. The only precious thing in life that has meaning.
For Jewels have brilliant fire but can offer no warmth.

Author's Note

I chose the title "Sweet Cornbread and Hot Green Tea" because it represents for me the sweetness we sometimes don't recognize in, out, and over our lives and the wellness the sweetest thoughts we bring to the brain and body - how the simplest things can bring us joy.

Life is an incredible and loving journey…

Take one.

Contents

Acknowledgments · xi
Author's Note · xiii

Wanting The Art of Desire · 1
Agape The Art of Love · 51
Struggle The Art of Survival · 155
Journeys The Art of Loss · 247
Storytelling The Art of the Griot · · · · · · · · · · · · · · · · · 337

Epilogue · 367

Wanting
The Art of Desire

Elliot and Brian

September 15, 2012

Get this:

About 9 months ago I'm on a business trip, you know the typical uneventful two-week business trip trying to make the best of it. I'm chillin with a couple of buddies who live in the city I'm sentenced to this month when all of a sudden, "BAM!!" out of the blue drops in the Beautiful Brown Brother - tall and sexy with a killer smile and eyes that'll make you dizzy if you stare too long.

So, I'm cool (or at least trying to be) 'cause the Brother is phine but then I start thinking that he probably ain't worth a damn! I know the type, ran into a couple of them before and ain't trying to run in that direction again.

But there's something different about this Brother. Something I feel when he asks me if I want to dance. His energy is alive. It's sincere. Simple. We hit the dance floor, chat it up for a minute and before you know it, it's time for me to leave. He tells me the hotel where he's staying, and I promise to call from mine to give him my info. I get to my room. I hesitate. "Remember your Peace... Remember your Peace", I keep repeating to myself. "You've had two failed relationships. Dare you risk a third?"

But suddenly and slowly, I recall this Brother's energy, his warm inviting light. I start to hear in my mind his smooth voice, silky, melodic, and commanding. I stub my toe running to the phone.
    That's Exactly How It Happened. I Have the Limp To Prove It!

Dear Elliot,

I don't even know how to begin this letter except to tell you it's not meant to be a mushy letter that pours out the heart and soul with cute epithets or corny poems. It's not one of those letters that tell you how you have awakened senses and sides of me that have long been buried, or how my thoughts about you turned on romantic feeling (candlelight, wine, and you) long ago forgotten.

I won't talk about how I light up at the sound of your voice, or how since I met you I've had butterflies in my stomach - stirring each time I think about you and the possibilities of a future.

This wouldn't be an appropriate place to tell you how I blush (like a damn teenager) when you tell me you miss me and my smile. I'll try to think of the appropriate venue to let you know how I long for your touch, how I long to touch you, hold you, protect you. I'll look for other ways to let you know that I've known you all my life but searched to find you for a very long time.

I'm racking my brain to find the best way to tell you how amazing it's been, the last several weeks, rethinking my life and future, knowing you'll be a part it - of everything beautiful and good. I asked a friend where would be a good place, space, or time to let you know that I want to be the best thing that's ever happened to you; the first to encourage and the last to condemn. He drew a blank.

So, I asked a Sister-friend where she thought a Brother like me could express to a Brother like you how he wants to and is willing to work on a future with him; openly, honestly, sincerely, lovingly, and spiritually. She was no help!

So I prayed for direction. I asked that you would come to know these things daily and that you and I would always feel the same excitement for each other as we are feeling now. And then the answer came.

It wouldn't be words over the phone, gifts, or letters I needed to write to explain to you how I feel. I simply need to show you. So I will. And I'll be a Man about it!

Always,
Brian

September 22, 2012

Dear Brian,

Yo man! You had me cracking up with that story! Stub your toe? Yea, right! Well, I couldn't tell. I didn't notice a limp when I saw you again. Tell me anything!

Seriously, I was just lying in bed last night thinking about you and how we met. I have a hard time believing it's only been six months and on top of that who would have thought we would have met in Dallas of all places while we were both on business trips? Same time, same club? Man, talk about fate!

Your letter was deep, man. It made me smile and feel warm all over to know that you were thinking of me too. I especially like the part where you said, "and I'll be a man about it?" Dayum! That's wassup! You know what I mean? Well, in case you don't let me explain to you just how deep I think that is. In a matter of six months you've broken barriers and broken records.

Since I met you I know what's been missing; what *I've* been missing all this time. I know the difference now between dating a Brother with issues - who doesn't know he has issues - and dating a Brother who knows he's been wounded - that he is wounded - but trying to do something about it. Bottom line, I know the difference between dating a man and dating "little boys" dressed up in a grown man's body. Thanks for reminding me that there's still some good left in all of us.

You've opened me up to a whole new world. One that I'm not afraid of anymore. One that I'm looking forward to sharing with you. Your commitment is to be a man about it and you just don't know how much I appreciate that. And so I'm offering you the same. I'll be a man about it too! And with that, how can we lose?

See you soon, beautiful!
Elliot

p.s. where have you been all my life?

October 1, 2012

Dear Elliot,

Where have I been all your life? Right here, man. Right here waiting, preparing, and hoping that you'd show up. And here you are and it's most definitely been worth the wait!

I feel you on the dating thing, man. I've been there too. Now at 27, I think I finally got some shit figured out. I'm not trying to make it sound like I'm some kind of angel or nothing. There was a time I was out there, too. I was in the game breaking hearts and finding my heart broken. I used to love them and leaving them but not on purpose. I'd get into these situations thinking that this Brother was "him", the one I waited for only to find out he wasn't.

But it was my fault really. All the time I was looking for the wrong things. I was looking for them to give me something I had all along. Love. And once I found it inside myself I knew it wouldn't be long before it would find its way to me - like now…with you.

So although I've had my share of troubles, pains, and drama, trying to love another Brother, I can't say that all of them are full of shit because now I've found you. I waited a long time for it to happen.

I made a commitment to myself a long time ago to "show up" exactly as who I am and forget about being who I'm not. It's a lot easier for me to do this now. I can admit that I don't have all the answers, that I'm not perfect and that I have a lot of shit with me that I'm trying to work out; all the shit I've share with you, the good, the bad, and the ugly.

I know my hurts and I know I'm jaded in certain places especially when it comes to loving and trusting a Brother with my heart. But the good part in knowing this is that I can't punish you in my present for the shit that's happened in my past.

I'm just trying to show up, man. I know I have issues but I also know that it's these very same issues that I have to be o.k. with showing you knowing that you won't run when you see that I'm human - just another Brother like you and a whole bunch of others, struggling to find some rhythm with the process of life; a Brother in the grips of understanding that part of the purpose of us being together is for us to help heal each other. And that can't happen unless we are allowed to be just who we are. No judgments. No shame. That's just the way it's got to be.

So if you ever find that in the middle of this healing we're about to go through that I've in some way jumped out of the box being selfish, angry, difficult for what you may think is no reason at all I'm asking you in the name of brotherhood and love to slow me. Ask me to take pause and offer correction and I'll listen because sometimes I'll tell you shit can just pop out of nowhere and can be triggered by most any dayum thing. ☺

I'm missing you and want to see you soon. And know this: I'm falling in love with you and I can't help myself.

Always,
Brian

October 5, 2012

Dear Brian,

Wassup, man! I got your letter this morning. I smile every time I see one from you. They mean so much to me. What you said makes so much sense. You put into words thing that have been on my mind that I have trouble getting my tongue to express. But the fact is I feel you. I really do.

One of the first things that attracted me to you, outside of your sexy good looks, was your energy - your spirit. I can't describe it but it was something I felt drawn to. And as we began to conversate (is that a word??) I was immediately charged by your self-confidence - a confidence that in no way suggested conceit but the kind of confidence that said, "*Here I am. Take all of me or none of me!*" Man, from that moment on I knew I wanted to be a part of your world. And you know what? I know I'm ready.

I've spent the last several years single, some by chance but mostly by choice. Seems I kept always running into the same kind of Brothers, the kind you said you once were, the love 'em and leave 'em type. The Brothers who'd come on strong in the beginning, only to suddenly and without warning pull back. Every time it happened man I'd be hurt and emotionally devastated so much so that it would wear me out physically.

I couldn't figure out why I couldn't find a Brother who could commit. Then one day after the hundredth time trying again with a Brother who pulled the same stunt it finally dawned on me. It wasn't that I kept running into these Brothers who couldn't commit. The real problem was I kept giving them my phone number!

Do you see what I mean? The problem wasn't that these Brothers were finding their way to me as much as I was finding my way to them. These were the Brothers *I* was attracted to. So after I thought about that I started asking myself, "*Why?*" And you know what the answer was? It was because I wasn't as ready as I thought I was for a commitment. Ain't that some shit?

So that's why I feel like I'm ready for you, man. I'm ready to give and receive love because I know now that I'm lovable and I deserve more than just quick flings and fixes, one-night stands, and temporary relationships. I know I'm ready because I'm not afraid of myself anymore. This isn't to say that I'm perfect either. I know I'm far from it but what I can say is that I'm healing.

I know we've got work to do but to get to love I mean real love individually and collectively just means that we keep our focus on loving and supporting each other through it all; not losing ourselves in the process but finding a medium - a place to balance each other without feeling that anything about us is being compromised. With you working on you and me working on me we automatically work on us.

So Brother correct me too when I'm wrong without anger, argument, or attitude. Let's find a way to correct each other lovingly and kindly. I don't know exactly how to do it but I want to find out. You're important to me and I want to make sure we get it right. I'm crazy about you and I know we can do this.

Always,
Elliot

p.s. You say you're falling in love with me. Well, Brother, I'm already there!

October 17, 2012

Dear Elliot,

I hear you loud and clear man and we're making progress with us. Good progress, and I've got to admit I'm loving it! It's exciting to me because I feel like finally I'm doing things the right way.

There is ease with you, man. There's ease and there's calm. Years ago for me to date a Brother long distance would have me upset and paranoid all the time - wondering and worrying if he was being honest, if he was being faithful, or if here were just stringing me along. I've never once had those thoughts about you.

I know that to trust you I've got to trust myself and I do. That's why you've never experienced the wrath of the old me. I'm so much better than I was three years ago. Better in every way. Better. Not perfect (but close to it ☺).

Admittedly, I have my moments when I start thinking of experiences in the past. I guess it's to be expected. But those painful feelings; the jealousy and insecurities, when we can't be nearer to each other don't visit with me that often and they're not as intense as they used to be when I didn't know any better. But when they do creep up I just remember who I am and who you are and I release them as quickly as they come.

So now that it seems that this relationship is moving onto another level, my feelings intensified, and we're feeling each other like that, we have to now shake hands and agree - agree to being committed to the process.

You say you want to know how to keep the bullshit at bay and keep peaceful communications between us. Well, I don't have all the answers either. I can only offer you my honesty and integrity; my promise that I will never lie to you and that every thought, action, or decision involving me will involve you.

When there are times when things stunt our communication and our growth; the distance between us, interpretations of things said or things done, or we're hindered by life's stressors unique to us as Black men and intensified as Black men loving each other we can't be afraid to allow the feelings - all of the emotions - to flow. If it's like that it's got to be like that. We can't kid ourselves into believing that at times we won't get mad or upset at each other. Anger's going to show up. It happens in the best of relationships. But as long as we make a promise that no matter how much confusion there is, no matter how much it brings us to explosion, no matter how much kicking and yelling there may be going on, not one of us is leaving the room. We remember that underneath all the shit there lies love. Just love. If we remember this we'll be just fine.

Hey, listen! I got a couple of weeks of vacation I have to use or lose. Maybe I can tempt you to meet up with me somewhere - somewhere warm, tropical, and sexy? Let me know what you think. I'd love to see you. I need to see you.

Always,
Brian

October 29, 2012

M'man, Brian!

I'm committed to be committed. You got that, man. No doubt! And I ain't tripping off the distance either. Right now we're just in our "meantime", the time we devote to learning about each other and not giving into suspicions, jealousy, and other shit that could destroy us. We just relax into this man. I'm here and I'm not going anywhere. My mind is focused and it's focused on you. It's focused on us.

So where do we go from here? Where do two Brothers, different experiences, different lives, different states, go from here? I was thinking about that the other day, you know, trying to figure out what the future holds for us.

I think one of the greatest challenges in relationships between Brothers is that we don't look ahead. We don't look to the future or think of ourselves being together in the future because we don't really see ourselves together for very long.

We don't think about the seriousness of commitment; shit like marriage, moving in together, homes, investments, combining finances, or even the possibility of raising children together. We stop short of making adult decisions about our lives together for a number of reasons I know but I wonder how much of that kind of thinking affects our actions in the "now" of our relationships? How much does belief in temporary destroy our futures before our present has time to take off? I'm determined not to let that happen to us.

In keeping you and me in mind I'm thinking about long-term. I'm thinking about lifelong commitment, partnership. I'm not talking about just being my lover, or my boyee, I'm talking about you and me maybe even marriage someday. I know that thought barely pass the lips of most Brothers today but that's what I'm talking about for us - a lifetime commitment and I don't think that it's too soon to start planting the seeds into our minds.

Others may disagree. They may think that we should be worried about getting past the introductory stage, the stage where we're fascinated with each other just long enough to check each other out and feel the vibe. But I'm saying to you right now is where it all begins. There couldn't be a better time to look ahead.

I'm committed to being committed. We can't make it easy on ourselves to just walk away when trouble brews, to find comfort in the arms of another Brother in the face of challenges. So, no! No matter how much we come to words, I'm willing to work it out. If we argue, we argue. We'll just let something greater than us guide.

So here are my pledges to you, simple edicts but important decrees nonetheless: Number 1 - I'll never go to bed angry with you especially now with you on one side of the world and me on the other – or so it seems. Number 2 - I'll never hang up the phone on you, ignore your calls, or play any other bullshit, childish games with you. Number 3 - I'll never, ever, ever lay a hand on you except to hold you, caress you, and love you.

I don't believe that what we've found in each other is special. Specialness isn't what I'm after. It's not something we should want. I believe that those kinds of relationships, special ones, are based on fear. A relationship like that seem to suggest that there's a person, one "special" person who can complete us as we join for a relationship. But to do so suggests that I'll look for you to do things for me that you cannot. In looking for you to give me these things I'll look for everything but love from you.

I don't want this relationship to be special. I want it to be ordained because I know that after years of looking for completeness from people that only God can complete us. We've been joined together to learn, love, teach, and heal each other. That's all. I'm agreeing to that commitment, to Him and to you, with a pledge that I won't ever fight for this relationship. I will always love for it.

I'm taking the next steps with you, man. Side-by-side.

Always,
Elliot

November 1, 2012

Dear Elliot,

I'm taking that step with you. I don't know what tomorrow brings but I agree. It's what we're thinking now, the stuff that's going on in our heads now, and what we make up in our minds in this moment that will save us or separate us.

Since we have no rules or regulations about how we are supposed to date and since the word dating has no real definition between Brothers we'll create some of our own to use as guidelines for how we'll treat each other and commit during this important time of commitment between us. The three you mention in your last letter is a perfect way to start. You have my agreement on that.

So now we make plans. We make plans and consider. We consider that we won't be guided by superficial wants or desires that may never be fulfilled. We'll hold tight to what we believe; the power of love and forgiveness and what it will mean for us as we make a life together. We'll make plans and consider what it would mean for us to someday bridge the gap of distance and live together - to share the same space with your things and mine, your quirks and mine, your taste and mine, your dislikes and mine.

We consider that our differences are nothing to fear but to rejoice in knowing that it's our individuality that makes us who we are and our differences that bring us closer together.

We plan and consider that somewhere down the line; weeks, months, or what have you that we'll have to let our families know about us and consider what it will mean if one or all on both sides - yours and minds - decide they can't handle it and reject us. Would love be strong enough to keep us together when others try to break us apart?

We consider what happens when family visits. Does one of us move into the guest room like "roommates" or do we stay close at night holding and loving? And we plan and consider that our families won't reject us but welcome us and acknowledge who we are together and we take part in family reunions, and graduations, and weddings, and funerals, and childbirths.

We plan and consider that they will want to come, all of them, your side and mine on the day we make our love known and sit to the left and to the right of us while there in front you and I stand in the presence of God - black tuxedos, white smiles, and dreams - celebrating Black love, Black sexuality, Black culture, Black heritage, and Black spirituality in a religion of our own - one we'll create when others reject us.

And they will all want to be there to see us and they will come. All of our ancestors, generations long gone, friends and family joining hands in a circle around us in celebration of what is.

We plan and consider to settle down in a house - urban style- in the hood, our hood, loving openly and honestly - a part of the community. No hiding but taking part in its growth and protection; block parties and the things that remind of us childhood.

And when we've grown in our love, when we've been able to clear our conscious of guilt, fear, and shame if any at all is present, we will welcome children with no home into our home and they will know love, and grow in it and from it.

They will be proud of themselves and of us and proud that we found each other in blessings and love, comfortable believing that we will be there for each other, loving each other until death us do part. We plan and we consider.

I Love you,
Brian

November 12, 2012

Dear Brian,

I'm making plans, man. I'm making plans and I'm considering all you've said and I love the sound of it!

So let's make plans and consider our first vacation together, the first of many to come, the first before it all comes into existence; the challenges, the family, the neighborhood, the children, and the rest. Let's plan and consider taking the time now to plan and consider; to ground each other in love and happiness - in each other's love.

And let us document for our family, our friends, our ancestors, and our future, pictures of us on a beach, somewhere beautiful, hand in hand, smiling, glowing in what we've found in each other. Let's scribe this now so that we can all look back each time we may forget, separated by distance or whatever, and remember the love, remember who we are as manifestations of the Divine - the hope and the promise.

Let's make plans to consider to plan and consider that what we do now, what we think and what we believe in this moment will forever root us. These are the things we think and believe - the very things that life and memories and love are made of.

I love you, Brian.
I really, really, do!!!
Elliot

November 20, 2012

Dear Elliot,

Let's make it happen!

I love you too, man. No doubt about it!

Always yours,
Brian

p.s. Shall we say Bermuda?

What Would You Say

If
I asked if
You ever knew
The Strength of Sentiment
The Beauty of Love's Truth
Everlasting
Eternal
Unchangeable?

What Would You Think
If
I asked you ever if you've ever known
The Depth of Compassion
The Boldness of Love's Promise

Its Soul
Its Dignity
Its Integrity
Its Importance

What Would You See
If
I asked you to close your eyes
As I described Shangri-La
A place
Warm
Exciting
Enticing
Passionate…

Where for a lifetime
You seek Love not solely
For its physical pleasures
But beyond
Into the Confounds of
Peace and Understanding
Where safety overwhelms?

What Would You Feel
If
I took
Your Hand
Looked Deep into
Your Eyes
and Offered
You
All of these things?

Would you say
Yes?

Brutha

Brutha was
phine
spittin' lines at me
I usta use to bed down
the Sistahs

He was good
two days before tonight
chillin' at my cousin's crib
he walks in
sparkin life into a boring ass set

Brutha's with his other half
wife
year 5
clinging like a unripe peach
staking claim

aware of desires from the crowd
of Sistahs
unaware of this man's desires

never ever thought about being
with another Brutha
never ever considered the possibility
never ever thought I thought that way

I'm with my girl
year 3
and summer brings the bell's toll
jumpin' the broom
her and me

But tonight's somehow different
longings for her softness
replaced
longings for his hardness
discovered

never wanted to kiss a Brutha
like I wanted to kiss him
never wanted to hold a Brutha
like I wanted to hold him
never wanted to taste a Brutha
like I wanted to taste him

he knows I wanna know
don't know how
but he knows

sly glances and smiles later
digits exchange
promises to call made
can't get Brutha outta my head

wishing
wondering
thinking
contemplating
dialing ain't easy

next day
noon
Brutha calls
get together…u know
hang out
maybe grab a bite
or do something?
Cool…I'm game
hoping he'd try
hoping he won't
he knows I wanna know
don't know how
but he knows

Brutha sittin' in my livin room
rollin a blunt
looking good
smelling good
seein' right thru me

starting slow
gentle words
accidental touches and
incidental stares
not seen from my other niggahs
my boyz
my crew

Brutha starrin' me down
looking for objections
and warnings
not found
he knows I wanna know
don't know how
but he knows

shotgun?

Cool
tells me to suck
he'll blow
Awww hell!

Brutha moves closer
eyes locked onto mine
I can't help but swoon

holding breath
face to face
lip to lip
not moving
not wanting to

smoke clears
convincing me
I want this
and he knows

he knows I wanna know
don't know how
but he knows

The Water Poured
For Kelvin

At first it was
sweat
I felt
trickling down the side
of my face
down my spine

the water poured
it was you

the sweet morning dew
met with the sun

I closed my eyes
and let the water
from the shower
beat onto my shoulders
and onto my chest
watching it roll off of me
not watching where it was going

I remember thinking
Who Is He
I smile

I stood on
the edge of the rocks
at the very top
under the surge of
the water fall

for four days its
warmth kept me there
not touching
        these waters are forbidden to my touch
not tasting
        these waters are forbidden to my taste
lingering
not wanting to move
knowing that I must

the water poured
but I don't get wet

these waters
are on a course
not of my own
but of another
hampered only by a dam
stopping only to gain
momentum

off in the distance
I hear a splash
I leave my place
on the rocks
and find there is a pond

the waters are calm

I see your reflection in it
in the water cool
I smile
and kneel down
in the sand
cupping both my hands together
to take a drink

but I cannot hold you
you trickle through
my fingers
leaving my hands
moist
with your goodness

I am reminded that
you
are not mine to taste

I stand
watching
you flow into
another
and continue my swim
alone
upstream

Nubian

He's there
Out there
Somewhere

Nubian

Waiting and wishing
Hoping and looking
For me

In between
Solo breakfast
Solo lunches
Solo dinners
Solo slumbers
I prepare

My mind to accept him and the gifts he brings
My soul to connect with his spiritual wonders
My body Temple Sacred
So sacred
For no other to touch or know
Except
Nubian
He's there
Out there somewhere
Preparing

Learning lessons of love lost
Building bridges to mend his character
Healing his life to walk into the light
Leaving behind adolescent insecurities
Growing into his spiritual nature
Rediscovering his morality
To reawaken nobility and honor

I need not look for
Nubian
I need not voice the desire
We will join in the appointed time

And when we are found
Amidst the backdrop
Of endless longings
Wanting
Cravings
Yearnings

We will take in our
Magnificence
And build in the center
Of peaceful deserts
A home
Where Self
Is relinquished
And we become fused

In all
Equations of life

Proclaiming undying love to the world
We will cut through the water
With a sword and receive
The blessings of the Nile

Its sacred waters will baptize
Us and shroud our affection
Protecting us
Aiding us
In
Negotiating
Conquering
The most difficult times of pain
With laughter and with love

Two Nubians
The most just of all men
Shall we will be

Carriers of ancient cultures
Filled with the knowledge of
The ages
In scribes
Leaving behind a legacy of love
Transcending

I knew

The moment he walked
into the room

I knew

Something about
his presence
Brought out years of yearnings
and desires
to be held
to be loved

Not a word did he say
not a glance in
my direction
Yet
I knew

Douglas & Irving

Subj: Hey You
Date: 9/12/2010 8:15 AM Eastern Standard Time
From: DougLove@oneonone.com
To: IrvingII@unknownlove.com
Sent from the Internet See Details – Click Here

Hey Baby!

Got your message last night. Didn't' get in until around mid-night from the airport. Spent the last two days after you left with my cousin looking at houses. Nothing I liked so far with only one possibility that I might take if nothing else comes through. Looks like I'll have to make at least one more visit up to secure a place before the end of the month. I'll keep you posted.

Anyway, as usual it was good being with you this weekend. Thanks for coming down. I know the road trips are getting hectic and I promise you that it won't always be this way. The distance is kickin' my ass too but I'm trying not to let it get the best of me. I waited over 12 years to fine with the PHINEST Brother on the planet and I'm not gonna let miles stand between us (B'lieve that!!!). We'll figure something out.... don't know what....but we'll figure it out. Just hang in there with me baby.

All right, I don't want to get too heavy first thing in the a.m., so I'll give you a call tonight. Have a beautiful day and know that somebody's thinking about you STRONG and ALWAYS!

Miss you baby!
Douglas

P.S.

I forgot to tell you yesterday that my neighbor brought over a belated birthday gift...guess what it was? Can't guess...o.k., I'll tell you...a movie...The Sixth Sense....So I got brave last night and decided to watch it....I was scared outta my mind! You're right. It was a good movie but my scary ass slept with every light on in the house!

Subject: **Hey You**
Date: 9/13/2010 2:15 PM Eastern Standard Time
From: IrvingII@unknownlove.com
To: DougLove@oneonone.com
Sent from the internet See Details – Click here

Douglas:

Now c'mon. I told you that the movie wasn't scary. What's there to be afraid of? Now how are you gonna be able to protect your family when you get married someday? (That's what my childhood friends used to say to get me to do "manly" acts when I was young). Man, they would coerce me into doing all kinds of deviant deeds with that line - even when I knew what I was doing was wrong. I don't know why I always felt I had to protect my manhood and masculinity. Even back then. I guess it hasn't really left me, even at thirty-five.

Which brings me to something I've been wanting to say to you. And please forgive me for getting a lil deep at this time but I feel like I have to. Something in me says that it's now or never. So here it goes: It's about our relationship, Doug. I'm not exactly sure how to say it or put it into words but I do know that I have to say this. Douglas, I don't believe this, our relationship, is what I want right now. In fact, I know it's not.

Now don't get me wrong, I've always been very, very fond of you and I do care for you. I could even comfortably say that I love you. But the truth of the matter is I don't believe we're equally yoked. We're not equally yoked in this lifestyle and I don't know if we're strong enough to survive it.

Our lives differ so much, Douglas. Most everything about your life is about being who you are; Black and existing as a same gender loving Black man. And I'm not faulting you for that by any means. I think it's the most unselfish and giving thing anyone can give to another.

What you are doing by showing your face and by working in the community is saving lives. It's giving people reason to pause and rethink their whole perception of what they think black and homosexual is. I think there should be more people like you in the world! You're brave, so much braver than I am. And free. So free! I mean, you are totally free to be who you are and that's a beautiful thing. I wish I could be as honest.

But I can't be and I, as you're aware, have lived with varying degrees of comfort and insecurity about my sexuality. I haven't found a comfort zone and I don't think I ever will. And surely, the fact that I haven't means that there are things in me I've yet to confront or can't confront for whatever reason. I'm not exactly sure where they come from. But I do know this: these demons would only surface in time, in me and in our relationship, and only cause more problems - superficial problems - between us in the future. Trust me. I know how I can be.

Let me give you an example. I'm not sure if you even noticed my fucked up attitude or anti-social posture the other day at brunch with your friends last Sunday. I was uncomfortable and didn't want to be a part of that scene so I kept to myself saying very little if anything. But that's the type of shit I'm capable of. And the funny thing is I'm sure those guys are probably very cool. I know, I know, I know, a stank, stank, stank attitude for a grown man, right?

Doug, I don't know. I'm just not where you are in this lifestyle which you must admit would make for a very ugly situation between us down the line. There are parts of me and my sexuality that I'm cool with, and then there are certain things that I can't even phantom giving in to. So it's not you, Doug, and it's not the distance between us. It's my inability to love myself.

We'll talk soon
Irving

Subj: **Hey You**
Date: 9/13/2010 8:26 PM Eastern Standard Time
From: DougLove@oneonone.com
To: IrvingII@unknownlove.com
Sent from the Internet See Details – Click Here

Irving:

Whoa… Am I mistaken, or did you just break up with me in an e-mail?

What am I supposed to say? Dayum, Irving! I thought we were better than that man and I believed, no, in fact, I'm sure that I deserve better than a "Dear John" e-mail and a "We'll talk!" You're right. We do need to talk.

I just got back from Chicago earlier this evening and leaving town again Wednesday morning - the day after tomorrow. Please contact me as soon as you get this and let's talk. But if I don't hear from you before I leave I will take it to mean that you've said everything you wanted to say in the manner in which you chose to say it.

Peace,
Doug

Subj: **Hey You**
Date: 9/14/2010 8:31 AM Eastern Standard Time
From: IrvingII@unknownlove.com
To: DougLove@oneonone.com
Sent from the Internet See Details = Click Here

Doug:

I am a better man than that. In fact, I'm a dayum good one! And it wasn't like that. I was reading my emails while at work (much like I am now) and replied back to you. I thought that it was as good as time as any to let you know my thoughts and my feelings.

But you're right. You deserve a form of communication that's much more personal. If you recall I did say that we'd talk and we will.

Peace
Irving

Subj: **Hey You**
Date: 9/14/2010 4:17 AM Eastern Standard Time
From: IrvingII@unknownlove.com
To: DougLove@oneonone.com
Sent from the Internet See Details = Click Here

Irving -

I'm not questioning whether you're a good man or not. You are a good man and I know this. It's what attracted me to you in the first place. You obviously misread my message. What I said was that I thought that "we" were better than this, meaning that we could have talked about your feelings and your concerns last week when I saw you.

You could have even said something when we were talking about our relationship when I point blank asked you were you still feeling "us". I'm just trying to understand. Help me out here.

Peace,
Doug

Subj: **Hey You**
Date: 9/15/2010 1:26 AM Eastern Standard Time
From: IrvingII@unknownlove.com
To: DougLove@oneonone.com
Sent from the Internet See Details = Click Here

Doug,

I see. What can I say? I have to admit there are times when I don't always say exactly what's going on with me which accounts for why I end up doing more damage in the end than I imagined. I am sorry for not being open with my feelings when we were together...if that helps at all.

And I really must apologize for the "Dear John" letter. As silly as it may sound, I really didn't know what a "Dear John" letter was until my friend, Maurice, explained. He too was very disappointed in the way I communicated to you via email. I tried to explain to him, just as I am to you, that I wasn't trying at all to be cold nor abrupt in my delivery of my feelings.

I was reading my emails and came across yours. You spoke of how you understood how hard the distance was between us and about me hanging in there. My mind started spinning about what you were saying. That was all. You mentioned your move to D.C. too and how it would at least bridge the gap between us. Do you remember? Well, it was at that time I just thought I should tell you what I was feeling. So I replied.

Again, I apologize I really didn't intend on appearing like this nasty, heartless Brother. I'm not that type of Dude! And I certainly wouldn't do that to you. You've been nothing but the best for me. Besides you're much too good, too beautiful a Brother for that.

Now you're probably wondering why you haven't received a phone call as I promise. Well, it's my phone service. For real. Its outta control...and off. Service is supposed to be repaired today. But I will call. I remember something about Chicago. Did you go? For now I must get back to the grind.

I'll chat with you later.
Love and Peace,
Irving

Subj: **Hey You**
Date: 9/16/2010 11:43 AM Eastern Standard Time
From: IrvingII@unknownlove.com
To: DougLove@oneonone.com
Sent from the Internet See Details = Click Here

Dear Irving -

I don't know Maurice but please let him know that I am eternally grateful to him for helping you to understand where I was coming from.

I'm hoping that we'll have an opportunity to talk soon, Irving, but until we do, there's something I want to put on your heart and mind. You're right when you say that we are unequally yoked in this "lifestyle". But we're not only unequally yoked in this lifestyle (I have found peace - you haven't) but we're also unequally yoked in our personal lives (you eat meat - I don't), and in our professional lives (I have found my passion - you're discovering yours), in our spiritual lives (I understand the magnitude of God's love - you're working on reconciling it), and even in our physical appearance (you claim you're taller - I disagree).

So what we're unequally yoked! We're different people with different experiences, different outlooks, and different beliefs. But these differences are nothing to fear. We should celebrate them. The beautiful part about this is that our only role is to love and support each other in everything. Everything!

Irving, I know exactly where you are. I understand your insecurities and your concerns. I know that you fear being "exposed" and what that may mean to you. I know this pain all too well. It took a lifetime of experiences to find resolve though I never imagined my life would turn out the way it has where I have been cast into the forefront of this lifestyle.

Believe it or not I'm still closeted in many respects. There are family members and friends who have not been informed and who I stand to lose once the truth is finally known. Yet, it is a small price to pay for peace of mind. After all, what's the sense in living if you can't feel alive?

But that was my journey. You are on one of your own and whether it takes a day, a month, a year, or a lifetime, I have to accept you and support you. And I do, Irving. I accept you and support you - just as you are. There's been no pressure, no expectations. There are no demands. There is only love here.

But you're giving up on us. You're giving up on us without realizing that it's all right for us to be unequally yoked. You're giving up without the benefit of discussing it. After all, I should be the one person with whom you can share your feelings with especially when it involves me.

You're giving up without an attempt to work through this with me. You're giving up without understanding that this, our relationship, is one of the safest places in this world for you to be - a place where you will just be loved...never judged. You're giving up, Irving, and I'm just asking you not to.

I got back this morning from Seattle. I understand your phone situation so as soon as it's repaired, and as soon as you feel comfortable call me... please.

Peace, Blessings, Love,
Doug

Subj: **Hey You**
Date: 9/18/2010 7:43 AM Eastern Standard Time
From: IrvingII@unknownlove.com
To: DougLove@oneonone.com
Sent from the Internet See Details = Click Here

Dear Doug:

It's me. Please know that I haven't been avoiding speaking with you. The phone situation has been corrected but I've been soooooooooooo busy running around with my 'lil cousin, who got in Friday.

He's here from Kentucky, doing this basketball camp here in New York and it's been hectic, so hectic that I haven't had a moment to connect with you. I've had to escort his ass everywhere. It's his first time to NYC--need I say more? It's been fun but none stop!

So what I'll do as soon as I get into tonight (which will be late because I have to attend a meeting at 6pm) is call you.

Talk with ya!
Irving

Subj: **Hey You**
Date: 11/3/2010 8:31 AM Eastern Standard Time
From: IrvingII@unknownlove.com
To: DougLove@oneonone.com
Sent from the Internet See Details - Click Here

Dear Irving,

Well, it's been nearly two months since I've heard from you. I waited all night that night for you to call but something in me knew you wouldn't. Perhaps it wasn't as easy as you imagined it to be to dial my numbers. I understand. I really do. The more time that passes the more difficult it is to call.

I want you to know that I'm not angry. I'm not angry nor am I mad. It does no good. And even if I could be angry who am I to be angry with? You for not loving yourself? Society for not allowing you to, or homophobia - internal and external - that whispers to you that there's nothing worth loving? How can I be angry or upset at that which I cannot control or correct?

There is a slight tinge in my heart; the pain of breakup, the pain of wanting and desiring something that cannot be yours; the pain of accepting that we were not meant to be. All these pains I will swallow up, knowing that in time - with time - I will heal and become stronger by this experience.

I wish, Irving, things could have been different. I wish things could have worked out between us. I wish we had an opportunity to talk and try at least to work through all of your fears and mine. But we are where we are and there's no sense in having regrets. I can walk away from this thankful that I had the opportunity to share in your world, however brief, however short lived.

I hope that you someday find the strength to finally live for yourself; to give yourself a break from expectations and start loving who you are. As you are, you're not living. You're existing. It's a horrible way to live like that, Irving, but an even more horrible way to die.

Don't waste any more time wasting time. You've got too much to offer to yourself and to this world. Loving yourself is a simple message with a powerful effect. Life is so much better when you do. You'll see one day. You'll see. It is my warmest prayer for you.

Know that you take with you all of my love and compassion. Use it however you see fit, however it will best serve you. I loved you from the first time I saw you until now and I will always love you, Irving. You can always count on that.

Peace and Love
Doug

I Bought This Ring in Mexico

"I bought this ring in Mexico"
Is the Line I use to explain
To those who inquire
Of the ring on my finger
And why on my left hand it remains

This ring was given me by someone special
Whose love once reigned supreme
Someone I loved with everything I am
And with whom shared all my dreams

Our love was a beautiful love
The kind that most can understand
But what many find difficult
And even hard to accept
Is that it was given to me
By another man

I'll never forget the space and time
When he gave this ring to me
In a crowded cafe
On the north side of Philly
With him on bended knee

He took my hand
Placed it on my finger
And asked if I'd stay forevermore
I smiled, said Yes, feeling his vibe
And as he raised himself from the floor

We kissed a kiss
And embraced an embrace
That only two men can understand
The wanting desire
The feeling
The warmth
Of loving another man

But since that time
Our love has faded
And now that we're apart
The love I had, the Passion I knew
Remains forever in my heart

I'm reminded each and every time
Someone questions me
On the position of my ring
I simply say,
"I bought this ring in Mexico"
And my soul begins to sing

Other times I'm saddened
By thoughts of lost love
And how it all began
And then I wonder sometimes loudly to myself
If I'll ever love again

But then I gaze at this ring
I bought in Mexico
This symbolic band of gold
That stands as a symbol of the
Love I once had
And the dreams I still do hold

Adored

Didn't want to hear from you
wanted to leave it where
it was
a beautiful weekend spent with a
Brother I adored

I know nothing can come of this
the writing is on the wall
just as plain as day
far too many hurdles to jump

Somebody else commands your attention
Jump 1
Don't know if you got in mind
What I got in mind…
about me…
about us
Jump 2

But I do know
that weekend
Dayum!
that weekend
Showed me
things I had longed for
not requiring moans
groans and nakedness
under the cover of darkness

kindness
consideration
attention capture mine
treating me like I treat myself

I was amazed
captivated
thrilled
excited
hopeful
awakened

all at once

Funny thing is
it comes so natural
you didn't know what you were doing
to me
for me

You weren't looking for love
neither was I
you were looking for a friend
needing to talk
get a couple things off your chest
off your mind

I was there
a good listener
heard you talking
felt your need
wanted to melt away your pain
confusion
erase it - erase him
from your memory
from your heart
offer a fresh start
a better way

Lying in your bed
head to feet
the night before
convincing myself to
leave it where it was
for us
this was not meant to be

told myself
be thankful
grateful
for the experience of this experience
nothing more nothing less

too painful to think what it would be like with him
too painful to think what it will be like without him

Days turn into weeks
thoughts of you subside
out of sight
out of mind

I carry on with life
lists
calls to make
calls to return
planning
scheduling
traveling
working
remembering
forgetting

Played messages
today
and here you are
sounding like you're in
the next room
calling my name
Dayum!

It all comes back
just as fresh

I listen over and over
and over and over
confused
what next?

call?
Naw…can't do that
don't want to get my hopes up

not call?
Naw…can't do that either
don't want to miss an opportunity

ignore the message?
pretend as if it never happened?
Maybe…

Didn't want to hear from you
just wanted to leave it where
a beautiful weekend spent with a
Brother I absolutely adore

Dayum…I hate this shit!

      Call him ____   Don't Call Him ____   Maybe ____
                      (Check One)

Allowed

my mind is at work
thinking,
how to make my move
on you
to you

in my mind, a thousand times,
i've imagined us together
turnin' heads everywhere we go
are they together? together, together?

yes, together
finally home, finally free

I imagine soft pillow talk
long nights of love making,
Sensuous touches, Sensual smells
feeling safe when you hold me

allowed

to feel what I need to feel
wanted
needed
loved

allowed

to be who i am
and forget about
being who I'm not

but it's all in my head

allowed

Agape
The Art of Love

Love Dances

Love Lives Here
    In this House
        In Our Heart
            And It Dances

It Dances
Soft in the Rhythm of Your Eyes
Warm in Your Arms and Natural Highs
And When We Make Love and Earth Touches Sky
In the Midst of Deep Slumber With Soft Gentle Sighs

    Love Dances
        Because Love Wants To Dance

            It Dances
      Overwhelmed by the Magic Behind Your Smile
       Blessed by Your Peace As Calm As The Nile
      Breathless Like A Saxophone's Smooth Satin Style
      Forever Like the Trumpet of Dear Brother Miles

                Love Dances
            Because Love Wants to Dance

Pure Emotions Take Over and I'm Rocked to the Core
I Take Your Hand in Mine and Lead You to the Floor
Play Your Favorite Song with Not a Crack in the Door
Lock Out the World It's You That I Adore

        Love Dances
       Because Love Wants To Dance

A Lover's Waltz We Dance in Heels or Bare Feet
Faithful Hearts Pound When We Dance Cheek to Cheek
Holding You Closer When eyes and Lips Meet
In Syncopated Rhythm Loving You My Sweet

Love Dances
    Because Love Wants to Dance

It dances

Slow and Loving in Tender Situations
Fast and Eager In Anticipations
Funky and Wet in Soul Reverberations
Safe and Excited in Love Sensations

Love Dances
Because Love Wants to Dance

It Dances Right Here in What We Found
Even In Absence of Music and Absence of Sound
Like the Scent of a Flower Plucked Straight From the Ground
And When My Nose is Wide Open Like a Swiss Basset Hound

Love Dances
Because Love Wants To Dance

Completing our Love as Two Become One
Is The Sweet Sultry Vision of a new day's Sun
And a Whole New World Of Love Has Begun
And We Love More Deeply Because of What We have Become

Love Dances
Because Love Wants to Dance

So Strike Up The Band No Doubts No Cant's
Take It From The Top
We've taken this chance

Let the Music Play On

Love's Taken Its Stance

And Turn On Forever

Because Love Wants to Dance

The Brazilian Café

I was chillin like mad in Dallas
Just chillin, not causin no malice
Hip hopin' to a groove in a club called Smooth
On the corner of Wynnewood and Palace

In between dances, phine Brother's glances
And kickin' it with my crew
Made my way through the crowd
Pumpin' music is loud
And I'm ready for drink number two

Got bartender's attention
Lookin good I must mention
"Yo' pour me a double Vodka on ice"
With money in hand, crowded bars I can't stand
He yells to me "Just a minute" twice

So I'm cool, you know, just waitin' my turn
When suddenly right out of the blue
Out the corner of my eye, I swear - no lie
Came my very first sight of Dude

Stay calm, stay collected, I tell myself
Can't let this dude see me sweat
But Brother is phine, and he's dressed to the 9's
Did he wink when our eyes just met?

Oh yea, he did, cause now he's smiled
And he looks like he's makin' his way
Over to my side, and my smile's getting wide
"Well, Dayum!!!" is all I can say

Dude's bout six-foot four, 32 waist
Probably a 46 or 48 chest
With locks to his shoulder, 32 no older
Rockin Tim's and Slims by Guess

Yo, this Brother is tight and his stylo's just right
And he's Blacker than midnight blue
                              He extends me his hand, says, "Wassup, I'm Sam,
                                    Been tryin' all night to get to you!"

"Say, Word?" I ask, and tell him my name
And smile to let him know that it's cool
                                "Nice to meet you!" he says, "Likewise!" I respond
                                      Then he pulls up these two bar stools

Dude buys my drink, orders one for him
And asks me to raise my glass
He offers a toast, and says,
                                                      "To the most
                                          Beautiful man in the class"

So we got through the normal intros, you know,
                                    Where you from and what do you do?
                          Who you here with? Are you havin' a good time?
                                        Is anybody here with you?

We click right away and chat up a storm
Chillin it's all a good time
Feelin' like I've known this Brother forever
Is it the music, him, or the wine?

Naw man, it's him, and I'm sure of it
Cause he just put his hand on my lap
And I let it stay, not movin, no way
Cause I'm really gettin' into his rap

"Awww dayum, that's the beat,
Wanna dance with me man?"

Well, I've been waitin' for that question to pop
So we hit the floor, six dances or more
And now I don't ever wanna stop

Sweat drippin all over, movin closer and closer
Eyes locked hard into this trance
Can't see nobody else, it's just me and this Dude
Celebratin our very first dance

But in the middle of glory, our fairytale story
This Brother walks up, he's pissed
Grabs Dude by his shoulder with the strength of a boulder
I'm like, "What the fuck is this?!"

Not causing a scene, he calms this queen
And excuses himself from me
Walks off to the corner with little jack horner
But nothing else could I see

So I kept my groove, not pressed, I'm smooth
I knew it was too good to be true
Besides, there's other Brothers around
And I'm new to this town
I mean, shit! What you expect me to do?

But no sooner than that's said, he's back and he's red
Hot from this scene, I can sense it
I ask "Are you cool, he's like,

                                          "That boy's a fool!
                              Can we go back and sit for a minute?"

And just like that, Dude's smile is back
And we pick up right where we left off
But back on the stool I explain my rule
About the danger of a flame and a moth

See I'm the type of Brother who won't mess with another
If the Brother already has a man,
"So check it, no matter, enjoyed our little chatter
Nice to meet you, take it easy, Brother Sam!"

He says,

                                  "Hold on, slow down, hold up, Yo',
                                        this is really easy to fix
                                I'm single, I told you, explained it already
                              And I'm sorry for twistin you up in that mix"

                            "See that Brother's obsessed and he's really a pest
                                          I was only tryin' to be nice
                              When we met last month, he bought me a drink
                                    And danced with me once or twice"

Well, I heard that before, a hundred times or more
So, "If that's a line I'm really not bitin
'Cause I'm feelin' too good to spoil my mood
And with your ex niggah I'm not fightin!"

"Tell you what," he says, "let's blow this joint
How bout coffee or somethin' to eat?
'Cause I'm tired of this place and these Brothers in your face
When I'm tryin' to sweep you off your feet"

"Well, that's cool", I say, "I'm feelin' you too
But I need to state one simple fact
There can't be expectations of sexual relations
A Brother don't get down like that!"

"I respect that man", he said with that smile,
"In fact, I think that's deep
But I'm feelin' your soul and I wanna know more
Let me say good night to my peeps"
"We'll meet at the door - five minutes no more
'Cause tonight's about me and you
I want you all to myself not nobody else
We could be jump startin' somethin' new!"

Well, we shared our souls 'till 6 I'm told
'Cause time meant nothing to me
In the Brazilian Café as night turned to day
Over Black coffee and Chai tea

That was a long time ago and here you should know
That Dude and me are still together
We committed our lives to stand side by side
Through good times, bad times, whatever

Now this ain't to say that it's bliss everyday
Cause sometime it's like total doom
But no matter how much yellin' and screamin' there is
Not one of us is leavin' the room

You see, we decided to remain undivided
And to keep this promise true
We focus on love and the Good Lord above
To ensure that we see it through

        So here's where I'll end, where this story began
        Tonight's our 5th anniversary
        And we're meeting today at that same café
        For Black coffee and Chai tea

Kelvin and Karl

August 12, 1996
2:48 a.m.

Wassup Baby!

It's almost three a.m. and I can't sleep. Again! I'm lying here in my bed, restless, wishing you were here next to me. Dayum, I miss you, baby! I don't know how I'm going to survive your being there and me being here. It's only been a couple of months but it feels like it's been much, much longer.

Besides that, even though we never actually lived together I always knew that you were just on the other side of town. Now your 4 hours by plane, 35 hours by car, and 123 days by foot (yea, I actually calculated it). Is it always going to be like this? Me wishing that you never left and you wishing I had come with you? This is really hard on a Brother!

Well, aside from missing you like crazy everything is o.k. I've been spending the time I'd be spending with you volunteering more time in the center and painting (finished two new pieces this week as a matter of fact!) other than that nothing special.

All right. Let me catch you up on things: Richard and Joe are still having problems but what else is new! Sheila and Terry said to tell you hello and not to forget Terry's birthday party next month. Greg met this Brother at Ryan's party a couple of weeks ago and hasn't been seen for weeks! Anthony's doing better - as well as can be expected. He's still in treatment but you know that crack shit had him bad! I drove up to see him this past Saturday at the facility. He looks good and seems to be doing all right but his fat ass must've gained about 20 pounds! Anyway, he's got about another two months left and then he's back home. All in all everybody's hanging in there.

Now I've gotten to the point of the letter that you've been waiting for. So let me answer the big question that I know is looming in your head: have I given any thought to moving there to be with you? You know I have. Of course I have. I think about it constantly, baby, more than I really want to admit. Day and night, night and day, I think about it. But as much as I do think about it I still have no answers. You don't know how much I wish I could tell you that I'm coming but I'm still not sure. Baby, I just don't know.

Let me say again that the fact that I'm still weighing this decision has nothing to do with the love I have for you. You should know that. You know how much I love you, man. You have to know. These past two years with you have been the best two years of my life and now that you're here I can't imagine it without you. It's just that moving there and giving up everything I have, everything familiar to me, to be there with you is a major decision. It's a life altering decision and there's so much more we have to consider.

I know I hurt you when I told you I wouldn't be coming with you but it hurt me too. It's just that your transfer couldn't have come at a worse time with my new promotion and all of the other things — friends, family, and commitments that keep me tied to this place.

We've talked about this before, baby but it's moving for a relationship that scares me the most. I've seen what can happen. I've watched Brothers do it all the time; giving up everything to be with another Brother only to have the relationship fall apart and having to start everything over again.

Baby, at 32, I feel like I'm too old to start all over again. I'm too old to find a new beginning. I love you, Kelvin but I'm wondering if love is enough. I know I promised you an answer by year's end and I promise that you'll have it. Just be patient with me, man. I just need a little more time.

I'll close now with sweet thought of you in my heart and my mind. Write back soon and let me know how things are going with you. I miss you, Kelvin, and I love you twice as much.

Love always,
Karl

August 16, 2003
3:14 a.m.

Ey, Baby!

It was soooo good to get your letter! I was missing you bad today man and feeling kind of lonely when I got home from work today. I miss you too, man! You just don't know how much. This bed is way too big and way too empty without you in it. I've been having trouble sleeping too. I wake up in the middle of the night and roll over hoping to put my arms around you only to feel the cold empty space. I just roll back over and try hard not to think about it too much until I drift back off to sleep.

It's not like on those nights when I could call you and ask you to come over or hop in my car at 3 in the morning and crawl up next to you. You know I never did like sleeping alone baby and now that you're not 20 minutes away anymore it's kickin' my ass! And I'm not even going to mention how horny I am! I tell you baby cold showers ain't going to do the job forever (smile)!

Listen baby, I know that this transfer came out of nowhere. It happened so quickly that we really didn't have a chance to think things through or work it out like we probably needed to. But it was an opportunity of a lifetime. It was hard for me to make this decision but I made it for the both of us. I did this because I knew it wouldn't just be good for me but for us. I was thinking about our future man because I want to spend the rest of my life with you. It's a lot for me to ask of you to move here with me but hell I'm selfish so what can I say? I love you and I want you here with me. Is that so wrong? I know your career is stable and that your job is important to you. I know that and I would never ask you to compromise anything for this relationship. You know I only want the best for you, Karl. It's all I ever wanted.

This decision wasn't easy for either of us. The hardest thing I've had to do at this point of my life was to leave the most important thing in my life - our relationship - You. But I know how independent you are and I knew that getting you here would be a long shot. You've always been your own man baby and that's what I love most about you. The discussions we had about you relocating with me reminded me of the discussions we had when I told you that it didn't make sense for both of us to pay separate rents when we spent as much time at each other's apartment as we spent at our own.

I remember clearly how you told me that a year in a relationship wasn't enough to move in together and I remember how you also told me that two years wasn't enough time to move in together. Having your space and your own life is important to you and I respect that. Now here we are about to celebrate almost three years together still loving as if we just met and what I think I'm hearing you say is that it still isn't enough. Baby, just when is enough going to be enough?

I was really happy for you when you got your promotion too. It was something that I knew you deserved a long time ago. And you're right my transfer and your promotion although tremendous blessings for the both of us couldn't have come at a worse time. But I still can't help but wonder if it would have made a difference or not.

Well, regardless baby, we find ourselves as close as two people can be but on opposite sides of the world. We probably still need more time but we'll have to come to some decisions before the end of the year. As much as I love you, Karl, and as much as I know you love me I just don't know how long our relationship can survive the strain of distance.

Let's promise to give this some serious thought baby and try to work it out. You know I'm committed to do whatever necessary. I love you, Karl, and I miss you like KRAZY!!!!

Love you, baby
Kelvin

p.s. The job is everything I expected and more! Challenging and nerve racking at the same time. You know, just like I like it (bigazzsmile). I fill you in later.
K.

August 22, 2003
2:21 a.m.

Dear Kelvin,

It's hot as hell in the city tonight. Right now I'm out on the fire escape, our favorite spot, listening to the sounds of the city. Just before I started to write this letter I wondered to myself what we would be doing tonight if you were still here. Would we be sitting out here sippin on some Hennessey in our boxers steeling kisses between the trains roaring by? Or would you be engaging me in long conversations about computer chips, CPUs, and memory cards? Better yet, would you trying to break my two-year winning streak in chess and make me play until sunrise? Naw, because if you were here we'd be back in my bedroom or on the living room floor in front of the fan making love against the sounds of Kitaro on the stereo! Dayum! My mind started racing so much that I had to go back inside and handle mine (you know what I mean).

I'm glad to know that this new position is working out for you. Sounds like you have quite a challenge on your hands. But I have faith that you'll dazzle them with your creativity and brilliance. If no one else in the world realizes it baby I know you're equal to the task. You're the smartest Black man I know and there's nothing in this world that you can't do. Keep giving them hell baby and if it gets to be too much just call me with some names and I'll come down and shake up a can of "whoop ass" on 'em!

Babe, I read your letter very carefully the other day when I got it. In fact, I read it three times. Something about the tone of it made me concentrate deeply on what you were saying. In one voice you seem to be saying that you understand where I'm coming from and in the next voice it seems you're trying to say something without really saying it. I know the strain of distance is taking a toll on the both of us baby and neither of us would have ever thought that we would be here in this place. But I can't take the full brunt of the decision about where we go from here.

One part of me knows that your taking this new position was for the both of us. For our future. The other part of me knows that this was something that you always wanted. You've always seen yourself standing at the very top of the corporate ladder. Baby, I know that this was a dream come true for you. I've supported you since the first time we met but I don't want you to turn this all on me. The fact is that you made this decision of your own free will and even if I did object or protest, which I never would have done, it wouldn't have really mattered. You had your heart set on this and I would never even as selfish as I am about you, ever consider giving you an ultimatum. I love you that much.

Kelvin, baby, you know how I am about things like this. You know how I hate to put myself out there. My independence over the years has been a result of not being able to ever depend on anyone for anything. You know how it was when my family found out about me and how hard I had to work to get through undergrad without any financial support from them or anyone. You know how difficult times were trying to finish school, feed myself, and just make it through another day. Everything I have I've worked hard to get and I can't afford to let that go. It's always been hard for me to depend on anyone because no one has ever been there before. All I've ever had was me. I've never had a safety net before. I'm trying hard to realize what I have with you. Baby, it's just hard.

Every time I think about moving to be with you I get overwhelmed. Moving there would mean living together, maybe even buying a house together, and we've never lived together before. I think of all of the Brothers we know who shacked up and broke up and it scares me. I don't want that for us. I don't know if I want to take that risk. Moving there would also mean giving up my position and looking for another job there. It may even mean that I would have to be unemployed for whatever length of time and baby you know that would drive me crazy. I've never been unemployed before and I've never lived off of anybody. And what happens if I did get a new job there and your job decides to move you again or my job decides to transfer me someplace? What happens then? You see, Kelvin, these are the kinds of things that run through my head man and sometimes I feel like I'm losing it.

Now on the real this distance is trippin me out too! Not only do I miss our conversations (read: arguments), your company, your smile, and your smell but it seems like my sex drive hit the roof when you left. Not that I took you for granted while you were here baby it's just that I knew you were here and nobody does me like you do. If I don't get my hands on you soon I'm going to explode!!!

We made a promise to remain monogamous and I've lived up to that promise. But it scares me to think that you're in a new city - the new face in the crowd (read: fresh meat) and I can't help but to think that the fellas are pushin up on you left and right. Shit, I know I would! Let's make a promise that before either of us start to lose control that we will discuss it first. Promise me that?

Well, I have to close now. Don't forget that I have a business trip to Philly coming up in a couple of weeks. Looks like I'll be there for about a week or so. I'll keep you posted. Well baby, I miss you but I love you twice as much!

I Love you, Baby
Karl

August 30, 2003
6:15 a.m.

Hey Man,

I've had the most amazing idea and I want you to hear me out. I also want you to think about this before you say, "*No*". O.k., here it goes: I know how much you love to paint and I also know how much you always wanted to devote yourself full time to seeing where it would take you. Well, I've been thinking. Arizona is beautiful man and I couldn't think of a more beautiful and inspirational place for you to paint. Don't you love it?

Man, look! You're so dayum talented! This could be the break you've been waiting for-the opportunity to practice your first love, painting, instead of wasting your talent in a mindless ad agency that could give a fuck about you! Now before you get ready to go to blows on me with this I'm not trying to down play the significance of your job or the fact that you're good at what you do. You, my love, are the best thing that ever happened to that fucked up place. What I'm saying is that this is the time, man. You can finally turn you hobby into your life's dream. This must be it. It's just got to be!

Now, look. I know you're thinking dollars now so check this out. With this new promotion I make enough to support us both until things take off for you like I know they will. And even if they don't, Karl, this is what you said you always wanted to do. Besides I know you got a stash you've been saving forever so it's not like you'll be completely dependent. You can pay yourself a salary and give it say a year or so to see what happens. And sometimes you have to rely on people to help give you a jump-start. Here I am baby! Your ticket to the big time!

I can't imagine what life must be like not realizing your dreams. You helped me to realize my mine. Now it's my turn to help you realize yours. Just think about it. Promise me and I promise you not to mention it again until you're ready to talk about it.

I love you,
Kelvin

P.S. Ain't nobody touching this body, baby. It belongs solely and exclusively to you. Only you!

September 22, 2003
7:44 a.m.

Kelvin –

Wow, man! I wish everybody believed in my art as much as you do! But I have to admit you really made me think. A full time artist, hmmm? "*The Kelvin Baker Gallery*"! Kinda has a ring to it, huh? I haven't thought about branching out on my own for a long time. I guess after a while you get used to a steady paycheck.

    I know a couple of people like my work but they're all friends of ours and I'm not sure if you've threatened or bribed them into buying my stuff. Don't get me wrong. I know I have talent but with no formal training I don't know if people would take me seriously or how successful I would be. Anyway, you're right about my stash. I have saved some money in my "*Just in case a Brother gets fired or tired*" fund that could keep me steady for a while. So money ain't the problem the real question is, "W*hat next?*"

    So I promise that I'll think about it. Gotta go baby. Don't want to be late for my plane. I'll talk to you from Philly.

Love Ya Baby,
Karl

P.S. I don't need Arizona to master my stroke…you are my greatest inspiration!

September 28, 2003
8:00 p.m.

Kelvin -

It was good seeing you in Philly this weekend, man! You have no idea! Thank you baby for that surprise. To open my hotel room door and see you standing there after the day I had was like, Dayum!!!!! You must have known that I was feelin' you in the worst way! I had been jonesing for you for weeks!!!! You're lucky my coworker was standing behind me or I would've tore your clothes off at the door!!! Seriously, baby thank you for that. I needed that man - mentally, physically, and spiritually I needed that (especially physically☺).

I'm glad that we could talk this weekend without one single argument or disagreements about the current state of you and me with this distance and everything. Thanks for not bringing that up. I didn't want to spend a single minute on that subject. Thanks for just giving us some time to enjoy each other.

It's funny, man, this weekend was just like old times. Just like it used to be. Holding you, kissing you, sleeping next to you, and your familiar scent in the room; your voice, your eyes, your lips, your skin (your lousy chess game – don't you know you will never beat me?). I even enjoyed your talking me to death about e-commerce after we made love. I tell you what baby you have sweetest pillow talk (not!). On the real, I loved every single second of it. Every single second!

Baby, seeing you this weekend not only reminded me just how much I love and miss you but how much I want to be with you. How much I *need* to be with you. It's funny how I never really recognized how free I am with you. I just feel safest when you're around me, safe and free; free to just let everything go and know that it's cool to. I always wanted to be in a place with somebody where I could just be me you know - to not have to pretend and just be. That's what you allow me baby. You have given me a safety net – a place to rest after all my battles (and there have been many). I feel like for the first time in my life somebody's got me and I have to say that it dayum sho feels good!!! Did I ever tell you how much I love you?

Well, I do and I love you enough to know that no matter what my decision I'm determined to make this work. My heart tells me, "*Yes!*" but my mind still tells me that there's too much risk involved. I'm still scared, baby. I'm scared as hell! I thought after seeing you this weekend it would make my decision easy but it just made it more confusing. There's a lot at stake. You know this. After all these years I'm starting to feel like my career is finally taking off and I'm positioning myself to do the things I always wanted to do. You know I never really saw myself doing this for the rest of my life. You know there are things I want to do outside of this neurotic world of corporate America. There's something else waiting for me and everything I need to do it is here. Everything except you.

Well, I'm not going to ramble on anymore. Just know that I'm still working on figuring this whole thing out. I know I'm running out of time but remember our agreement. I have until the first of the year to make up my mind right? O.k. then baby, I'm working on it. I really.

I love you and I miss you.
Karl

October 15, 2003
12:00 a.m.

Dear Karl,

Boy, if you could have seen the expression on your face when you opened the door and saw me standing there! I thought you were going to have a stroke or something! And I hate to tell you this but I think your coworker knows. How could she not after you jumped on me and kissed me the way you did?

I had a good time with you too, baby. I miss you so much and being with you only made me miss you more. I hated to leave you. I didn't want you to drive me to the airport that morning because saying good-bye is way too hard. It was hard when we were in the same city so you can imagine what it's like for me now. Karl, we just got to do something about this. I know it sounds like I'm pressuring you man but I'm really trying not to. I understand more than you would imagine that this isn't an easy thing to do.

I don't want to be selfish about this. Please don't think this has been easy for me either man. Don't you think I wonder about this all the time? Well, I do. But we can only have faith that we are going to work together. I only want you to see like I do just what we have here. We've built a beautiful relationship and I don't want to blow it. We just can't let fear in any form ruin us or keep us from being happy together.

You talked about the tone of one of my last few letters. About how I seem to be saying something without really saying it. I didn't want to bring this up in Philly because I didn't want to spent any time in an argument or debate either. Be assured that there was no hidden meaning in what I was saying to you. The last thing I would ever do is to give you an ultimatum.

But since I've been here man I've discovered so many new things. Arizona is a beautiful. So centering. It's like the center of the world and you know what? When the sun sets here it's like the world comes alive. All of the colors that you see in a crayon box suddenly dance like watercolors pasting themselves perfectly in the sky. All you can see is the shapes and shadows dancing onto the backdrop of the atmosphere. For a minute or two it seems like the whole world stands still while each color finds its place. Right there - right in that precise moment - its validation. I know this is where I belong.

But it's not just Arizona that I'm discovering baby. I'm discovering me. You can't help but do it here without the distraction of the city, the noise, the trains, the people, and the appointments. It's like I woke up and realized that there's a part of me I never knew existed.

I've discovered a side of my spirit that has calmed me and given me new direction. I'm learning how to trust it.

I know you're probably falling out of your chair right now because you know how I feel about religion and stuff like that but it's much more than that man. It's like I've evolved into this new awareness and found this incredible strength. It's a strength that tells me that things are not in my control or yours. It's a strength that's slowly melting away everything I've ever feared. I'm starting to accept that there's a divine plan for everything that happens. The only thing I'm trying to say, Karl, is that this new outlook has made me realize that whether we are together or apart, I'll be fine. We'll be fine. My tone in my last letter is only an indication of how I'm feeling and the consciousness that I'm discovering.

Don't read anything into it. There's nobody else. You know that. I love you and only you and I still want you here more than anything. But what I don't want is for you to move here out of sympathy or pity. I don't want you to move here because you're afraid of losing this relationship and I don't want you to move here because you know this is what *I* want. You have to want it, too. If you decide to move here I want you to do it because *you* want to. Your happiness and our peace are my only concern baby. I want us to both be o.k. with whatever happens.

But I have to say man that something tells me that this is the place for us – the place where we belong. Don't ask me how I know. I just know. I see us in a big house, the kind we always talked about having, on a hill with a southern exposure and a bedroom where we could wake up with the sun. Can you imagine how sexy that would be? We could make one of the rooms into a studio for you or we can build one on the property if you want to.

Tell you what: I want you to come out here next month and see for yourself what I'm talking about. You know it's our anniversary, number 3, and we can spend it here - maybe drive up to Tempe for the weekend and then you'll see what I mean. Besides, I've only got another 2 months left in corporate housing and I need to start looking for a permanent place to live. We can look for a house for us ☺…or an apartment for me☹. Let me know if you can arrange the time. I'll even spring for the ticket! Now that's an offer you can't refuse!

I love you, baby.
Please try to come. Please baby, please baby, please…
Kelvin

October 30, 2003
9:35 a.m.

Dear Kelvin,

Sorry it took so long for me to get back to you baby but things here have been real hectic and I can't seem to get a hold of my schedule. This new job is really kickin' my ass right now and I'm running from meeting to meeting from state to state to stay on top of it. Sometimes I swear they're trying to set me up for failure. And you know how it is. They assume that just because I'm not married (well…not in the legal sense) and have no children that I can take all of the shit assignments. Doesn't look like I'll be able to get there this month but I'll do everything I can to get there next month. Besides it's you I really want to see anyway and you're coming up for Terry's birthday, right? I promise I'll try to get down there one weekend next month. I promise baby.

Your description of Arizona makes it sound like a paradise on earth. I bet it's beautiful. I remember only passing through there years ago on a family vacation and being mesmerized by the sunset. That was the best part of that cross-country hell with my family in a camper and my urban cowboy father playing Charlie Pride the whole dayum trip! I would never put my children through that torture (that is if I ever have any).

I'll admit that I was a little freaked out by what you were saying about awakening your spirit. That's beautiful, Kelvin. I'm really happy that you've awakened that side of you. I know the issues you have with religion and stuff like that being a preacher's kid and all but I couldn't be happier that you're starting to realize the power of the Spirit. I always told you that there's a difference, a big difference, between religion and spirituality. This new found insight could only make you more beautiful and sexier and I'll be really scared of you then!

You know, Kelvin, I've had a couple of revelations over the past couple of weeks myself. For months I have been in turmoil about what to do and how to do it. Endless questions and drills with myself about whether I should leave or whether I should stay here? If I go what will happen? If I stay here what would happen? Is this the time that we should be going our separate ways or is the time where we should be together beginning a new chapter in what we already started?

I've been weighing the odds, counting the positives, stacking the negatives, and almost sick to my stomach when I don't get any answers. I don't want to keep you or me on hold forever. So last week I decided to do something I haven't done in a while. I decided that I should pray about this situation and about us.

Now you know that I've always been a praying man. It's what's kept me out of trouble in my life. But you want to hear something funny? I never prayed for anything for myself. It was always for somebody else; for you, for my family, for my friends but never for me. I never thought I could pray for anything for me because in some way I thought God wouldn't listen to the prayers of a man like me – a man who's in love with another man – especially if they were not for other people. But last night I had a long conversation with God and totally surrendered this decision. I've asked for divine intervention to see where it leads me.

It's a big relief not to have this weight on me anymore. Getting the monkey off of my back. Not that I'm just forgetting about it because I know that God helps those who helps themselves but like you I realized that everything that happens is predestined. We're just walking our natural paths. Where we'll be in the next several months or even the next several years has already been determined. So really, baby, it not our decision to make. We have to wait and see what happens. Where we'll be lead and what we'll be led to do only God can say. Isn't it amazing that we both ended up here at the same time? Do you think it's a sign?

I'll keep you posted about my schedule and about the date of the party. I can't wait to see you, man. I miss you but I love you more!

Yours truly,
Karl

November 7, 2003
10:00 p.m.

Dear Karl,

You're absolutely right! This is not our decision to make. It's all in God's hands. But I sure do hope that He's thinking the way I am!

We'll talk about it some more when I see you at the end of the month. Better than that what we'll do is pray together about it. But we won't pray about whether you should come or whether you should stay.

What we'll pray for is that we are both at peace with whatever the outcome. So this letter will be short since I won't have to try to con you into getting here. I'll just leave you with a big, "I love you!", and I'll see you in couple of weeks.

Love always,
Kelvin

November 14, 2003
5:00 a.m.

Wassup Baby!

Today I woke up with you on my mind – strong and heavy on my mind. Last night before I went to bed I prayed hard for peace and after all this time it came to me. It finally came. It was just crystal clear to me what I have to do. I tell you man prayer and surrender gives you everything you need. Finally, clarity!

I've realized that I spent most of my life planning and postponing. I'll do this when this happens or when I make a little more money I'll do this or that. But I never would do any of the things that I really wanted to do. It seems I was always waiting for life to begin at the start of some momentous occasion.

First it was school, then it was a job, then it was my own apartment, then it was a relationship and even with everything I have been blessed to have in my life, including you, it still seems like I've been waiting for something to jump-start me. It's almost like I've been living for a moment rather than living in it.

For years I wondered what kept me from being completely happy and from enjoying life to the fullest like everyone else seems to. Then I realized what it was. It was me, Kelvin. All along it was me. I've been my worst enemy because I never really trusted anybody especially myself. I mean, sure I know beyond a shadow of a doubt that I can take care of myself and I've done well in my career but I haven't been happy in it for years. I was too scared to do anything else, especially paint.

I was scared of being a success as much as I was afraid of being a failure. All this time I've been thinking, '*Who am I to be a brilliant artist? Who am I to be successful?*', when the real question should have been, '*Who *am I not to be brilliant? Who am I not to be successful?'* I've been sipping life through a teacup when I could have been drinking from a river.

Then I thought about you. About us and about all of the things you've shown me over the last couple of years. I thought about how you have been able to affect me in ways I never thought possible. I thought about allowing time, space, and distance destroy the one person who has been a constant in my life. The one person who has shown me love in its most pure context. I never knew this kind of love before, Kelvin, and I feel sorry for whom it never comes. In the overall scheme of things love is the only thing that matters. Love is always enough.

It's amazing how just a simple shift in your mindset and a whole lot of prayer can change your outlook. The instant I changed my mind about me it was like a light bulb went off in my head and the answer came. I want to paint, Kelvin. I've always wanted to paint. I believe it's my life's purpose and now I'm going to do it. I love you and I want to be with you. So, I'm coming, baby! I'm coming to Arizona. With you is where I belong and I'm not afraid anymore. So whether that's in Arizona, or New York, or Katmandu it doesn't matter. I know this now and I'm more certain than I've ever been before. I'm resigning in December and starting fresh in Arizona with my art and with my beloved. So baby, here we go! A new beginning. The beginning of the rest of our lives together!

In the meantime, I'm going to get the moving process started. I have a lot of planning to do. I don't know what I'm bringing or if I'm bringing anything at all except my artwork and supplies. I don't know whether to sell my stuff, hire movers, or rent a truck. So many decisions but I'll work it out. I guess I need to schedule a trip so we can go house hunting, huh? Well, if the offer still stands for you to spring for the ticket I'm all yours. Just let me know when's a good time and I'm there! I haven't told anybody yet. I wanted to break the news to you first before I start alerting the troops but I can already smell a bon voyage party in the air!

I love you, Kelvin, and I thank you from the bottom of my heart for everything but especially for loving and believing in me. I'll see you soon.

Love Always,
Karl

p.s. You know, the most beautiful part about life is not having a purpose…..but finding it.! Thank you for helping me see that. I love you.

November 20, 2003
7:15 a.m.

Karl,

My sweet, sweet, baby. You have made me the happiest man alive!

Hell yea, I'm springing for the ticket! I'll make the arrangements and call you with the flight schedule in a day or two. I'll call a realtor too and have some appointments set up so we can find OUR house.

I love you, man and I have faith that we're doing the right thing. I can't wait to see you.

All my love,
Kelvin

p.s. If there's gonna be a party, you know I'm in there! If you decide to keep your stuff we'll rent a U-Haul and drive cross-country. You and me on the road? Hmmmmmmm!!!!!!!

p.p.s. I love you, I love you, I love you!!!!!!!!!!
K.

Be Still

What is it that you need
What is it you're looking for?

What's become your passion
Exactly what is your quest
To find love and validation
To help you become your best?

    Well, did you really think you'd find it
    In the places you've been
    The countless beds you've slept in
    The nameless, faceless men?

        In dark rooms with naked strangers
        Pawing at your gifts
        Taking turns with your body
        Like the changing of a shift?

            Or in a relationship you're glued to
            With a lying, cheating man
            Molding your insecurities
            Like footprints in the sand?

                Or did you think you'd find it
                In his strong Black arms
                Between his strong Black legs
                Or in his masculine Black charms?

Did you think it would be swimming
In the bottom of an empty glass
Drowning pains, sorrows, and unresolved wounds
Grounded in your past?

Was it in the pills you popped, the weed you smoked
Or the purple haze of trips
Puff, puff passin the blunt
Withering from your lips?

Could it be you thought it was hiding
Behind protein shakes and pumpin weights
In skin you never really loved
And Blackness you were taught to hate?

Or maybe you thought you'd find it
On 900 thread count sheets
In a penthouse overlooking the city
Or in a corner office suite?

Well…
No matter where you were searching
No matter where you've been
The true search for love
Always starts within

Be still

Beginnings

When the dawn begins to break
the sun starts to rise
and the moon makes way for the sun
a new day is born
of promise
and hope
because of what your love has done

You see
I never really noticed
how beautiful life really is
how special each moment can be
not the chirp of a bird
the scent of a rose
or the curvatures in a tree

It wasn't until I first met you
that my world took shape to expand
you made me see
the beauty in the oceans
and feel the softness in the sand

I was blind to the puff
of the cumulous cloud
resting high against a clear blue sky
and the magnificence of leaves
changing colors in the fall
somehow always escaped my eye

But with you now I can hear
the laughter of children
playing carefree in the park
and the rhythmic sounds
of the cricket's cry
against its loneliness in the dark

No more do I take for granted
God's gentle breath
In the form of the morning breeze
nor does the majesty of the setting sun
longer pass my mind with ease

You've awakened my senses to season's change
and the scent of spring's first bloom
your touch stimulates sights and sounds
and excites me in rainfall's gloom

Neither the brilliance of stars
moonlight's glow
nor the serenity of stillness in the night
escapes me now since we fell in love
I've climbed the highest heights

You've made life worth living
My love
by shining your love my way
I've basked in its glow
and welcomed the light
it brings each and every day

You are so much more than my lover
you are my very best friend
the first to encourage
my hopes and dream
and the very last to
condemn

I look forward to the rest of my life
with you
and new experiences to begin
but mostly
what I want you to know
my sweet baby
is

I'd do it over and over again!

Fantasy

In My Fantasy
We are free to love

He holds my hand as we walk
And my waist when we stand still
I call him in the middle of the day
Just because

We plan vacations
The two of us
Exotic destinations
Lover's holidays
Leaving the stress of our lives
To toil among the neurosis of miles left behind

Long baths
Long slumbers
And longer conversations
Lost in the pleasures of our souls
Where lovemaking makes love
Deepening communication and
Commitment

I hear him laugh and smile
A brilliant smile
As he suddenly changes face
To kiss me passionately…on my lips

Blessed to have found me says he
Loves me says he
As he pulls me close

We laugh and talk
Nights into mornings of
Safeguarding intimate secrets
Keeping us at the forefront
Of mindful thinking
Ours a holy union

...And I'm loving me loving him

What Would They Say

What would They Say
If They Knew

That You And I Are Lovers
Sharing More Than Just This Apartment

What Would They Say
Our Family
Who Think We're Just Roommates
Who Think We're Best Friends

What Would They Say
Your Co-Workers and Mine
You're Straight Friends and Mine
Who Think We're Cousins
On Our Father's Side

What Would They Say If They Knew
That We Know Every Intimate Detail,
Every Secret
Every Inch
Of Mind, Soul, and Body

That We Love Each Other
In Ways Thought Unacceptable

What Would They Say
If They Knew

Or
Do They?

Dear Diary

August 1993

Dear Diary,

I'm sitting here in the dark in my dorm; my first night on campus. It's quiet and dark. And hot! I don't think I ever remember being this hot before! It must be 100 degrees outside and 120 in here. But still I'm glad to be here. I'm blessed to be. This I know. I'm a college man now. It's official. I'm an adult.

My roommate hasn't gotten here yet but it's still two days before orientation so I suspect he'll be here sometime tomorrow night. He's an upperclassman I found out today - a sophomore this year - so he doesn't have to be in the meeting tomorrow. It's just for incoming freshman of the swim team. I wonder what he's going to be like. It doesn't really matter. I just hope we get along. I'm a little nervous about it. A whole year living with somebody I don't know is nerve racking. Well, if nothing else at least we have the swim team in common so it shouldn't be that bad.

It's so quiet here tonight. I thought it would be noisy and unruly. Maybe that's how it is over in the freshman dorms on the other side of campus. But here in the athletic dorm it's almost spooky quiet. I know everybody hasn't gotten here yet but this afternoon when I arrived I saw a whole lot of people. It was so busy; cars with license plates from all over, U-Haul truck, and vans.

There were a lot of mothers crying and a whole lot of proud fathers, uncles, and grandfathers carrying suitcases, boxes, computers, refrigerators, and all kinds of other stuff. Some of the Brothers looked happy, some nervous, and some not so happy. Maybe like me this is their first time living away from home.

But I'm way too excited to be unhappy or nervous about being on my own! I waited for this all my life it seems; independence and a college experience and so had my mom. She worked hard to get me here. Real hard! Sacrificed a lot. I know she wanted to be here with me today to settle me, and make sure I was o.k. but we just couldn't afford it. Besides she knows I can handle myself. I'm not a baby anymore or needy like these other Brothers seem to be. I've been the man of the family since I was eight. She knows I'll be alright.

Mom cried all the way to the airport. I imagine she was crying for a whole lot of reasons; crying because she couldn't be here or that my father showed no interest in being here. Hell, he hadn't shown interest in any of us since the divorce ten years ago. It's not easy for her to see me go - to let me go.

She cries for me and she cries for her. Her tears were mixed with a lot of stuff of what was and what could have been. It was tough on us when he left but we made do. Always plenty to eat, warm winters, and cool summers. My part-time job helped too. I had enough money to buy a used car to get back and forth to school, buy my own clothes and even some for my little brother. Still I wonder how different it would have been had they stayed together or if he had at least helped out. My mom worked hard, too hard, to keep the house and keep us together. She worked too hard and too much. No time to rest her feet.

Anyway, I'll help her more once I finish school. I'll definitely help. Take her off her feet - rest them - to thank her for all of her sacrifices. Well, at least I took the burden of college off of her even though I wish I could have done more. I did alright getting this scholarship to swim so she doesn't have tuition to worry about and I'll get a part-time job to help with the rest. I worked hard all my life. I'm not afraid of that. And now I'm going to work harder.

Oh well, I'm going to try to sleep. Between the heat and my tears I don't know how I will. And I have to admit that I'm feeling a little lonely…and strange. Kind of unsure but sure, happy but sad, angry but not angry, and the truth is I really do miss my dad. I never realized it until today. I miss him. Seeing all those fathers with their sons this afternoon reminded me. It hurts.

But I'll never admit that to anyone. Not anyone! All the anger and hurt I feel I'll use for all my goodness and he'll see one day the mistake he made not being a part of my life. He'll see just what he's missed out on. In the meantime though I thank God for getting me here, for keeping me out of trouble and for keeping me focused. Thank you, God, for everything!

Cedrick

September 1993

Dear Diary,

Well everything's going o.k. I'm getting used to college life and being independent. Classes have started and I have a heavy load but not too heavy where I'm worried about it or nothing. I got this covered and in four years I'll be out of here and in eight years I'll be a doctor if I stay focused.

I'm keeping focus too. I'm not letting anything take me away from that. I'm on a mission. A serious one and I've got a lot of responsibilities weighing on my shoulder. Everybody's depending on me. Some know it and some don't. But I know they are.

Mom's doing o.k. though she misses me. I can hear it in her voice. We talk once a week or so. I don't want to run up her phone bill. She's still working hard and getting used to the idea of me being 1500 miles away but she sounds good - sounds strong. She's always been. My brother's doing all right too. He misses me too. He won't say it but I know he does. It was hard to leave him too but it's all for the best. It'll all work out in the end if it works out in the beginning and now's the beginning!

But so far so good! My roommate is cool as hell and we vibe like we've known each other all our lives. His name is Kahlil. From California somewhere in the hills outside of LA. He swims the third leg on the relay team and he's just as focused as I am on school and swimming so we've been getting along good. He says now that since they've recruited me it looks like we'll have a championship team this year. He also said the whole team had been watching my high school career and begged the coach to recruit me. I was amazed. People were watching and wanting me when I thought nobody could see me except my mom of course. Anyway, he's as confident in me as the coach and the rest of the team is. They've all been cool helping me get adjusted to collegiate competition. They've been real cool!

I know I won't disappoint them. I'm confident too. After all the anchor leg on the relay team is my specialty. I broke all kinds of records, even college ones, with my speed in 100-meter free style and on the relay team. Nobody can catch me once I get in the water. The water is my freedom and my jail if that makes any sense. It's like when I'm in the water I'm swimming to live, to break free, and every stroke and every breath I take feels like it could be the last one. My heart pounds like it's going to explode out of my chest and I pull harder and harder to get to safety. I swim fast to keep from drowning; drowning in disappointments and anger, and sadness. I swim to survive. But nobody knows that nor do they need to. It's my best weapon when I'm in the middle of competition.

Anyway, we'll dominate in those events and we're putting a lot of work into preparing now. In fact, we've been here almost two months and I haven't even seen the pool yet, except when they gave us a tour of the campus. Right now it's all about conditioning; running and lifting weights before we hit the water. Coach says we have to be in the best condition we can be - expanding our lungs, increasing our endurance, muscle strength, and stretch. And he's right. A half-inch stretch to the finish line can make all the difference in a meet - the difference between first and second place. I'm all right with that - at least for now - but I'm ready to hit the water. I'm ready to break free.

Kahlil's ready too. We talk about it all the time. Since he swims the third leg he and I will have to get our timing down to a science! Once we get in the water man look out! Until then we just talk finding a rhythm on morning jogs with the rest of the team and we talk about it more during the weight sessions in the afternoons after classes.

We're determined not to be second anything Kahlil and me! We're becoming real good friends. We have a lot in common. We hang out all the time even outside of practice so he's a perfect roommate. I'm glad too because I was worried at first. But only after a couple days it was all-good. He's easy to get along with and living with him ain't as hard as I thought it would be. He's a little sloppy but not in a dirty kind of way. Just unorganized. Like he'll step out of his gear and leave them right on the floor where he steps out of them. His clothes are thrown everywhere around the room. But it's cool. When you've picked up after a little brother all your life you get used to it. So I don't mind it. I just pile it all in a corner - his corner - of the room and look right past it like it ain't even there.

He has a girlfriend, Monica. She's cool as hell too! A real southern belle kind of girl - dignified and beautiful. They've been together since freshman year - two years now and I can tell she loves him. He worships the ground she walks on! She's smart too. Studying engineering. And man is she dedicated! Dedicated to her studies, her family, and her friends. She's completely dedicated to Kahlil too. I think it's her dedication that helps keep him focused. It's rubbing off on me I can tell.

We're all cool and hang out all the time I mean between practices and studies but we even do that together although we're all majoring in different things. It helps. We're like a family. She's always bringing one of her girlfriends around trying to get me hooked up. But I'm not ready to settle down just yet. I'm really trying to keep my focus and not trying to get all twisted up in the love game like I did in high school. I got hurt one time - in my junior year - but no more. This one friend though, Cynthia, is real cool and we've feeling each other. We've been hanging out, the four of us, and it's cool. She's nice - a good girl from a good family and ain't interested in no boyfriend-girlfriend situation either. So that works well. No stings, no pressure. Just the way I need it.

Cedrick

October 1993

Dear Diary,

Well, after all these weeks we're finally in the water practicing. I'm back in the pool and feeling alive again! We've got a meet in a couple of weeks – a preliminary competition that really doesn't count for anything but I'm a little nervous nonetheless. Kahlil tells me not to be. Says I have nothing to worry about. He thinks the relay team with me as an anchor is the best this school's ever had. We'll see.

But just to be sure we've been spending time in the pool after practice trying to shave off a few seconds off our time. We're finding that rhythm that we always talk about and already we've shaved off about two seconds from our best time. He thinks if we keep it up we can break the collegiate record. Practices are long as it is but he keeps on pushing. Sometimes we're in the pool until midnight or later depending on what time I get there after work. I've picked up a part-time job cleaning office buildings downtown in the evenings. He thinks I work too hard but I need the money. Its shit work but it pays. Books and other stuff are expensive - sure gives you an appreciation for free books when you're in high school but I've been buying everything myself. Mom can't send money though she tries to. I tell her to keep her money and do something for herself. I'm doing o.k. Besides I don't need much.

Kahlil tries to give me money all the time. I've had to borrow some on occasion but I always pay him back. He says I don't have to but I don't feel right taking his money. I mean I know we're friends and all and he gets a lot of money from his parents but it's his money not mine. And like I said I don't need much. He gets upset when I pay him back always saying we're friends and that's what friends do for each other. I know he's right but I don't want him to feel like I'm taking advantage of him because I'm really not. I'm independent and want to pay my own way. I think its good discipline for me. It'll pay off in the future.

He's real kind hearted. I mean he really is. He's even asked me to come to California with him for Thanksgiving next month since I'm not going home. He said his mom and step dad will pay for the ticket. I told him I'd think about it but I really need to work during the break. Next semester is almost here and that means more dollars for more books. But I am thinking about taking him up on his offer. I've never been to California and always wanted to go. We'll see. I know he really wants me to go. For some reason he doesn't want to be there by himself.

I think it's because he doesn't get along with his step-dad. His mom married him a couple of years after his father died. He told me one night while we were talking that he never got along with him. I don't know why. He seems nice enough to me. But then again I only met him briefly when they came up to bring him to school. They only stayed a couple of hours though. Long enough to unpack the rental car and head back to the airport. They were off to New York to catch a flight overseas.

Kahlil says they travel all the time like that. Always calling him from some part of the world. I think he feels like they don't really want him around. Like they use their money - and they have plenty of it - to love him and control him at the same time. He seemed so sad when he was telling me this - sad like crying sad. I could hear him trying to fight off the tears in the darkness.

He doesn't like to talk about it either. Kind of like me not liking to talk about my father. He says he's never talked to Monica about it either. Says she comes from a perfect family. Her mother and father are real close to her and her sisters and she'd never be able to relate. But I think he trusts me because we have that in common. He said he misses that family thing like he had when his real father was alive. I told him that I do too although my father's alive. I guess it's a lot different for him since he's an only child and doesn't have any relatives to speak of.

But it's cool. We're supporting each other and we've made a promise that we'll always be best friends no matter what. We laugh and talk at night when the lights are out and the room is dark. We talk about finishing school, marrying Monica and Cynthia, having children and living next door to each other. It all sounds real cool until I start thinking about all the responsibilities I have once I finish med school then marriage and children seem a long way away. I never tell him that though. I don't want to disappoint him.

A couple of days ago we were sitting on the floor eating apples and talking about nothing in particular when his mom called and said they weren't going to be in California for thanksgiving. His step dad has business he has to attend to in London. He owns his own company so there was nothing he could do. Business first is his philosophy. Kahlil was disappointed but not in a mad way. I think he was kind of expecting something would happen but I also think he was expecting them to tell him to come to London instead. But they didn't invite him.

He was real sad when he hung up the phone. I told him not to worry about it. We could spend Thanksgiving at school and use the time to practice and catch up on some studying. Besides the coach invited those of us on the swim team who aren't going home to have dinner with him and his family. I told him it was going to be cool and not to worry. It seemed to make him feel a little better but he's got something inside of him that hurts so deep.

After that, while we were sitting on the floor he kind of broke down. He was talking about everything that was bothering him about him mom and step-dad; how much he missed his real father and about how much he was hurting. He started crying but didn't want me to see until they just broke away from him and he let it all out. I grabbed him and held onto him telling him that it was cool to let it out; to just let it go. He had his head on my shoulder and we hugged each other. I felt so bad for him. I wished I could erase all the pain he was feeling. He's such a cool Brother that it hurts me to see him hurt. I walked him over to his bed after a while - after he calmed down - and told him to lay down. I sat on the edge of his bed patting his shoulders until he drifted off to sleep. He's most at peace with everything when he sleeps.

The next morning he was up early. He'd gone to the cafeteria and grabbed up some breakfast. We gripped and hugged, and he thanked me for listening. He kept apologizing for breaking down. I told him not to. I didn't mind it. In fact, I was glad in a way he got it out. I always knew something was bothering him but I didn't know how to get him to talk about it. I told him that it was our secret and that this room we lived in was our safe haven. The place where we'll get our lives right. The place where the future begins. No need for bad feelings or regrets. I think he's feeling better now.

Cedrick

December 1993

Dear Diary,

We had a good time over Thanksgiving. We went to Coach's house for dinner (which was slammin!) and spent the weekend working out, running, and swimming. I don't know but ever since that night Kahlil seems freer and we're even closer than before. We're still studying hard, swimming hard, and dating hard. The girls are cool too. We're all still having a good time. We went to a party the other night together. Coach had given us the day off from practice since we killed everybody in our last meet so we didn't have curfew or have to worry about getting up the next morning.

We went to Kahlil's frat party and it was off the chain! We drank, danced, and hung out all night long. I haven't had fun like that in a long time! I think he wants me to join his frat although he's not pushing me and even though half the team is in it. So I'm thinking about it. I've been invited to a lot of frat parties lately but he tells me not to go to too many. He says that if I do it will give an appearance that I'm checking each one out - which I would be doing - but he says that's not cool to do. He says I should show interest but not show interest. I don't know what that means exactly but I'll follow his lead. I trust him.

Grades were posted a couple of days ago and we aced all our classes. But we put a lot of studying into the semester and into finals that just about wore all our asses out! We all made Dean's list. All of us! Me, Kahlil, Monica and Cynthia, and have been celebrating ever since. We've got a couple of days left before we leave for Christmas vacation and I'm excited about going home. I miss my mom and my brother. Besides, I could use the rest. I'm worn out.

Monica and Cynthia left this afternoon and Kahlil and I leave the day after tomorrow. He's headed to California although he doesn't seem so excited. He says it's because Christmas in California with his family is fake - more like obligation than anything else. He wishes he could come with me and of course I invited him to come. But he has to be home for Christmas. He's got to be at His step dad's company party and all the other parties they get invited to. He's got to smile and charm, and act like they're the perfect family when they're really not. I feel bad for him.

I keep reminding him that it's only for a couple of weeks. The swim team has to get back two weeks earlier than anybody else on campus because of our meets in January. I told him to hang in there. He said he would and then reminded me that this is the first time since we got to school that we're going to be separated. I never really thought about it that way until he said it. But he was right and after I started thinking about it I started to really feel bad. I was going to miss him. I really was and told him so. I knew he was going to miss me too. He said so.

We took the train to the airport this morning, gripped and hugged, and said our good-byes with promises to call. I'm hoping he'll survive it without having a breakdown. I'm hoping he'll deal with it and come back o.k. I'm praying that he will.

Cedrick

January 1994

Dear Diary;

Well, the holidays are over and we're back in the water. Kahlil managed somehow to survive and I had the time of my life with my family. It was so good to see them. We didn't do much of anything except eat. I visited a couple of friends from high school but other than that I didn't hang out that much. Most of my other time was spent sleeping. I didn't run, swim, or lift one single weight! I needed to be lazy for a while and my mom let me. She's very proud of me and I'm glad I can make her happy.

I talked to Kahlil most of the break, every day, sometimes three times a day. He was dealing with the family as best he could but I know our conversations kept his mind off of being at home. He said he was swimming every day and still working out (which is easy to do when you have a pool in the back yard and a gym in the basement) and was running in the evenings. He laughed when I told him I hadn't done shit but sleep and eat.

I hadn't really talked to Cynthia at all but we don't do a whole lot of the phone stuff anyway. He hadn't really talked to Monica much either but he didn't seemed to be stressing over it. I think they're so grounded in their relationship they just trust each other. Anyway before I knew it, it was time for us to go back to school. I don't know where the time went but I was so glad to see him.

We got right to work as soon as we got back. We had already pre-registered so all we needed to do was buy books and stuff like that. In the pool we picked up right where we left off. Surprisingly, I hadn't lost any of my time like Kahlil thought I would from being so lazy. In fact I shaved off a second on the 100-meter freestyle and the relay well we just tore that up. We won our 6th consecutive meet and now half the conference is in fear. We're unstoppable and undefeated so far and doesn't look like we'll have much competition left on the schedule. Regionals are coming up soon so we're preparing to whoop ass! We're going for records at the regional meets. We're taking no prisoner!

I have to say though between school, work, and practice, I'm really starting to feel it. I mean my classes are getting a little harder now and I know Kahlil and the girls feel it too. We don't study as much together as we used to because everybody's always being split up into study groups with people from our own classes. But we still make time to hang out in between.

Kahlil and Monica are still hanging in there although something seems to be troubling both of them. I don't think they're as close as they used to be. They're starting to seem more like brother and sister rather than boyfriend and girlfriend. I don't know why but it just seems that way. I mean they're still close and have a good time together but things are changing. I think we all feel it. Cynthia and I are still cool but even we don't hang out as often as we used to either.

A lot of people said that it would happen eventually - that there'd come a time when all of your relationships change in college and you'll see them for what they really are. Not in a bad way but in a good way. All of our changes are good; good for all of us so we're not panicking. It's just life is evolving and we're a part of that evolution I suppose. Anyway, whatever happens we're all friends and I have a strong feeling that we'll be that way for the rest of our lives.

Cedrick

March 1994

Dear Dairy;

From regional champs, to State champs, straight to the National Championships! We did it and we did it breaking records in the process!

All the hard work paid off and we walked away undefeated. This has been a dream come true! We medaled in every single category and swept the gold at the national championships. Man! the whole school showed up to cheer us on and we didn't disappoint. The 100-meter freestyle was the easiest. I broke the record like Kahlil expected I would and he was so siked! It's like he's my biggest supporter outside of my mom. I have to admit I kicked ass in it!

I was still nervous going into the relay but Kahlil calmed me down right away. He said to keep my focus on getting back to the podium. We gripped and hugged like we always do and agreed we would win and break records. It was all we could think about. It all started our just like we planned but somehow our second leg got behind by a couple of seconds and we looked like we lost our momentum. By the time Kahlil got into the water we were almost five seconds behind. But he was killing it. I mean the Brother was working hard! I don't think I ever saw him swim so fast. On the final turn we were only two seconds behind but as much as he was pulling past the water he couldn't catch up. We were cheering and hollering like mad! About half way to me he looked at the clock and on the next stroke he looked up at me and in that one second – in that one glance – he told me that it was all up to me. His eyes said it. They said he was depending on me to pull this off - that he was depending on me period! I gladly took the responsibility off his shoulders and put them onto mine.

When he touched the podium it was like he was touching me and I stretched into the water like a wave finding its way back to sea. When I hit the water I could feel myself joined with it - in perfect syncopation with it and every single stoke blended into the rhythm of it. Every breath after every other stroke was life breathing into me. I kept my form and kept my focus not on the time or the other lanes but on his voice. Kahlil's voice. I could hear him calling to me even through the cheers and screams from the team and the crowd. I could hear his voice encouraging me like he had done so many night before in the pool practicing for just this kind of scenario.

He kept calling to me and I kept listening for him - hearing him - trying to get back to him. When I made the final turn and felt the rush of the water push me forward I felt like there was nothing or no one around but Kahlil and me. I could still hear him calling to me - calling me to him - and I sliced the water faster and more precise.

I looked up midway to see him standing there aside the podium waving to me, smiling, cheering, and glad. On the next stroke I met his eyes and we locked in almost the same moment as when he was in the water and before I knew it I was there with him. All I heard was bells and whistles and cheers. I looked up into his eyes for a sign and he gave it to me.

He smiled and nodded his head, "We won. We did it. We broke the record!" he said as he knelt down to help me out of the water. He grabbed me and hugged me as the rest of the team ran over to us to hug in celebration. We did it. We won! The team and me and him. We won! We celebrated for days after that! The school had a parade and an award ceremony and the whole city was on us for interviews and appearances and other stuff. We met the mayor who declared an official day in the city for the team.

They called me and Kahlil the "Dynamic Duo" and we're starting to believe it. But it hasn't gone to our heads. We put a lot of hard work into training and finding our rhythm. And I know our friendship helps that out. We're best friends without a doubt and we love each other. We look out for each other and push each other to be our best and over the last year since we've been friends we've come to depend on each other for everything. I know I'm blessed to have him in my life and just thankful that he's here. He fills many voids for me. The places where I used to miss my father I don't miss anymore and the places where he always wanted to have a brother has been filled. We're as thick as thieves!

We've got exams coming up in the next couple of weeks and we're trying to decide what to do for the summer. Coach has been getting a lot of interest letters about us possibly training for the Olympic team.

We're both siked about that. That would be off the hinges if that could happen! But we're not thinking about that too hard. Right now we've got to make it through finals and see if we can figure out our next steps. Whatever it is though we want to do it together. We're a package deal. We tell everybody that.

Cedrick

May 1994

Dear Diary!

Finals are over and we're free for the summer. My first year of college was everything I expected and more. I had an unbelievable time. My grades are through the roof I've broken all kinds of records my freshman year and I have a best friend I can share this all with. I don't know what I've done to please God but whatever it is I want to keep right on doing it!

Kahlil blew up the spot too! Things couldn't be better. Monica and Cynthia are still hanging in there strong though it's pretty official that Monica and Kahlil aren't dating anymore. They made that official right after nationals. Everybody's life is getting hectic and we're finding no more time for dating and stuff like that. They'll be plenty of time for that later on in life. Right now we all have to stay focused.

Monica and Cynthia are headed to Paris for the summer in an exchange program and Kahlil and I are headed to swim camp. We won a scholarship sponsored by the U.S. Olympic committee. It's a hook up deal too plus there'll be money left over to pay for school next year. All of it! So goodbye to cleaning offices! I can relax and be just a regular student now. We had coach and the schools lawyer look at it before we committed to taking it. We wanted to make sure it was just a scholarship and it is. It doesn't lock us into any obligations to try out for the Olympics but does give us first priority option at the trials if we decide to do it.

I'm really looking forward to camp because it's in California! Another dream come true. Two months in LA! Kahlil is even excited. I tease him about it because this is the first time he's gotten excited about going to California. But he says it's different because we'll be staying in dorms at the facility and he doesn't have to go home except on weekends if we want to. It'll be cool because there'll be swimmers from all over the country - some we already know from meet but I'm sure there'll be new people too. Besides, he says, we're rooming together so we get to spend the entire summer together with the exception of the two weeks we have before we have to report. I'm going to see my mom and he's headed to Cali. I agreed to come a week early to hang out with him so he can take me around. His parents will be there so I'll have a chance to spend some time with them too.

I feel like I'm on my way. I've managed to do everything right. I kept my focus and my cool and it all worked out for the best. One year down and three to go. I feel like me and my best friend are going to conquer the world!

Cedrick

July 1994

Dear Diary,

I've been in Cali for almost two months now and feel like I was born to be here. It's so beautiful like I never imagined. I got here a week before swim camp began and been rolling non-stop since my feet hit the pavement. Kahlil was at the airport to meet me and we went straight to his house to get me settled.

His house is amazing! I don't think I've ever seen anything that big before. I mean you could fit 5 big houses into it. I can't tell you how many bedrooms it has just say a whole lot and seems like every door I open is a bathroom. His mom's decorated it nice too with stuff from all over the world; places they've traveled to I'm sure. But it's not cluttered or anything. It's very nice. What impressed me most was the outside. I mean they have a tennis court, basketball court, and a big ass swimming pool - about as big as the one at school. This is a whole lot of house for three people; well two when Kahlil's at school.

Anyway, his parents have been real nice to me. I think they're glad he brought a friend home so they don't have to feel like they have to entertain him. I can tell there's distance between them. In fact sometimes they act like total strangers - like they don't know each other at all. I feel bad for Kahlil. You can tell he wants to be closer but they seem to like things the way they are. But like I said they're nice to me and made me feel very welcomed. They didn't stay all week though. In fact they left two nights after I got there. They've got business somewhere. I don't know where and I didn't ask. But Kahlil had plans for us to explored Cali.

When I first got there his parents told me I could sleep in any room in the house but we're used to staying in the same room so I'm roomed with him. We're too used to each other to be separated like that and anyway his room is about the size of my mom's living room or bigger with a balcony and a big ass bathroom with a sunken tub. I was like dayum! And to be honest the house was way too big for me to be on the other end of it. We were cool sleeping the same room in the same bed. I mean the bed was so big - bigger than king size - if that's possible. It's like we were in our dorm sleeping in twin beds anyway. We'd spent a couple of weekends there between camp working out in the gym, sitting out by the pool, and talking. We did lots of talking especially at night when the lights are out and it's dark.

Camp is cool as hell! We met some cool as people and learned a lot from the coaches, some of the best in the world and some former Olympic swimmers. We were like celebrities when we got there too!

Everybody wanted to see who we were, the Dynamic Duo, and wanted to know what we did to train. Some of the younger cats followed us everywhere we went and took notes every time we got into the water. But we shared what we did to train. I mean it's not like we did anything special except practice hard dedicated ourselves to practices and conditioning and found our rhythm. I didn't share with them that when I make my final lap in competition I search out Kahlil - his eyes and his voice - to bring me home. They don't need to know that our spirits are connected in ways we don't know or understand and I couldn't possibly explain it. Besides, some things you keep to yourself.

Anyway, we leave the day after tomorrow to report back to school. We're taking back what we learned here and sharing it with the rest of the team so we can prepare. We've got a tough schedule coming up this year. A real tough one and because we're the national champs you can best believe there're people trying their best to get us! They've been training all summer and out to make our last season seem like a fluke. But we're not worried. We know we've got one advantage. We've found our rhythm, me and Kahlil, and nothing can stop us. Not nothing!

Cedrick

September 1994

Dear Diary,

We're back on campus. It's been about three weeks now and we're back in our groove. The team is all hyped for this season of meets and me and Kahlil have been named co-captains of the team. We haven't seen the pool yet as usual because we've been busy conditioning; running, lifting, weights, and stretching. Coach is proud of us but hasn't let up. You'd think we lost every single meet last season instead of being national champs. He keeps telling us that the past is the past and we have to look ahead. I hear him! I feel the same way. We've got a lot of work to do. The team believes it and we're all in sync - like a well-oiled machine. Even the freshman came in and got into the groove. I think that has a lot to do with Kahlil. He's good at motivating the team and they all respect him.

I didn't spend as much time with my mom as I would like to this summer but she understood. We still talk once a week and I still miss her but things are getting so much better for her. She's even met a nice man she's dating now and I'm happy for her. She deserves somebody nice in her life and he's real good to her. I like him. I had a chance to meet him last time I was there and kind of told him in so many words that if he even thinks about hurting my mom I'd kill him! I think he got my message. My younger brother is behaving and doing his thing in school playing football this year and focused like I am. I'm proud of him.

Classes this year seemed to get tougher. I'm glad I don't have to work because I don't know how I'd survive it. Kahlil's got a heavy load too and always has a paper due or something. I've been helping him as much as I can with them but he keeps telling me he has it all under control. We see the girls from time to time on campus and at other school events. They're still doing their thing and had a good time studying in Paris. Monica is dating a brother on the basketball team and Cynthia, well, Cynthia's always going to be Cynthia. She's not trying to let anybody lock her down. I tell her she's a player. She agrees.

We're back in our same room this year and because we're captains we had our choice. We both thought it would be bad luck to move or to change anything so we decided to stay put in our same room. He's still sloppy and I'm still picking up after him but we're so tight now it doesn't matter. I mean we're so tight that I can tell what he's thinking or what he's feeling without us saying a word. He still has his moments when his mother or father calls and cancels their plans to visit or get together but I keep him diverted from that.

In fact, I invited him to come with me to my mom's for Thanksgiving and he said he was coming. His parents didn't even object. They just said that they would take a vacation somewhere since he wasn't coming home. He didn't care too much this time because he knew he was going to be with me. I can't wait for him to meet my mom. She's going to love him.

Our first meet is in a couple of weeks so we're trying to stay focused. Our new goal is to break our old record so we got our work cut out for us. But again he tells me not to worry and I don't. I find it so easy to relax when he tells me to and I seem to have the same effect on him. I mean we get into it sometimes - we always have disagreements - but nothing serious. We never really get mad at each other. We always try to find the best way to do things that work for us and for everyone on the team we're responsible for.

We're connected and getting more and more connected as time goes by. It's strange, but it's like that connection is rooted in our souls. I don't know how to explain it but it's like we're always trying to make things good for each other. We have a special bond. We need each other.

Cedrick

December 1994

Dear Diary,

We just got back from the Thanksgiving holiday and had a ball! My mom loves Kahlil and him and my Brother are like best friends. We ate like crazy and slept our asses off! It felt good to be home. We hung out with some of my friends from high school and a couple of my cousins. The time went by too fast though. I could have used another week. Kahlil says so too.

Before we left for Thanksgiving break though, we had three meets that we slaughtered the competition in. Me and Kahlil kept our focus and I kept swimming to him in the relay. We haven't quite broken our record from last year in fact in one meet we came in under the record time by 1.5 seconds but we won anyway. We didn't have much time to prepare for that meet and didn't spend as much time as we did last year practicing after practice. We agreed when we were at my mom's to correct that and we have. Already we're feeling the syncopation again and just in time for our last meet before the semester ends. Time flies so fast.

We got finals coming up in a couple of weeks and we're both ready to get that over with! We're all set. We have no choice but to be! All we've been doing is swimming and studying. We did hang out with Monica and Cynthia last weekend - went to a movie but that's been it as far as a social life is concerned. We usually don't leave the pool until around 11 p.m. or so and then study for an hour, talk for about an hour more in the room in the dark and then we pass out. Our days begin at 6:00 a.m. so every break we get we just sleep. Especially on Sundays. It's the only day we don't practice. We'll get up early enough to get to worship service on campus, grab something to eat on the way back, and pass out again. But Christmas vacation is coming soon so that means nothing but rest.

Kahlil's headed to California for the "fake out" as he calls it and I'm headed to my aunts. The guy mom's dating is taking her and my brother on a cruise. They invited me along but I really didn't feel like being on a boat in the middle of winter no matter where it was headed. So I'll hang out at my aunt and uncles and catch up with my cousins. Kahlil's not looking forward to another temporary separation. Lately he doesn't look forward to breaks where we can't be together and the truth is neither do I. He's like my strength and my inspiration, and I don't like to be away from him for any length of time. It doesn't seem natural that we'd be so close or does it? I don't know. I just know he makes life good. He makes all of what we're going through worthwhile. I'm just grateful to have him.

Cedrick

January 1995

Dear Diary,

A couple of days before we were supposed to leave for Christmas vacation Kahlil's parent called and said they had to leave the country for Christmas. They didn't invite him to come along. He was devastated. I know he hates going home for Christmas anyway but I think to him it's his only link to his mom and step-dad. I was upset for him.

He tried not to show that he was upset but I know him. I know him better than he knows himself. We were sitting on the floor and after he hung up the phone he just put his hands over his face. So I sat next to him on the floor and put my arm around him and he laid he head on my shoulders. I kept telling him it was cool that we'd figure something out but he just sat there crying. I kept rubbing his shoulder and head trying to reassure him and calm him. After a while he did. We sat there holding each other like that like we belonged - together in a warm embrace.

When he was calm enough to talk he looked at me and said that I was his best friend in the world and that he didn't know what he would do without me. He told me that before we became friends he was thinking of committing suicide because his pain was so deep. He said I saved him – that I made life worth living. He stood up and stood me up with him and told me he loved me. He looked me dead in the eyes and told me he loved me. And then he kissed me - on the lips.

He kissed me on my lips and I kissed him back, melting into him - melting into us. Breaking all barriers if there were any that existed between us. We kissed each other long and hard and soft and tenderly, and held onto each other, soul-to-soul; heart-to-heart, beating from the known and the unknown. We kissed and held onto each other not knowing what to say. Not feeling we needed to say anything. We stared into each other's eyes not looking for anything but finding it anyway. It's like we found freedom - freedom for our secrets and a secret place for our freedom. All of our pains, regrets, longings, and desires seemed to gather together in that moment and we heard each other calling though we spoke no words. And all of the places where our fears and hesitations were hidden; where misery and disappointments were once swallowed now leaped out and we cut our spirits free.

That night just like every other night since we held onto each other and slept peacefully in each other's arms. Kahlil didn't want to be alone for the holidays and I didn't want him to be. I changed my plans and we spent many nights in each other's arms at his house in California in his bed. We were like newlyweds on honeymoon, him and me, loving each other beyond description. Discovering something new in us; something we never knew but glad we found. We ran in the mornings and worked out in the afternoons. We'd swim in the evenings and at night we made love. Melting into each other and cutting our spirits free.

Our lovemaking brought us so much closer. It was sacred to us. Much more than just sex but a unification of sex and spirit - interconnected and divine where we found this kind of transformative light. It streams from his body and mine like an energetic force of love. We feel fulfilled and enlightened. It's our divine celebration of life - like when we swim and we only hear and see each other.

We've established a deep karmetic connection that extends itself beyond who we are alone and apart, and who we believe we are alone or apart. All that's exists is mutualness - mutual love, mutual support, mutual care, mutual tenderness, and a mutual appreciation that we are love itself. In our lovemaking we transcend everything we know or think we know and we heal. We love. Just Love. I love him and he loves me. I feel it. He does too.

Cedrick

August 2004

Dear Diary,

It's been over nine years since I've written you. I couldn't find you for a while. In fact I thought I had lost you forever. I was so relieved to find you packed away here in one of my old boxes from school. So much has been gone on and it seems like the years went by way too fast! I'll try to play catch up now and promise not to let too much time pass between us again.

Since the last time I wrote I've finished medical school and I'm now a practicing physician. I graduated with honors from undergrad and opted to go right to medical school as opposed to taking time off to prepare for the Olympics. A lot of people were disappointed with my decision but I was o.k. with it. My mom made both my graduations and was so proud. She came with my step-dad. I guess they were dating the last time I wrote but they've been married for several years now.

She's happy and in love and he's crazy about her. She deserves it too. He rested her feet. In fact she hardly works at all anymore. She spends the majority of time volunteering and working for different charities keeping herself busy and traveling all over the country following my brother's college football career. He's the number one running back in the nation and looks like he'll be a number one draft pick after he graduates next year. I've caught a couple of games when I could in between school and other commitments but he knows I'm still proud of him.

Well enough about them. My last entry was Christmas of 1994. What an unbelievable and unforgettable time! It was when Kahlil and I fell in love. We found a way to understand what had happened between us. I think it was confusing for us both only because neither of us expected that we'd fall in love. Especially with each other! Who would have guessed? We'll, we did and I realized that we were in love the whole time. We just didn't realize it. The good thing is that it was just as natural as it was normal for us. We just found ourselves there. The best part was that we didn't have to change a thing between us. Everything was already there. We were still who we were; friends, best friends, who cared about each other and loved each other. The difference - if it was a difference at all - is that we were *in love*. I guess we had always been. We just needed our spirits to be cut free.

We stayed together in that dorm the entire time we were in undergrad. At night we would put our mattresses on the floor and laugh and talk, and hold each other in the darkness. I pledged the fraternity, his fraternity, that following year. Our swim team went undefeated all four years we were on the team! We were co-captains until we graduated. We won all kinds of awards, broke all kinds of records, and had all kinds of celebrations. They wanted him for the Olympics too but he opted to go to law school instead.

After we graduated we moved into an apartment close enough to both of our campuses. We still ran in the mornings, swam in the evenings, and at night held onto each other. We were in love and didn't care who knew it. We told Monica and Cynthia who were a little surprised at first. I guess their surprise was mixed with relief to know that it happened a long time after we all kind of went our separate ways. But they were cool with it. They really were. So were our teammates. A couple of them even told us they thought we were lovers long before we became lovers. We thought that was odd!

Our coach said he didn't really give a dayum! He's so funny. He said he didn't care if we were loving each other or loving goats as long as we kept winning. And we did. My mom and step-dad were cool with it too. My mom had grown to love Kahlil like a son so to her it was no big deal. My little brother, on the other hand, had it rough for a minute but he eventually came around. He's a major player and all the girls are always on him so it was nearly impossible for him to get it but he respected where we were coming from.

We were going to tell Kahlil's parents but sadly we never got the chance to. On their way from a safari in Africa their plane went down. He was completely devastated. I know he had always believed in the back of his mind that there'd be a chance they would get closer. Sadly, that was the end of his dream. I'm sure he's still grieving their loss though he won't admit it. We flew to Namibia to identify their remains and escorted them back to the states. We buried them here in California next to where his father is buried. He was their only heir so everything was left to him. He moved back to California to finish his last year of law school and run the company. He makes a fantastic CEO and the company is more profitable than it had ever been. I decided to move with him and finished my residency here. Things have been great. We even opened a free clinic in honor of his mother and father that I run in one of the more underserved communities in LA.

And as for us we're as in as much love today as we were long before we learned to cut our spirits free. We've been through a lot to get where we are to keep each other loved and protected but somehow we've managed to do it. I think it's only because we kept on loving throughout and despite. I love him and I'm very proud of him. And I know he loves me and is just as proud.

This month makes ten years exactly that we've been together and we decided to celebrate by jumping the broom. That's right! We're getting married and it's going to be huge! We've invited everyone; family, friends from school, former teammates, people who work for the company, and people who work at the clinic. My mom and step dad are here and so is my little brother with his girlfriend. He's my best man. Most of the Brothers from the swim team are here with their wives or significant others and Coach is here too. He's Kahlil's best man. Monica and Cynthia are here with their husbands. I can't believe Cynthia finally decided to settle down so you know I'm dying to meet that Brother!

Well, I'll close here until next time. I hear him calling for me. I think our guests have started to arrive and I have to finish getting dressed. He tells me all the time that I've gotten slow in my old age, always running late, but he can't prove it. He still can't beat me in the water though no matter how hard he tries. And he does try! We had the pool expanded out back and every day he tries.

But it doesn't matter really. We both won really! We have each other and that's the greatest prize of all. We're still holding each other and loving each other, and still talking in the darkness until we fall asleep. Still talking, laughing, and loving just like we did all those years ago back in college when we first learned to cut our spirits free.

Cedrick

No Fear

I am lost
Pieces
Of hopelessness
Fear, despair

They said
You
Wouldn't love me
Couldn't love me
Cause I love another like me

Should I fear to love?
Or is the blessing
In the feelings themselves?

Take this hand
Show me…Show them
They were wrong

Lead me on
To where love roams
Where peace abounds
Heart, mind, and soul

I am a fragment
Pieces of You
Your love
Mercy
Compassion
Grace

I am still your son
I know this now
I surrender

No fear

At 30

My Dear Friends:

Today was no different from the rest. This morning I woke up - grateful as always. I watched the sun slowly rise, replacing the darkness gently with the light of a new dawn; the air thick with humidity even in the early hours and sat down for my morning prayer and meditation.

Yet, something was different about this morning. The chirp of the birds seemed louder than I can ever remember and the smell of spring in full bloom was just as loud as it permeated, awakened, and revived my senses.

I sat on my deck as one by one three red Robins visited me, resting comfortably on the railing, unafraid to bid me a good day and to share in the delights of my sweet cornbread - as is our daily ritual - while I sipped on hot green tea. Then, like a ton of bricks, it hits me. Today is the anniversary of my birth. Today I turned 30.

I kept my kewl (did I say 30????) as I rushed to the kitchen in a panic for the Vodka and the Bloody Mary mix stopping short of pouring and gulping to remember... *"Hold up,"* I say to myself, *"It's not all that bad! I'm still grateful! Yes, I am!"*

I'm Grateful because there were times in my life where I never thought I'd be here. Unwise decisions, unhealthy choices, black on black violence, HIV, prison lockdowns, or natural disaster could have been limiting of life and of promise. And still there are no regrets when I think of the years since passed when life was confusing at most and uncertain at best. I'm still here. I have survived...we all have....what a blessing!!!!! I pour my cocktail down the sink. I decide to pray instead.

This morning, my first day At 30 I take a deep breath. A cleansing breath. I close my eyes and fall to my knees petitioning Jehovah in prayer. I thank Him for so many opportunities and the many, many blessings that have been presented on my journey. Most thankful am I that He has allowed me to understand and surrender to the Power that shapes my way. The message here: Find your way back!

At 30, I venerate peace; peace with myself and peace with the process of life realizing dreams, desires, hopes, and ambitions, stopping only to raise the bar as I start anew with fresh ideologies and mindset. The message: Join Me Here!

At 30, I celebrate my health; physical, spiritual, and emotional. Finding myself in the best conditioning I've ever been. Refreshed, revived, and renewed. Standing ready, front and center to rest arms of others weary from battle deserving of a place to lay peacefully after years of struggle and of sacrifice. The Message: Treasure your Health! Nurture Your Spirit! Pick up the Spear! There's So Much More To Be Done!

At 30, I rejoice in family; those here and not, and relish in love that has surrounded, engulfed, and protected me since before a word I could utter. I use what I now know to express it freely to the young who once played around my knee as they move onto womanhood and into manhood - coming to grips with life and with themselves; finding their own voice to footnote history. Keep Giving Back is the Message..."*What Kind of Ancestor do I want to be?*" is the question!

At 30, I delight in memories though bittersweet of friends as I recall painful times when ravens dropped Black feathers at my door. I remember Anthony, Kenny, Charlie, Billy, Tim, Steve, Milton, Arthur, Leonard, Stacy, Donna, Yvette, and the other named and nameless beautiful souls stolen by HIV and AIDS - forever etched in my heart and in my mind. The Message: Remember least we not repeat!

At 30, I revel in the boldness of love's promise; its strength and its sentiment. The beauty of its truth; exciting, passionate, and enticing for it has arrived - in me and of me – in a time appointed time where I seek not solely love's pleasure but pass outside its earthly restrictions into peace and understanding. It is in this place where it is safe to hope with all my hopes, cry all of my tears, and laugh all of my laughter. The

Message: our relationships - all of them - are Holy Given to us by God for His purposes. Not ours. Know this and you will always be at Peace!

At 30, I indulge in the beauty of my friends. A beauty beyond the senses - a beauty like the still of water; like the green cedars in Zambia; a beauty unworthy of simple description. Because of you I am. You have shown me the true meaning of love. Teaching that love is not an art. Love is life. I am forever in debt to you for validating that material possessions mean nothing - only love does - for jewels have brilliant fire but can offer no warmth.

At 30, I thank you for being here with me on this ride through this life. I celebrate each day that you have unselfishly shared with me and the light and love you've brought to them. I thank God for your presence and thank you for answering the call to come here; to bless me with you. I could never repay you for there is no price worthy of your love, belief, encouragement, and support. In return I can offer you little but offer all that I have.

Peace, Blessings, Light, and Love,
Sundiata
At 30

Tell Him

You must have loved a Brother
With no conscious
With no soul

Who Was He?
Who did it to you?

Your heart
Closed
Your Love
Unreachable
Shuddering at the slightest touch
Drawing In and leaving alone
No one knows you
Not even you

Tell Him, Brother
        Tell Him you want you back

Uncertainly
Perplexity
Make you fall apart
Thinking you're together
But you fall apart
Insecurities pointing
To the places of your wounds

Maybe you weighed your ability to love you
On the scales he weighed his love for you
Your self-preservation became
Your self-deprivation
Cause he stole your soul

Tell Him, Brother
        Tell Him you want you back

You built a fortress
To protect your heart
Kept yourself hidden for so long
And now the forest is bare
Hollowed

How many promises unkept?
How many chances granted?

Tell Him, Brother
        Tell Him you want you back

When he left you
Alone and Broken
You stood at the closed door
So long
You didn't notice the window
Open behind you
Where I stood
Waiting

To know you
To hold you
To love you

Tell Him, Brother….Tell Him Now…

    Tell Him you want you back

If My Brother Is In Trouble

Never Have I Walked Alone
You've Stood Always By My Side
My Warmth, My Strength
My Confidants
And My Ever-Constant Guides

In Infancy
My Lowest Times
When I Could Barely Crawl
You Laid Down A Cushion
Held Out Your Hand
Made Me Steady, Straight, and Tall

When I First Stood On My Own
Whether To Protest, Object, Or Deny
There You Were Each Step Of The Way
Standing On Either Side

When I Took My First Steps
To Know Who I Am…To Love, To Live, To Be
Each Time I Stumbled And there Were Many
You Came And Lifted Me

As My Stride Became Greater, A Quickened Pace
And I Was Far Too Ahead Of Myself
Gently You Slowed Me And Made Me See
The Power Of My Self-Worth

Your Wisdom, Love, and Dedication
Has Brightened Many A Darkened Day
And I Owe You In No Uncertain Terms
And In Many Desperate Ways

If My Brother's In Trouble…..So Am I

If My Brother Is In Trouble

Never Have I Walked Alone
You've Stood Always By My Side
My Warmth, My Strength
My Confidants
And My Ever-Constant Guides

In Infancy
My Lowest Times
When I Could Barely Crawl
You Laid Down A Cushion
Held Out Your Hand
Made Me Steady, Straight, and Tall

When I First Stood On My Own
Whether To Protest, Object, Or Deny
There You Were Each Step Of The Way
Standing On Either Side

When I Took My First Steps
To Know Who I Am…To Love, To Live, To Be
Each Time I Stumbled And there Were Many
You Came And Lifted Me

As My Stride Became Greater, A Quickened Pace
And I Was Far Too Ahead Of Myself
Gently You Slowed Me And Made Me See
The Power Of My Self-Worth

Your Wisdom, Love, and Dedication
Has Brightened Many A Darkened Day
And I Owe You In No Uncertain Terms
And In Many Desperate Ways

If My Brother's In Trouble…..So Am I

Gary and Taylor

June 15, 2011
Yo, wassup Taylor!

Well big brother, I've finally done it! I got my MBA, man, and you don't know how happy I am - even happier then when you got your J.D. times two! Graduation day was off the hook! The only thing missing was you, big bro! But I understand. Working a cushy job for the JAG and the military's "God and Country" mentality keeps you doing what you've got to do. I get it! But I sure missed you but hopefully you'll be stateside soon (next month is what ma said) so we'll celebrate then.

I'm actually headed home next week for a couple of days of R&R. I need to let my brain rest a minute. You didn't mention that grad school would take so much out of me. I mean I'm fried, man! So I'm just planning to lay around for a while and let mom spoil me with her cooking before the "real world" gets a hold of me. I'm headed to another celebration tonight so I'm going to cut this short.

But before I go, I just want to say this to you: Gary, you've been the best brother a man could hope to have. You've been my mentor and my hero (and on more occasions than *you* care to count, my financier ☺). Everything I am, I owe in no small part to you, man, for keeping me focused and for keeping my ass out of trouble. You really are my best friend and I love you for always being there. Thanks, from the bottom of my heart. I owe you big time!

I love you, man.
Gary

P.S. I took your counsel, Counselor, and took the job with Xerox. As always you were right. This was the best offer. Thanks for the advice!

June 30, 2011
Yo, Gary!

My man! You finally did it! Congratulations, man. You know I tried everything in the world to get there (short of lying – but you know – integrity) but to tell you the truth I was tempted to just to see my lil' brother do his thing and walk across the stage. Although I couldn't be there physically I was there in spirit. I woke up at the crack of dawn; right about the time your graduation was starting there and proposed a toast here. So congratulations again! You've worked hard to do what you've done and you don't owe me a thing! I was glad to do it. So… uh…when are you going to start paying me back? Just kidding!

So you took my advice and decided on Xerox, huh? Good choice, lil' brother. I think they did make you the best offer plus the benefits package can't be beat. Check it out for a couple of years to get your feet wet and then see what happens. If it doesn't suit you roll out but at least you'll have a couple years' experience under your belt. Either way you can't lose.

Now, schools out of the way the job secured, so wassup with your romantic life? You're an educated, paid brother now so you're a hot commodity. The sisters are going to be all over you! Give 'em hell, lil' bro but remember you made it this far without creating a junior or a burn in your piss so don't fuck it all up now. Date and do your thing, man. But keep it wrapped the hell up! You're still young and got some time - not much - but some time to play the field. Weed out the females too man and find you a loving supportive sister that wants nothing from you except your love.

Trust me when I tell you that it takes time so start now. I know I must be nuts trying to give Casanova himself advice on the ladies but I can't help myself. Remember how we used to run 'em back in the day? Man! Those were the days. But I'm a happily married man — five years next month but dayum! The memories, the memories, the memories! Well, I better close before Debra comes sneaking up on me and reads this part. It'll be hell to pay! She sends her love by the way.

So check it - I love you lil' brother and I'm so, so proud of you. You've done well. We'll see you in a couple of months and get our swerve on to celebrate. Keep me posted on the new gig. I want to know how it's working for you.

Peace,
Big bro. Taylor
p.s. You didn't say anything about the gift we sent. Did you get it?

July 7, 2011
Taylor —

Aww man, bruh. My bad! I guess I was so wrapped up in graduation that I forgot to say thanks for the briefcase. I was hoping you'd spring for a coach! And the tablet hidden inside was a nice touch. Thanks, man. It's perfect. I appreciate it. Thank Deb for me. I know she was the one who picked it out ☺.

Yo man, loving Xerox! Got my own office with a door and windows, and an assistant too (check me out!). I'm working with some real cool people and on some real interesting projects. Still trying to get used to the daily grind which all of sudden seemed worthwhile when I got my first paycheck. Dayum! Even I was impressed. When I checked my balance the other day online I just stared at it. It feels good to have more than 20 bones in the bank.

But don't worry. I didn't go crazy or nothing. I just bought a couple of things I really needed (o.k., I bought a lot of things I really didn't need: a new stereo, surround sound theatre system, a 60 inch flat screen, an X-Box, new computer, and a couple pairs of shoes…ok 4 pair). But I only did this after I paid myself first with twenty-five percent of it stashed in the bank. See, I listen to you. Always did. I'm not going to lose my mind. I'm going to start saving for a house or a condo or something. You know, invest.

So mom tells me that you and Deb aren't coming home after all. Dayum man. That's messed up! I was looking forward to seeing you - Deb too - but I really wanted to see you. It's been over a year and a half almost and since I'm still on probation with the new gig, I doubt if I can use any of the vacation time for three months. Do you have a new date yet? Let me know when you're coming. We've got so much to catch up on and all this writing back and forth is starting to cramp my fingers. Maybe I'll start having my assistant write for me ☺.

I'm still headed to moms next week since I already paid for my ticket and it's non-refundable. She promised to cook and I promised to eat! I'll miss you man but I'll drown my sorrows in mom's sweet potato pie. On the real let me know the next possible date. I have a couple of things I want to run pass you so get back at me soon. I'll holla!

Love,
Gary

July 25, 2011
Dear Gary,

I can't believe you threw mom's sweet potato pie in my face! That's foul man, real foul. I'd never be that cruel to you. You don't have any idea how much I miss mom's cooking. Deb tries but you know and I know she can't cook worth a dayum! But then again, I didn't marry her for cooking skills ☺.

I'm glad to know that you're enjoying the job (and the money – sounds like). Life's falling into place and everything's going according to plan but don't freak out over the commas in your check, man. Make sure you keep on a schedule to save, save, save. Now that doesn't mean you shouldn't enjoy the fruits of your labor. You should but save and invest so you can enjoy it more. I want you to make sure you call Terry Wright, my old roommate. You know he's an investment wiz at Merrill Lynch and doing some crazy things with my money. He'll hook you up. I don't have the number but mom has it. Call him next week. You know I'll double check to make sure you did so put it in your palm pilot to call him the first chance you get.

As for coming home, well...looks like it'll be about another nine months or so (hint...hint). Deb's doctors don't think it's a good idea for her to travel now (hint...hint...hint). They say women in her condition shouldn't travel after the first trimester (big ass hint). That's right, lil' brother we're pregnant and you're going to be an uncle! We wanted to tell you and mom at the same time but anytime we call you're missing in action – running around with some female no doubt. We told her last week and made her promise not to tell you. Sorry for keeping it a secret but I wanted to be the one to do it. I didn't want to do it by letter but the problem is you're hard to get by phone. This was the only way.

Man, can you believe it? We're so excited and Deb looks so beautiful – all glowing and sexy. And man is she nervous! She's like a mad women around here reading books, setting up classes, and changing our diets; low fat this, low fat that, no sugars, not too many starches, and all the rest. I tell you, man, as it is I'm already malnourished but now I'm dayum near wasting away! It's all for the best though. She's just trying to make sure the baby is healthy and I'm all for that.

I'm going to be a father - imagine that! To tell you the truth, man, I'm probably more nervous about this than she is. I don't know what kind of father I'm going to be. I don't know what to do or how to prepare for it. I just know two things; if I can be half the father dad was to us the kid is going to shine! And if he's anything like you he's got it made. I have no doubt in my mind that you going to make a great uncle. I just hope I can be a good dad. Dayum! This is some scary shit.

So before you go run out this afternoon to F.A.O Schwartz and blow your paycheck on toys think about this: Deb's decided to have the baby here as opposed to the states so her parents are coming and so is mom. Now you know I can't do this without you here so start planning your trip. The baby's due on the third of May – that's right, your birthday – so what better place to celebrate it. Now that you have loot you can afford the ticket and you'll be out of your probationary period so you have the time. What do you say? Can I count on you, Uncle Gary? Will you be here? Let me know.

Love, your big brother
Taylor

August 1, 2011
Dear Papa!

Man, I'm so siked! I'm going to be an uncle! Dayum! Man, please give Deb my best and all my love. Tell her I'm excited for all of us and to take it easy. Tell her I said not to let you get on her nerves. Poor girl. I know how your neurotic worrying ass can be, Taylor, so please cut her some slack.

My brother is going to be a dad and I'm going to be an uncle. Dayum! I waited a long time for this and I know you've always wanted this and here it is. You know what that means don't you? We're officially grown ass men! Where the hell did the time go? I remember being so young not so long ago running around driving mom and dad crazy, and getting into everything. I remember when our only care in the world was would we make football or basketball practice on time or who would run the most yards or score the most baskets. And now here we are; you about to be a papa and me about to have a nephew (yea man…I'm calling it…it's got to be a boy☺!). Wow! I'm so proud of you man, real proud – more now than I've ever been before!

Having children is a major responsibility. A huge one and I know you're worried. But I'm not. You're going to be an amazing father, man. After all, you've had some practice with me. You were like a dad to me when pop died, and I didn't turn out too bad. This child you're about to welcome will be so lucky to have you as his father. Just about as lucky I am to have you as a brother. Don't worry, Taylor. You'll be fine, man.

And don't worry about keeping the secret from me, either. You know I'd much rather have heard it from you. But your mom is a trip. I could tell something was up when I asked her if she had heard from you and Deb. She said she had talked to you and just said you were doing fine. But when she said it she had this kind of looked like the cat that swallowed the canary. You'd be proud of her though. She never let on. I didn't have a clue and as much as she wants grandchildren I'm surprised she didn't take out an ad in the newspaper announcing it! I don't know what you said to keep her quiet but she did. Did you threaten her by any chance? Well, in any event half the country knows now. She's been telling everybody so expect a truckload of mail and gifts from the U.S.

Now speaking of secrets I've been keeping one of my own. I know you've wondered about what was going on in my dating life so are you ready? Well, big brother, I'm in love. Yea, that's right, man. I'm in love. Michele and I met in grad school but we were just friends at first. Over the two years we kind of got closer and closer. I never said anything to you because I wanted to be sure, and now I am. You remember the "love sensation" you said I'd feel when I fell in love? We'll I got it! Actually I got it early on when we met but didn't quite know what it was so I let it go. But then all of a sudden it came back and Boom! Everything just sort of came together all at once. Out of nowhere it came back and I can't be happier, man.

We took it slow, you know, no rushing, getting to know each other and adjusting to each other but I think after about a year or so we found our rhythm. Yup! Baby brother's in love and everything feels so right. I find myself smiling all the time for no reason watching the clock all day long until I get off and we meet for drinks, dinner, or whatever. There were times when I thought it wouldn't happen for me like it happened for you and Deb but it's here man. It's finally here. I'm talking marriage, a home, and children - the whole nine. Who would have thought I would have met someone so warm, caring, sensitive, and a sports nut to boot? And you talk about smart! Dayum! And sexy! I mean the mind blowing kind of sexy with a smile that could melt the coldest heart. Everywhere we go, man, people tell us we look good together - that we're made for each other. Even mom thinks so, so you know the deal. I can't wait until we all get together. You'll see what I mean.

Anyway, since you can't be here anytime soon I was thinking that we both might come there for the birth of my nephew if that's alright with you and Deb. I'll have about three weeks' vacation, two to spend with you and then a week to travel around to a couple of nearby cities. How's that sound? Let me know if that's cool. I've got to close now. We're meeting for dinner and I don't want to be late. Congratulations again, big brother. When I grow up I want to be just like you! (smile).

Love Always,
Your brother,
Uncle Gary

August 20, 2011
Gary!

Is it cool? Is it cool? Are you kidding? Of course it is, man. We'd love that!

So baby brother is in love? Hot dayum! Congratulations. Really! I mean that. It's a good feeling ain't it? Man, that's the best news I've heard all week. And you say mom likes her? Well, she's got to be all that! You know what a cold shoulder mom gave to Deb the first year we were dating! She felt like Deb was stealing her first-born son away. I always imagined she'd practically kirk out when her baby boy brought "the" girl home. Tell your girl that Deb and I are looking forward to meeting her and since mom's the biggest hurdle she'd ever have to face, believe me, it's smooth sailing from here on.

So tell me, man, because you left out some important details, where's she from? How does she look? Does she work with you? What does she do? Have you met her family? Does she feel the same about you? I want answers and I want them in that order! Come on, man, give me the scoop. I can't wait to hear back from you and I really can't wait to meet her. Deb says to tell you congratulations! She said she's excited for you too and looking forward to another in-law to share mom with. Do you think she's being sarcastic? I think so☺!

Alright. Let me impart on you some brotherly wisdom and advice. You've done right to take it slow. Keep that pace. There's no need to rush into anything. You've found each other. That's the hardest part. Now you have to take time to get to know each other – I mean really get to know each other – before you make any huge commitments like engagement or marriage, and especially children. You're just beginning and need some time to enjoy yourselves together.

Remember, Deb and I dated for two years and then were engaged for another two before we felt ready for marriage. The time we took to vibe each other made all the difference in the world. I still feel the same for her as I did when we first met. I still light up when I hear her voice or see her walking towards me and as the years go by I fall more in love with her. Now that she's carrying my baby, my child, the love is more intense. It's unbelievable and unmistakable. That's love, lil' brother. True love.

I'm glad for you. I really am, and I hope she loves you just as much. You deserve that. So please bring her with you here to Geneva in May.

I'll give her the once over – I need to know that she really loves my little brother and has your best interesting mind. You know I've got see for myself that she has your back. I'm looking forward to having the family, both families, all together to welcome my son (yea…I'm calling it too!) into the world with all this love around him. And soon enough (but not too soon), you'll be welcoming a child of your own and we'll all be there too.

We're writing another chapter, Gary – another legacy of family name and new contributions to the world. I feel like I'm so ready for this, man. I'm so prepared for this. Keep in touch and tell the lucky lady welcome to the family and although it's a small one – you, me, and mom - there's a whole lot of love here.

Love always,
Your proud big brother,
Taylor

August 30, 2011
Dear Taylor!

It's always nice to get your letters big bro and thanks for extending the invitation to Michele. We're all excited to be coming now! But it does seem like I left out one important detail about Michele. I don't know how I forgot to mention this! Maybe I was too caught up in the moment of all the good news of my nephew or maybe just caught up in this new love thing but Michele's not a woman. Michele's a man.

The name probably threw you off but he's French-Canadian, from Montreal, and Michele is a common name for men. We met on an intramural basketball league I played on in grad school and were just chill friends you know hanging out and stuff like that. But then these feelings started to develop between us and then it just sort of happened. I was buggin out at first - feeling shit for a man that I had only felt for women before - but like I said something just clicked and everything started to make sense.

I'm in love with him, Taylor. I really am and, Yes! To answer your question there's no doubt in my mind that he feels the same about me. I can feel it you know? I can feel the love just like you said I would. He was just as bugged out about it as I was at first. This is a first time for both of us - being with another man - but we're over that now. We were both like, "*Oh well, here we are!*" I think that's what I love most about him. He sees life so differently than I do. He just takes off from wherever he is, no stress, no "what ifs", he just goes for it. He's got that kind of personality and I've learned a lot from him since we've been together. I feel like I can rely on him and I know he's got my back.

We get along like you and Deb - like friends. We laugh a lot and can have a good time whether in a crowded club or just chillin in my apartment or his. We like the same things too; basketball, football - all sports - he's athletic and has a mean crossover (like you do) only he's a little slow (like you are ☺). Anyway, he's cool as shit and I know you'll like him.

And man, he had no problem winning mom over. I was a little nervous about them meeting at first but everybody likes Michele - you can't help but like him. Mom said he reminds her of dad when he was younger and she's crazy about him. She said to me the other day that we seem to be made for each other. He's hooked on her too. One taste of her sweet potato pie and that was all she wrote! You'd think they've known each other for years. Now all they can talk about now is the trip to Geneva to see you, Deb, and the new baby. This is his first trip to Europe so he's mad siked about it! They're making all kinds of plans so I hope you and Deb have the energy. I have a feeling they're going to drive all of us crazy!

So I'm sorry for the confusion. Give Deb my love and tell her I'm hoping she's doing well. I'll see you soon but not soon enough!

Love,
Lil' Brother
Gary

September 12, 2011
Gary —

When I first got your letter I thought it was a joke or something! I was telling Deb how funny you were but then she kind of looked at me funny, like she knew something but wasn't saying. So I called mom and I'll be dayum if she didn't confirm it. Michele is a man! A man. A man! A man? And she spoke about it like it was as natural to her as the recipe for her sweet potato pie. I don't understand. I don't know what to say. I feel like I'm losing my mind!

Man, what the hell is going on? What the fuck happened to you? Michele is a man! A man. A man! A man? Y'all need to quit playing man. Where did all this come from? I must be missing something. One day you're the Casanova king and the next you're in love with a man? A man? A man? And you were saying you were thinking of settling down; marriage, house, cars, kids, vacations, and all this time you were talking about a man? What the hell!

And what the fuck makes you think the name had anything to do with it? It wasn't the name that threw me off. You tell me what on earth would make me think that Michele was a man? You could have told me the name was Oscar and I would have thought it was short for Oscarina or some shit!

Somebody tell me this is a joke and if it isn't please explain this shit to me. Are you telling me you're gay? Help me out here lil' brother cause I'm freaked the fuck out!

Taylor

September 30, 2003
Dear Taylor,

Naw man. It's not a joke and I was just as surprised about it as you are. I don't know what happened. Maybe a lot of things, maybe nothing at all. I just know that it did and now we're in love.

The reason mom can talk about it so naturally is because to me it is and that's how I first explained it to her. I mean I was like "*Whoa!*" for a minute when we first started feeling each other like that but only for a minute. Then I just relaxed into it. It didn't seem abnormal or unusual to me. It sounds strange I know but I didn't feel like there was anything to hide or anything to be ashamed about. It's just what it is and that's how I'm approaching it. It just is as it is Taylor. I don't know how else to explain it.

And it's not like I feel like I'm gay or anything by societies perception of what a loving another man is and what the word is termed to mean. Honestly I don't see myself that way. Maybe it's psychological or something but "gay" to me means something else - I mean like flamboyant and feminine men or men who wear dresses or want to be women, rainbow flags, and parades and shit. But that's not me. I love being a man. Always have. I'm just a Black man who happens to love another man - without the need for labels or categories or stereotypes. I don't know many Black men who love other men because this whole thing is a new world to me but the few I do know are very much like me. I mean they're athletic, play sports, and naturally masculine. Not everyone behaves or dress flashy, wear heals and makeup or want to be women. But there are some who are. There is a community of Brothers who express themselves differently from other but that that's what makes this community so incredible. The diversity of it all is amazing!

Taylor, in the larger scheme of things and in the greater definition or perception people have about gay people, the label gay doesn't fit well for me or Michele for that matter although I am in love with another man. I don't really like the word "gay" and not solely because of the images that it congers up in the minds of people. Gay means happy and I'm just not happy all the time. It's the same reason why I don't identify as queer. Queer means strange and I don't find anything about me, my life, or the man I'm in love with strange. And the word homosexual doesn't suit me either. People tend to go right to "sexual" and for us and this community of Black men like me who love other men it is so much more than that. So if there is a label that is to be ascribed to me I would rather it be "same gender loving" because at least with that definition "love" is present. Do you see what I mean?

And I do still want to get married one day. I mean right now it's not quite legal to do it yet but one day it just might be. And if I could do it now I'd marry Michele in a heartbeat! And we would have children together. He loves kids and so do I and for us adoption or surrogacy would be an alternative. And I would want them to know their cousins - your children - and I would still want to live right next door to you like we always planned and go on family vacations, PTA meetings, football and basketball games, and graduations and all that! And we could sit back and enjoy our lives, watching our children grow; you and Deb, Michele and me, and mom. And we will all be proud, so grateful that we have what we have.

I'm not expecting this to be easy for anyone to digest. It took me a minute too. But you're my Brother - my best friend in the entire world - and I'm asking you to at least try to get used to the idea of it all. Honestly, it's going to be cool. Just trust me like you always have. Just trust me.

I hope this is making sense - some sense - any sense to you. But if it doesn't please let me know. I need to know that you have my back here, man, and if there's anything that makes you uncomfortable about this, talk to me. I love you big bro. I want us to get past it. We just have to, man. We just have to.

Love, Gary

October 5, 2003
Dear Gary,

I'm still freaking out here, man. Are you sure about this? I mean are you really sure this isn't some kind of experimentation, or phase, or something? I'm having a hard time with this, man, because it's a whole new world to me too and while I know I can be rigid at times in my beliefs and behaviors I'm absolutely stuck in this one! It's unbelievable to me. I don't think I can handle this. I don't know what to feel about it. I move from depression to disappointment and even anger. But I don't know who or what the depression, disappointment, and anger is directed at. One minute it's at you, then it's at me, then mom and dad, then gay people, and then the world. I'm just trying to sort it all out, man, for real – trying to figure out what all this means now and what it will mean for the future.

I don't know many gay people. I admit that. I see some from time-to-time in this section of Geneva where they hang out. Deb and I go through there occasionally to get to one of our favorite restaurants. It always looks so wild, so unrestrained. Decadent. I have a hard time now picturing you in that scene with all the shit that going on – men holding hands, kissing each other, and switching in tight pants and shirts, and some in heals, dresses, and makeup and shit. I think about that and then I think about you and my heart just sinks. I know you're not like that and don't feel like the word "gay" suits you either but it's my only association. My heart hurts and I feel ashamed.

I feel ashamed of you and then I feel ashamed of feeling ashamed of my little brother, my best friend, the only one in this world I know I can depend on. The little brother that always was a man about his appearance in this world; his words and his manners – respectful, sincere, a good brother, a good son, and a good friend to everybody. And likeable. Everybody likes you and every girl I know from high school until now wants to marry you and have your children. Even a couple of Deb's friends fell in love just looking at your picture over here and are ready to get hitched when you get here. To think that you've changed in that way and to know that everything I thought you were you're really not isn't that easy to deal with.

Deb tells me it's no big deal. No big deal. No big deal?! She talks about it like mom does – like it doesn't matter one way or another. I love her to death and you know I do but we're worlds apart on this one! Maybe it's a woman thing, a female thing, a natural connection or instinct or something that comes with carrying a growing child inside you – a human being developing in your body that you want to love and protect even now – not knowing who it's going to be or who it's going to love. Maybe it's a mother-to-be preparing herself to extend unconditional love. Maybe it's a lot of things to her but for me, a Black man, it's not so cut and dry.

I think about shit like how society reacts to Black men in general and then how they react to gay men in particular. And then I think about how they're going to react to the combination of both. I think about the rest of the family and how they're going to react and about how our friends will react and I get so worked up. I know I shouldn't worry about shit I can't control and I also know that I can't control how people are going to react and judge you, and then judge mom and dad for having a child like that or me for having a brother like that. I get worried that one or all of it is going to destroy me, you, both of us or all of us.

I just don't understand it man. I just don't. I've been in the military for ten years now surrounded by men but never once did I ever get the desire to be with another man. Sometimes I think it's a choice. What else could make another man attracted to another man? And what would make another Black man with all we already have to face in this racist world fall for another man? I mean, we've been blessed enough to come from a stable home; two parents, and a drive for education. What went wrong?

It's true that we have an advantage over some other Brothers but no matter where you come from or where or how you were raised, nothing means more for us – Black men – than our masculinity. It overshadows everything we are. It's all we have when you get right down to it – the only thing that garners a level of respect in a world that doesn't want to respect us or even acknowledge that we're here. It's the only thing left we have to hold onto – the only thing that keeps them from coming – from lynching us all over again. It's the only thing that keeps them at bay. Without it, we're lost. Without it, we go nowhere, we do nothing, and they control us. What's going to happen to you now?

Maybe that's what I'm worried about. I think maybe that's it but I don't really know. I'm still trying hard to come to grips with it all. Look man, you're my only brother. I love you. I do. We're all we got. I'm trying man. I am. I'm really, really trying to get with this.

Love,
Taylor

p.s. Deb is tickled to death and sends her congratulations.

November 18, 2003
Dear Taylor,

I know this is still freaking you out but man, I'm hoping with all I can hope with that you'll reach the point of understanding and once that happens you'll reach the point of acceptance. I know this is overwhelming and you're worried about a lot of things. To be honest, I'm glad that you are. It means that you still love me and that you care enough about me to go through what you're going through. That means everything to me, man. It really does.

Michele wasn't so blessed. His family has refused to see him or talk to him since he told them about us and his older brother threatened to kill him. For now it's not safe for him to see his family. But like he always does he keeps on. He believes that they'll eventually come around, maybe now, maybe ten years, or twenty years from now. But he's confident that they will.

So I'm blessed that you're at least willing to hear me out and in hearing me out there's one important thing that I want you to know; nothing has changed about who I am. I'm still Gary, you're little brother. The same one who kept your ass in trouble all the time when we were younger and the same one you always bailed out. The same one you depended on to make excuses for you when you were late for curfew and the same one you taught to play basketball, football, and how to pitch.

I'm the same little brother who kept your confidence and all of your secrets even until this day. I'm the same one who loves you and depends on you for your guidance, support, your friendship, and love. I'm still Gary, your little brother, the same one you used to talk to all night long; you in the top bunk and me on the bottom one, about your dreams and goals, growing up, college, the military girls, dating, love, and sex.

I'm still Gary, your little brother and nothing has changed about me. When I get up in the morning before I go to bed at night the first thing I do is pray just like we used to do together when we were younger. Even until this day I always imagine that you're next to me. After I pray, I go for a run just like we used to do and when I get back home I eat my cereal, Capt. Crunch real fast so it doesn't get soggy just like we used to and I drink my juice right from the carton like we used to. I take a shower and shave like you taught me to and then I put on my suit, and tie my tie the way you taught me to.

I treat people - all people - with kindness and respect just like you taught me to, and I'm fair and honest in my dealings with them - a man of my word - like you showed me to be. I still give time to the community, like you taught me, and tutor twice a week. I take care of my body, eat right, hit the gym three or four times a week, and get my rest like you taught me. I still got mad skills on the b-ball court and a wicked serve on the tennis court that you probably still can't return. Nothing has changed about me man. Not a thing!

Every single thing you taught me I remembered - I remembered and I applied. I remembered and I applied your philosophy that *it's not what we are but who we are* that makes us. I remember, too, that you taught me that the measure of success in a man is defined by his character. I believe that still. I'm not wild or decadent, Taylor. I still have the same moral fiber that you molded in me that makes me a man. Those people you see on that street and in that neighborhood, those images that frighten you are just a couple of the many expressions of this lifestyle.

They don't represent the total truth about what it means to be same gender loving and they don't represent me, Michele, or some of the others I've come to know over the last year. I never had a question about my masculinity, and I still don't. I'm a man and I love being a man. The truth is I never desired to be anything else. I celebrate my masculinity. So it's not a question of masculinity and it's not about sex. It's not about sex or masculinity, or testosterone, or cop outs, or weakness, or anything like that. It's just about love. Plain and simple, love.

I want to assure you too that this wasn't a choice, man. Believe me it wasn't. I never desired much less chose to love another man. I didn't chose this, Taylor. It's like it chose me. I don't know why or how but it did. The only choice I've made is to accept that this is who I am and to recognize that the change in me, the change I've come to understand and accept, isn't a change that occurred on the outside. It changed for me on the inside and when it did it opened a new world of truth. I felt free. I feel free.

Most of all, I still believe what you told me about love. You said, "*Love is active. It is a force within us that takes position - knows no limits and no boundaries*". "*It is what it is*", you said, and now I know exactly what you meant. I know who I am and I don't fool myself into believing that it's going to be all gravy living as a man loving another man. I know it won't be. But I'm o.k. with it and Michele's o.k. with it but everybody won't be and that's o.k. too!

As long as I am grounded, that I don't lose sight of my own love and acceptance, I have a feeling I'll be fine. And if I can look to my family for love and acceptance - nothing more - than the world can kiss my ass!

Michele is who I love, Taylor. He's who I want to be with and I'm who he wants to be with and we can do that without compromise. It's the only way we'll survive. I'm not trying to start a crusade to change the world or even change anybody's mind. For those who can't understand it, find it difficult to accept, or are revolted at the thought well, they can look the other way. I'm not trying to sway anybody to this side, rub anything in anybody's face, or demand that they respect me. I'm just trying to live and love with the hope that my obligation to heal the world can be gained in some small way by my example - just by love.

So don't let yourself become depressed about this or disappointed or angry. There isn't anything anybody did or didn't do that made me who I am and loving who I'm loving. It's not anyone's fault because "fault" in this would suggests that there's something wrong with loving someone else no matter who they are. It would also mean that I should be ashamed or afraid but I'm not. I'm not afraid to be who I am, Taylor. You taught me that too!

Take your time to get used to it and let me know how you want to handle it. If you think you need time and space I can give you that. If you don't think I should come next month or that meeting Michele may be too much for you let me know that too. We can postpone until you think you're ready - maybe until after the baby is born. I won't be upset. I really won't. Let me know what you want me to do and I'll do it. I love you, man, with all my heart. Give Deb my love, and tell her I said thanks. She's amazing!

Love,
Your lil' Brother,
Gary

December 1, 2003
Dear Gary,

Wait until after the baby is born? Do you really think I'm that f'd up? Man, I have a billion unanswered questions about this and I'm dealing with a whole lot of shit it's true but dayum! It's not so deep that I don't want to see you. I couldn't imagine doing to you what Michele's brother said he'd do to him. I would never do that too you no matter what I'm dealing with. I would never take it out on you and I feel bad for him.

So naw lil' brother. You'd better bring your ass as planned and bring Michele too. You know this whole thing is bugging me out and I know it'll take some time to adjust but you're not being here is not the answer. I want you here with me man just like we planned cigars and all. I need you here little brother. I couldn't do this without you.

I read your letter a couple of time and I have to say it made sense. You made it perfectly clear to me – although Deb had her hand in bringing the point home – and you're right. She is amazing! That's why I love her so much. But the point she drove home to me as only she could is that underneath it all – underneath anything and everything – I just want you to be happy. And she's right. That's all I ever wanted for you – to be happy and to be loved. So if you've found happiness no matter in whom you found it I'm just grateful that you did. I'm just grateful that somebody is loving you like you deserve to be loved. So if you love him, Gary, I love him for loving you. I'll see you in a couple of months man.

Love Always,
Taylor

P.S. Michele – French Canadian. The burning question on my mind now is: Is he white? I have to admit I've been afraid to ask mom or Deb.

January 1, 2004
Dear Taylor,

Thanks, man. I needed to hear you say that. You don't know what it means to me to have you finding a way to hear me out and understand where I am coming from. Consider me there and all of the hopes, plans, dreams, and goals for the future that we had when we were young I'll bring with me too. We can go over them again, revise the old ones, and makes some new ones.

I love you, man, and I can't wait to see you. Michele sends his best and says thanks for being so cool. Happy New Year!

Love always,
Gary

p.s. "*If she can't use my comb don't bring her home!*" You taught me that, too! A long time ago - back in high school - and the same rules apply. Yes, Michele is Black - Blacker than midnight blue. Black and beautiful!

G.

The Exchange

Dad, I'm gay!

                                        Say again, son, what did you say?

Dad, I'm gay

                                        'Scuse me, boy, what did you say?

Dad, I'm gay

                             I didn't raise my Black son to be that way!

Dad, I'm gay!

                                                    Uh, Uh, No Way!
                                                  It must be a phase
                                                   It'll pass someday

Dad, I'm gay!

                                                  Don't say that, No!
                                            It'll kill yo' po' mama
                                                 She can't ever know

Dad, I'm gay!

                                     But son, you're a good-lookin' man
                                            You stand 6 foot 3
                                        You're not what I know
                                             A gay man to be

But, Dad, I am
I've known all my life

                                                You'll feel different, son
                                         If you find yo'self a wife
                              Now go git' ya self a nice young girl
                                                And go on a date

No, Dad, I can't
It's far too late

I know this is hard, Pop
But I want you to understand
I have fallen in love,
And it is with a man

> I don't wanna hear this, Junior
> What done happen to you?
> Was it that fancy college
> We done sent you to?
>
> What did I do wrong? How did I fail you, son?
> I did as much as I could fo' ya'
> 'Cause you my only one
> Talk ta me, boy
> I want to know the truth
> Was it dem white boys dat done
> Dis ta you?

No, Dad, No!
It's not like that at all
You raised me to be a
Proud Black Man
To be strong and stand tall

The man I love is Black like me
And he reminds me a lot of you
He works very hard
He's honest and clean
He's kind and funny, too

You didn't fail me, Pop
This has nothing to do with you
There have been changes in my life
And things that I've been through

I tried for years, Dad
To hide from the way I felt
But you always said,
"Son, deal with the hand you've been dealt! "

So instead of resisting,
I just let myself go
And It was a big relief
Unlike you'll never know
And all of a sudden,
It was as clear as can be
And for the first time in my life
I finally felt free

                                                So wha'cha sayin' son
                                                Is that how it's gonna be?
                                                Am I 'spose to accept
                                                My son's a Gawd-dayumm fairy?

                                                Junior, the good book say
                                                It's a 'bomination
                                                I'm gone call Reverend Murphy
                                                Ta pray fo' yo' salvation

Dad, look at me
I'm not a fairy-I'm still the same man
Nothing has changed about who I am

I'm still Junior, your one and only son
Still playin' basketball, as fast as I run
Still pumpin' weights
Eat three squares a day
And every night before bed I'm on my knees to pray
I'm still as honest
As you taught me to be
I don't lie, cheat, or steal
It's not that I've changed, Pop
It's the way I *feel*

           Good lord, gimme 'screnff
            This is really hard to take
            Son, I thought I raised ya ta
          Be careful wit choices ya make

But that's just it, Pop
It's not a choice you see
I didn't *choose* to be gay
It's like it chose me

Believe me when I tell you, Pop
This has been really hard for me
I spent many nights praying
For these feelings to let me be

But the more I resisted
The stronger they became
And then I started hating myself
I thought I was to blame

The last thing I ever want
Is to disappoint mama and you
But Pop, this is *who I am*
Not what just something I want to do

                                 I think I understand, Junior
                              But cha' know I don't like this shit
                              Two mens ta' getha jus ain't natural
                                  Make me…make me wanna spit

                              Itz' gone take some time ta a'juss
                              But I know we gone' make it through
                                  Just promise ta be safe, son
                                  And no matta' what…I loves you

                                  Now git up and dry yo' eyes
                                'Cause we got real work ahead
                                Yo' mama's gonna flip her wig
                                    And just may fall out dead!
        What she gone tell dem church folk the way she brag 'bout you?

            …I'mma tell 'em how I always tell 'em
                    What else am I s'possed ta do?
          I'mma tell 'em 'bout how proud I am of Junior
                      And oh how I love him so!
        Grad-u-atin' at da toppa his class at law school
                          Chile, don't 'ya know
               I ain't shame of my baby, honey
                    No matta what he do
      'Cides, I been knowin' for a whole year now…

                    We just had ta tell you!

Struggle
The Art of Survival

Native New Yorkers
(For My Cousins Stacy and Donna)

the beat of the city
pulsed in the palm of your hand
you were the rhythm
you were New York
All over you

baptized by the noise of the subway
anointed by intoxicating fumes
from gypsy cabs
you gladly took in as an ocean breeze
from the beach at Coney Island
and Reese

your walk the walk of a Queen
you strutted your stuff
while the winds of Central
and Prospect
blew your natural a little to the left

every borough
claimed you as its own
the Grand Dame of Brooklyn
the Bastion of the Bronx
the Maharini of Manhattan
the Queen of Queens

every project
wanted you there
Marcy
Thompkins
Woodside
to create its identity
to keep it alive

the Village knew you by
first name
the dance floor at Roseland
felt your feet and peeped under
your skirt as you
hustled and bus stopped the night into day

you mastered circles
turns and spins
at Empire
in your halter top
bell bottoms
skates and Afro puffs

and you held New York
right there
in the center of your hand
pulsating, beating, and charged

everybody loved you
everyone cared
even you

but then you held out your hand
gave up the pulse
the beat
the charge
to a man
in exchange for what you thought he had to offer
stealing your spark
draining your energy
quieting your smile

you gave him your love
he gave you his fist

you gave him your mind
he gave you his insecurities

you gave him your soul
he gave you needles

you gave him your body
he gave you HIV

the city is silent now
the life has been choked
out of it
and the only sounds are the moans
and groans of pain
and longings
that seem to whimper your name

It begs for you
asks for you
looks for you
around every corner
anticipating your energy
your blaze
your fire
your beautiful face

the handball courts are lonely
the benches in the court
and turtle park
empty
with the absence of your laugh
your smile
your song

there are no bites left to
take in the Apple
the flavor is gone
the taste bitter-sweet
the shiny skin dimmed
forever

only lasting imprints
failing memories
scattered pictures
of the smiles
and love you left behind
too much
too little
too late
to prove

You were New York
All over you

Moses and David

March 7, 2015

Dear Moses,

How are you best friend? I hope you're doing fine!

Well, it's finally over! He moved out yesterday. Took everything he owned and left. Now I'm sitting here in a half empty house wondering what to do next. I don't know whether to laugh or to cry - laugh for my freedom or cry for my loneliness. Five years is a long time to spend with one Brother. Five years of loving is hard to let go of. I have mixed emotions about this.

It's kind of scary being alone again. You know how I feel about being alone. Never really like it! Still don't. But I guess in some way this is good for me right now. I know that time will heal this wound. I've got to hold on. It's just going to take some time to get used to.

You know he was my first everything. The first Brother I ever loved, the first I ever knew sexually, and now the first man to break my heart. Who would have guessed that my life would have turned out the way it has. Certainly not me! I would have never thought that I'd be sitting here with my heart torn into pieces because of another man.

I always imagined that by thirty-five I'd be married, have the house I always wanted, the career path of my dreams, and a couple of kids to raise. Thought there would be family vacations, barbecues in the park, PTA, baby sitters, family reunions and the whole nine. Instead, I'm getting a "divorce" and from another man to boot! Hiding this pain from my family, depressed, and confused about my future.

Life is very strange man. Lots of curves and dips in the road and way too many forks in it to know if you're doing the right thing. I came across way too many forks in my road but it seems that I never chose the path myself. Always seemed that I let others choose it for me. Now I guess it's my turn to grow up. For real, Moses, this is really scary!

When I think about this whole situation man. I get mad as hell! I think of what we had to do to be together. The sacrifices we had to make to stay together and all of the pressure we were under not to let anyone know. I think about all this and I get pissed the fuck off!

And to think that all we went through, all I went through, could be thrown away in a blink of an eye. How could five years be tossed to the side and forgotten in a matter of two weeks? How could he let somebody come between us like this? I guess I'll never really know.

Well anyway, I don't want you to worry about me. I'm doing o.k. This is just one more thing on my long list of shit I have to deal with. I don't have any immediate plans right now other than to get the house back in order. There are some things I have to replace you know, some furniture, kitchen stuff, sheets and things like that so I'll probably spend the next couple weeks trying to turn this house back into a home.

Well, I gotta go! Hope all is well on your end. Write me back and let me know. In the meantime, I'll keep you posted on my progress. Miss you man! Take care.

Love Always,
Your Best Friend,
David

March 11, 2015

Dear David,

I just opened your letter and a bottle of champagne at the same time! Congratulations, baby boyee, you're finally free!!! I know you're not in the mood for a celebration, so I'll do it for you! Hip, Hip Hooray! The niggah is gone!!!!!

Listen David, I don't want it to appear that I'm making light of the situation because you know I'm not. I just know that the mutha fukka didn't deserve you in the first place! I never thought he loved you the way you loved him. You were so good to him man and it never seemed to me like he cared at all. Besides, you know he never liked me so believe me there's no love lost! As far as I'm concerned the further he's away from you the better he smells!!

The sad thing is I always knew that it would come to this. There was no other way it could have ended. That fool always had a wandering eye and I'm sure - in fact I know - that this wasn't the first time he cheated on you or let another Brother come between you. There are some things I know you kept from me because you know I would have pimp slapped the shit out of him and probably you! But you know how this life is - telephone, telegraph, tell-a-sissy! Even though I'm way in California now I still get updates. My phone be ringing off-da-hook!!!!

The Brother had too many issues anyway. Way too many for you to erase. I know you tried hard for years and had this attachment because he was the first Brother you loved in that way but you should have been able to see through his shit. I know I could. That's why that trifling bastard never liked me!

That's also why he tried to get you to choose between me and him. Remember that? Well, I do. I'm just glad you had the good sense to tell him not to force you into making a choice. He would have lost hands down - I think (Smile)!

Nevertheless, I know you loved him and I was hoping in the back of my mind that I was wrong about him. That's why I backed off a little to give you some space. I thought it was the best thing to do. You have to believe that I really wanted things to work out between you and him. I really did. That's why I didn't mind that I had to limit my call and when you had to lie to him when you were coming to meet me I kept quiet.

I didn't trip (too hard) either when you two decided to buy a house together and I had to limit my visits to when he was gone did I? No. I held my tongue and I gave you space. I knew he would eventually show his true colors and you would wake up one day and see him for who he was. Now the day is here and I couldn't be happier!

So it sounds like you're keeping the house. Well, you should. You put a lot of time and energy into it so why not! I'm just curious as to how that's going to work out. Can you handle that house payment on your own? Did you get his name off of the mortgage and deed? I hope you didn't let his foul ass take everything with him either. I know how kind hearted you are and what an ass he can be. And what about all that dayum grass? You know you don't like doing yard work and shit like that and you know I can't help you. I have particular preference about where I sweat (smile). Maybe you should consider something smaller. Five bedrooms is a lot of house for one person. Well, whatever you decide you know I got your back. Just let me know if you need anything man. I mean anything. Don't be shy. You know I'm here for you.

O.K. I have to run now. I got a date tonight (You know how I roll!!) so I'm going to close. But before I do there are a couple of things I have to say:

First David, you know you're my best friend and I love you to death! I only want the best for you. It's all I ever wanted. Now you have this new opportunity to see yourself through your own eyes and do all of the things you put on hold for this relationship. It's your turn now man. I know this is the last place you expected to be at this time in your life. I know you like the idea of being settled and I know you expected this to last. Nobody gets into a relationship thinking that it's going to end.

But, oh well, it's where you are. Might as well make the best of it. That's what I try to do. I always thought I'd be married with children too but it just didn't happen for me like that. So I've made a good life for myself. I wouldn't have ever expected to be single at this age either but I know I won't be forever. In the meantime I'm enjoying my life and dealing with myself. So really single life ain't all that bad!

Take some time to get over this. Take some time to put all this shit in perspective. You need to figure out why you stayed as long as you did. Trust me. You'll find out that this had little to do with that gutter slime Brother you attached yourself to. This is about you! Once you work all of that out you'll be back in the saddle before you know it! You're beautiful inside and out, smart, intelligent, and attractive! It won't be long before the Brothers are lined up around the corner trying to get with you! He was an ass hole, David. Forget him!

Listen, if you want to come out here let me know. Some time away from the city and that house could do you the world of good. You probably need to feel the sun, sit by the ocean, and take your mind off of things - not to mention that you've been promising to come ever since I moved out here. That's been over two years now. Wassup with that? Let me know. In the meantime Brother I'll be praying for you. Call me if you need me.

Love Ya, Baby,
Peace,
Moses

March 21, 2015

Wassup, Moses!

Thanks for the words of wisdom (and the laughs). I knew I could count on you to put things into perspective and help me find some humor in this! Seriously, it means a lot to me.

Sorry it took so long to write back but as you can imagine I've been real busy. Between working and trying to deal with this it seems that I don't have a moment to myself. I'm working at home today waiting for some new living room furniture to be delivered so I thought I'd take advantage of this moment to update you on what's going on here.

First, I want to just say thank you. There haven't been many things in my life that have been constant with the exception of you. You just don't know how much I love and appreciate our friendship. Even during the time of conflict with Craig you respected my choices and kept quiet. Believe me I know how hard that was for you! I know you didn't like him (and still don't) but you knew how I felt about him and you supported me anyway. Those times, the ones when you'd let me unload all this shit on your shoulders and try to perk me up enough to leave him, are forever in my mind. I'm grateful to have you. Thanks for always being there!

So now to the real shit. First, the business side of things: You know I don't have a real good business sense that's always been your area but believe it or not I use to listen to the advice you gave me (well…some of it at least). Anyway, Craig has agreed to continue paying his half of the mortgage until the end of the year. At that point either one or two things will happen: we'll sell the house and pay off the mortgage or I'll buy out his interest and take him off the mortgage.

I don't know what I'm going to do at this point. I really love this house and I don't want to leave it. I can afford the payments on my own (thank you very much!) but you're right five bedrooms is a lot of house for one person. Besides there are so many memories here and it's still painful. Sometimes I'm comfortable being here other times I'm not so sure.

I do alright until I come back home. It's so different in here now. Not just because he took some of the furniture and shit but the energy is different too. I don't know but sometimes it's almost like coming inside of a house covered by an overwhelming sadness - like there's been a death. Except I know he's not dead - just in another part of the city starting a new life with somebody else.

When I look around the house and listen to empty sounds bouncing off of the wall I want to leave. But then there are times when I think he'll be back and we can pick up where we left off and I want to stay. I don't know. I'm still confused right now. There is a part of me that wants him back and another part that wants him to stay away. Is that natural?

On the emotional tip rest assured, Moses, it's getting easier day-by-day. I've been doing a lot of thinking you know, soul searching and I have to admit that the pain is subsiding. In fact I haven't cried in days and my appetite is coming back. Still, I can't help but take some of this personal and wonder if I did something wrong or if I could have done something more. I know I did what I could to make this work but sometimes I think that I should have fought harder. I don't know. I just need more time to sort it out. One thing's for sure I'm still mad as hell and trying to let that go. But, oh well, like you said this isn't about Craig. It's about me. I'm working real hard trying not to let this get the best of me.

By the way he called me last week to see if he could come by and pick up some stuff he left in the garage. I told him that he could and we ended up having a big argument. I opened the garage door and his new man was sitting in the car. Can you believe he brought his new man with him?

The Brother didn't get out of the car but I couldn't believe he brought him here. I told him that he had a lot of nerve but he just told me to, "*Get over it*!" He said that this was still his house and since this was the new Brother in his life and everything was out in the open he didn't have to hide him anymore. I told him I wasn't asking him to hide him but he shouldn't flaunt him in my face. Now get this, dude got out of the car and had the balls to ask me if there was a problem? He stepped up to me like he was going to try to whip my ass man!

Craig knew I was about to go off on both of them so he told the Brother to get back in the car and they left. I was like, "*Dayum*!!" You're right, Moses, I'm really starting to see him for who he really is and I swear I don't like what I see. I'm trying real hard not to hate him but it's a fine line between love and hate, and I can feel he's about to cross it. He'd better not ever try that shit again!

And thanks for the offer to come to Cali. I think I might take you up on it soon but now is not a good time. Work is hectic and I'm still trying to get the house together. Maybe I'll come in the next couple of months. I'll let you know. Furniture truck just pulled up. Gotta go! I'll holla. Write me back!

Love,
David

April 5, 2015

David,

Tell me that muthafukka didn't bring that boy to your house! Please tell me he didn't! See...all I need is a fuckin' reason! If that's how he want to play this shit out then so be it! You should have spit in the mutha fukka's face and beat his ass with them golf clubs you never use. Dayum! I wish I was there. It would've been blood, guts, and hair everywhere!!!!

All right, David, I realize that the relationship is over and shit, and you're dealing with separation issues but dayum!! That doesn't give him free reign to disrespect you and treat you like you a fuckin' stranger on the street. I'm going to tell you this too - don't be sitting over there like a pussy either taking that shit! You ain't never been no passive niggah so wassup? You need to lay the shit on the line to Craig and tell him to back the fuck off! All this shit ain't even necessary!

Do me a favor man and watch your back. You may not know what Craig's capable of but I do! He's probably enjoying this shit. Knowing his ass he might be even encouraging this new niggah of his. I know the dude is young too so he's trying to show out like he's all that. Stupid bitch!

I know you would never tell me but I know that wasn't the first time he flaunted that Brother in your face. You know I'm well connected and somebody and I won't say who (o.k., it was Dennis!) told me that Craig brought the Brother to his birthday party a couple of weeks ago. He said that you and Craig had words and that the Brother said something to you and you left.

Now look - I'm getting mad as shit! You know and I know that shit ain't cool! I'm telling you now, David, only one more report is all it's going to take and I promise you I'm on the next plane out there. Try me!

Chin up!
Love you,
Moses

April 10, 2015

Dear Moses,

Listen man. I'm cool. Really I am. I didn't tell you about all this shit because I know how you are and I don't want no shit. I don't know what's up with Craig man. He's tripping like you wouldn't believe. I don't get it. I'm just trying to keep the peace.

Leave it to Dennis to call you way in California to gossip. The incident at the party wasn't really about shit. Craig come over to me and asked if we could have dinner that next week to talk and settle our differences. I told him, "*No!*", and he got an attitude and stormed off.

The next thing I know his boy was all up in my face. I wasn't being a pussy because I left out of there bruh. I just needed to get out before I created a scene. You know I don't like situations man especially in somebody else's house.

Anyway, he's been calling me a lot lately saying shit like he doesn't know if he did the right thing and that he misses us. He even had the nerve to ask me if I still loved him and if things were different between him and his boy would I take him back. I told him that I did still love him but as far as coming back given all the shit we've been through over the last couple of months I wasn't too sure.

I don't understand why he's asking this shit. He and his boy are supposed to be all good and everything. I just don't get it. Anyway, stay put for now. I'll call in the big guns if I need them later!

Love,
David

April 20, 2015

Well, David!

If you don't get it I certainly do! I heard that there's trouble in paradise. There's a whole lot of shit happening on the other side of town. Seems Craig's boy is everybody else's boy too! He's been sneaking and creeping out on Craig and now Mr. Wonderful ain't all that wonderful anymore!

As I understand it Craig caught ol' boy with Cedric (you know Cedric, the village hoe - he'd fuck a snake if he could get down low enough!). Anyway, supposedly Craig came home early one day last week and caught them at his crib pants down and all. I heard it got ugly! I hear Craig and the dude had a big ass fight. Supposedly Craig put him out but I found out last night that they were seen at the club two nights later together all hugged up and shit.

But you can imagine Craig ain't happy with this shit and now he's looking to try to see where he stands with you. He knows in his heart of hearts that he should have never left his relationship for that young trick anyway. He can't be but about 23 years old. You know he ain't ready to settle down with no 35-year-old dude. Shit, you know what it was like when we were 23. Couldn't nobody hold these bodies down! Well, all I can say is good for Craig's ass. He's getting just what he deserves!

Now-as far as you're concerned you have to be strong, David. Craig is desperate. The Brother's sitting at the helm of the Titanic and knows the shit is about to sink! Ain't no telling the shit he's going to pull and the stuff he's going to say to get you to let him back in. DON"T DO IT!!! No matter what he says, no matter what he does, DON'T DO IT!!!!!

And for goodness sake, David, whatever you do don't sleep with him. Don't forget the heartbreak and all the shit he's put you through.

It's over. Let it stay that way. It can't be erased with a nutt! Remember, man, be strong!

Love,
Moses

April 27, 2015

Dear Moses!

You're right, as always! Craig called last week crying and begging me to see him. He says he wants to talk. I told him no (again) only because your letter arrived fifteen minutes before he called. Dayum! Your timing is always perfect!

 He didn't say that anything was wrong with his relationship. He only said that he wanted to give us another try. He sounded pitiful, crying and shit. But his words just rolled right off of me like a raincoat. I wasn't fazed man for real. I told him I didn't think it was a good idea for us to get back together and I could hear the hurt in his voice. Moses, I can't help but feel sorry for him. He sounded real bad, man.

 Part of me still wants him back but the other part is telling me to just let it be. Shit! Just when I was starting to get over his ass here he comes with this shit again! When He called the other day he was all broke the hell up asking me to reconsider seeing him on neutral territory, dinner or something. This time I told him I would. I'm going to meet him next Thursday night for dinner to talk. Just talk. I'll let you know how it goes.

 I know I have to be strong and I will. I promise to be. And I'm not going to sleep with him (I don't think - smile). But you know the Brother does things to my body that no one else has ever been able to do. He makes me feel things. I don't know man I can't describe it but I tell you what my body needs this! It's been about 3 months now and I'm about to lose my mind. Besides, I don't think there's anything wrong with a bump and grind for old time sake do you? I'm not saying that it would happen but if the opportunity presents itself I don't know how I'm going to resist. Shit, he owes me at least that much!

O.k. I'm out. I'll keep you posted. Miss you man.

Love,
David

May 1, 2015

David,

I just got back in town today to find your letter and a stack of bills waiting for me. I had a conference in San Francisco (and a couple of dates lined up - I'll fill you in on that later) so in case you're wondering why I sent this letter FedEx. It's simple. I'm coming to town tomorrow - that would be Thursday.

My plane gets in at 3:00 in the afternoon. What time did you say we're meeting Craig for dinner? Give me a call so I'll know what to wear!

Love Always,
Moses

A Heart Broken

What Becomes Of A Heart Broken?

Does it
sit idle rested in pain
break and tear as easily as a bubble bursts
allow pain and hurt to eat at it as does a cancer
Does it dwindle
Shattered until there is nothing left?

Does it
stop beating
pulsating
Leaving it all
Body and soul
To die?

Does its
immunity
instinct
protect it from betrayal
veins and arteries survive
tears and tears of love lost

Does it fight
For survival
For beat
Rapid
Rhythmic
Steady?

Does it love
Trust again
Heal?

What becomes of a heart broken?

Where

I was lonely
Without home
Without direction
When the Brother said, *"Come..."*

To a place
Where
The compass points
To sweet pleasures
Of fantasy and delight

Where
Secrets have a home and
Unspoken desires are voiced

Where unlocked passions
Savor flavors of brown
From touches to moans

Nothing begged
Beckoned me to stop
No alarms
No rules or regulations
Pulled me away
Nothing pinned me against tides of no

Thought love would be there
Somewhere
But there was none

No where
Yet I fell for it
All of It...

When he said, "*Come...*"

Still On The Stage

Act III - Scene One - Take 2

I call for my line

What do I say?
How do I move?
Who do I look at?
Who do I choose?

Let me set the stage for you

Three characters
Perfectly sketched
You, Me, and He
Standing on this stage
The next line belongs to me

You and him
Blocked
Stage right
Together for whatever reason
You've dreamed up now

Only you and I know the truth

I stand alone
Stage left
Back turned
Face forward of difficult decisions
Issues of my own Diaspora
I have now to confront
Thought I left this saga tides ago
But I'm still standing on the stage
In the first act –

Act One - Scene Two - Take 1

I did it all
Gave what I knew and didn't know
Parts of me I never knew I had
Loving every inch of who you were
Coming to my rescue
Thinking, hoping you felt the same
We could have written our own ending
You and me
A happily ever after

But I forgot about me in the midst of finding you

I neglected, I postponed, I reserved
Put myself and plans on hold
For hopes
Holding tongue, holding breath
Withholding words, disappointments, hurts
To keep you
Not knowing why or what
I was trying to keep

All through

Act One - Scene Three

You demanded, you expected, you pushed,
You barked,
You lied
I demanded, I expected, I pushed
I barked,
I begged
Wanted you to see what you could not
Something
Anything to let me know you knew

But nothing ever came
Except the star struck
You made a part of our story
Who became integral to our dialogue
As the drama unfolded

Writing in a crucial plot
Forever changing our script
Confirming my fears
Validating insecurities

Here in this space
Between orchestra, audience, and crew
We lose our voices
No longer can we hear
Words bounce back and forth
Projecting empty sounds
In a barren arena

Your light dimmed me
Hollowed my soul
Until we fade to Black
Exposing Me
Dark
Naked on the stage

Now that wounds have been revealed
And I see them
I need to see myself
A change
To change

A spotlight of my own
No longer a costar in your production

In the opening of

Act Two - Scene One

I said good-bye
The hardest performance I ever had to give
Confusion dominating my motivation
Unsure of exodus
Hoping somewhere deep
Something would change
Time
A challenge for us to recognize a healing
And mend what was started

Your lack of action
Prompted my reaction
I left
Disappointments in tow
Looking for somewhere to drop them
Before I rehearsed for a new role

My role - the best ever
A starring role in my own story
A One Man Show
Exclusive rights long ago granted
To produce and direct
You wouldn't
Couldn't
Can't let go
Friends we agree
Though never could I imagine
A New Dynamic

Enter Stage Right
A new character
An Understudy
Called to fill my role
To fill shoe and descriptions
That cannot fit his feet nor his tongue
No Ovations
No Curtain Call

Exit stage left?
That I already tried
Only your confusion
My vulnerability
Ties us
Bringing me back to center stage

Tension mounts
One more screen test
One more audition
Weakness prevails
We let it happen
My body needs this
You didn't stop it
I couldn't

Once more on the casting couch
Your body yearns
And my body craves
No regard for the understudy
Waiting in the wings

Recalling
What I've done to the understudy
Mirrors what you did to me

Discovering
The lighting isn't any different
The stench in the air any fresher
The set still the same
The role not mine to play

Epilogue

I stand here calling for my line
No response from the crew or the crowd
This line I must write myself
It's obvious to me

You and him blocked
Stage right
Me
Still standing on the stage

I turn to you
Not looking at him
Breathing deep
To deliver my line,

"There will never be a day that I won't
think about you or what could have been
but you and I can be no more
I know this now

Thank you
for helping me reach
deeper than I have ever before
to find love and forgiveness

I will never forget you
Good-bye!"

Amid music and applause
I exit
Stage left

Dutiful

Dutiful moves through life
Seemingly effortlessly to those who know of his nature
His soul
He's everything to everyone
But only he know of the sorrows of his heart
Unfilled desires
Years ago abandoned in his mind
His heart won't let go of

Dutiful performs obligations of a family
Acknowledging his existence
Knowing nothing of his life

No one's ever asks
Of who holds him
Of who's loving him
Touching him tenderly
With kindness
And care

Dutiful
Remains silent
Swallowing his pain
And hurt and loneliness
Speaking his isolation not even to
Friends blinded by their own
Not wanting to see the same loathing
In their own hearts
Mouths choked with cotton balls

Laced with shame in their throats
Clinging hopefully but superficially to each other
To fade away hopelessness

Dutiful
Keeps pace
With graduations
Finances
Needs
Advice
Smiling always
Pretending all is well

Taking in the harshness and tongue lashes
From others words or actions
Or both words and actions to keep him placed

Balancing spirit with sanity
And insanity
To keep himself moving
And forward on
As waves of destruction
And self-destruction
And waterless tears
Tear at him
Eating away at his love and his character

Wanting to lash back - hit
Strike at something
Anything
With hands tied to defenselessness

Dutiful
Lies in bed
Headful of remembrance
Of lost friends
Lost love
Lost promise
From he who could not love
And reflects on wrongdoings
Of his own

He wonders if this is penance
Settlement
And here in this life's station
He must remain

As disappointments surround
His heart and mind
He creates and thinks
What if he who could not love
Could love
Equally and strong

How different the sound
How different the drum
How different the heartbeat

At night he dreams
In darkness and
In turmoil
That he may never be loved

And when he wakes
From uncomfortable slumber
Heart filled with sadness and
Missings
He calls out to
He who could not love
And left him hurt
And in wonder
Longing to hear his voice
He who left him for another
And he wants to touch the other him
Who found no comfort in loving another
Like him
Or himself

And he wonders if he should have
Tried harder
Fought longer
Or submit to drama
Begging, convincing, conniving

Or that he should have allowed himself
To feel the feeling of vulnerability
Show tears and weakness
And complications
To guilt them
Each of them
To come back

Dutiful
Asks God to remove the
Hurt and the pains
Away from his heart
Asks God for the time to come
When love will be
While he wonders if peace is
Only in escape from his life
In another city
In another state
In another country
Or in death

Wherever it is
Wherever peace may be
He yearns for it
Comfortable to be with it
Wherever it is found
Whatever is required
To get to it

Part II.

Dutiful
Cries
His heart oppressed
His desires unspoken
Fighting
The breakdown
Remaining stable
Fragile

Though no one knows nor will they ever know
Of his wanting to
Scream, scream, scream
And cry
And break things
And say no to those who ask for his
Continued sacrifices

Say no to always being kind
And understanding
And say no to keeping silent
When targeted
And say no to looking for the
Loving way
The spiritual way
And say no to accepting lies
Deceit
And issues

And say no to thoughts helplessly
Tying him to this pain
All this pain

Dutiful
only talks to God
But not as often
Not as sincerely
Not as much as he should
He knows
For no one he thinks
Walks with him on his journey

Dutiful
Wonders if there is something
Not right
Something wrong with him

And he hurts knowing that he may
Never be understood
Or loved
Or touched
Or warmed
And kissed
And spoken to
Gently and with kindness
Or comforted
Or danced with
Or that he won't have him
He that cannot be loved
To stare in his eyes
And melt with desire
And love
With unspoken tongue
But knowing the feeling still

And he asks God
Again
To remove the burden from
To take away the desires completely
To leave him alone
Of thoughts
That it could happen
That it might come

He asks that memories are erased
Of recent and long ago
To clear his mind of
Remembrance
Of them that he loves
But cannot

Dutiful
Asks God to heal
Please heal
Heal
As he prepares himself for another day

Free Falling

This Brother
Strong, Sexy
Inviting
Echoing Sounds
And Vibes Of His Present
Preserving The Fragrance
Of a Past
That He Cannot See

                                  Free Falling

This Brother
Kind, Compassionate
Generous
Every Bit The Protector
Caretaker From Sun to Sun
With Nowhere To Lay His Burdens
Long After The Day Is Done

Longing For The Beat
Of Passion And Excitement
Long Missing From
Days Of Devotion

Free Falling

His Eyes Tell Of Confusion
That His Spirit Cannot Hide
Not Knowing the Sweet Passion
Of Peaceful Waters
Free flowing On The Other Side

His Eyes Hold the Pain And
Disappointments
His Lips Will Never Speak
Nor of the Freedom of
Love's Understanding
His Heart Desperately Seeks

His Soul Is In Limbo
And He Cannot See

His Heart Battles Confusion
And He Cannot Hear

Free Falling

But Fear Not, Brother,
Peaceful Waters Always Flow
But Inside Yourself
To Awaken Love's Senses
Is Where You First Must Go

The Wind, My Brother,
Is At Your Back
And The Sun
Always On Your Face
And If You Take A Moment
To Reflect On This
You'll Find a Peaceful Place

Where You Are Always Warmed
Against Brutal Cold
And Cooled
Against Scorching Heat
Where Your Soul
Your Heart
And Passions
Find The Place Where Love Does Meet

Uncertain Days Are Over
Troubled Waters Need Not Be Violent

You Must Yet Find
Quiet Space amongst The Noise
And Listen To The Silence

Your Eyes

I was looking for
escape
from my old self
to see a different self
in the mirror of your eyes

tired of feeling the same things
welcoming excitement
and passion thought lacking
in a pair long since gone
on separate paths

I left…him for you

he hated to see me leave
begged me not to go
cried a thousand tears
of a crocodile sort
falling upon deaf ears

couldn't see past offers you made
to save me from him
to save me from me

find happiness in my soul
search strengths
surface peace
breath harmony
slow quickened paces
remedy lesions
years buried
and unspoken?

not a chance
I was looking for
escape from my old self
to see a different self in the mirror
of your eyes

romance my first love?
discover what made me fall
the first time?
his smile
his humor
his command
his attention
the bend in his back
the touch of his hand?

the thought never occurred to me

a lover's holiday
a reprieve
a change of pace
a change of scenery
a change of mind
to see newness?

never thought of something
so simple

I was looking for
escape from my old self
to see a different self in the mirror
of your eyes

Didn't realize it at the time
But my eyes were never really open
And yours always closed
Opened only to the excitement
Of stealing me from him

And once you did
And the hunt and chase no longer exciting
I saw nothingness
And emptiness

There were only lies in your eyes

Promise

He was life
Promise itself

Tall
Sexy
Charming
Strong

For years and more years
I was captivated by
Promise

his presence
his greeting
his warmth
his smile
never letting known my secret affection
for fear of rejection
in chance meetings of five minute no more
conversation maybe twice a year

for years and more years
I loved him
Promise
Never told me of secret affection
for fear of rejection
Promise believing I was
too together
not knowing I was
falling apart

So young were we then

Then it happened
twelve could be thirteen years down the line
Promise
voiced his attraction
I echo the same
We discussed
Promise and I
his excitement for us
in future plans laid in both our minds

timing felt so right
no longer young but seasoned
in the middle of life
are we

placed aside are the longings and desires
of free love
mindless
loveless
pursuits of flesh
and of parties
and of clubs
and of the next good time

we find ourselves here together
matured in life
in self
experienced enough
to experience this experience
so I thought

for months we share
life
hope
plans
future
Promise

we hold
hug
kiss
dream
plan
sleep
wrapped in the warmth of love
of love's Promise

Then it happened
Promises Broken
Promise broke
himself
me
us
Promise
can't be with me
it's not distance
or even another's Promise

Promise can't be with himself

unequally yoked
he says we are
in accepting who we are
in loving who we are
in loving another Brother
in loving himself

tells me so in words not easily spoken
written
on a blank screen
delivered
with a click of a button
cutting
me to the core

Promise
is Broken
and I feel for him

Poor Promise
Broken Promise
Will never be fulfilled

I feel for the lovelessness in
Promise
Empty Promise

And I miss you
Promise
and all we had the potential to be

I Want To Tell Her

I want to tell her
but I don't want to make her cry
that the son she raised
the son she loves
has been living a lie

how disappointed I imagine she would be
to know the truth about her fourth child,
her second son, me

that I'm a Brother loving Brother
a same gender loving Man of Color
and all her suspicions were true
that the son she raised to be a Black man's man
has loved other men too

my reasons for not telling her the truth
for not sharing that part of my life
is to spare her the hurt and burden of failure
knowing I'll never have a wife

will her eyes well up in disappointment
and tears roll down the folds of her soft brown face
will she hold her head in her hands in disgust
and think my life's a waste

would she, too, tell me I've lost God's favor
that I've condemned myself to die
would she ask that I leave - to never darken her door
and not kiss me good-bye

would she be ashamed or embarrassed
and never speak of me again
in public or private
in her heart or in mind
or to family or to friends

I want to tell her
but I don't want to make her cry

it's too much for her heart to take
so I'll live in silence and never let on
and spare us both the heartache

Break Up To Make Up

This break up to
Make up
Is tearin my Black ass up

Same shit, different day
What was it this time?
        Your ex or mine
        Your laziness
        Or my expectations

You're lack of communication
Or my "fuck it! "attitude?
Your friends
My friends
Your lies or
My half-truths
The brother I swear you were crusin
The brother you swear I winked at?

Who knows?
It always ends up the same

1 a.m. - 2 a.m. attitude in the club
2 a.m. - 3 a.m. arguin all the way home
3 a.m. - 3:30 a.m. yellin, screamin, bitchin
Waking up the neighbors
With our shit again
We stopped caring long ago bout that

4 a.m. grabbin the shit you brought over
The last time we broke up and made up
4:15 a.m. last minute jabs and punches with words
4:18 a.m. you slam the slam the door behind you
With a final
"Fuck you! I'm out. Peace!"

But you can't stay away
Cause you know wassup
Ringin me at home every hour on the hour
Blowin up my cell
Wantin to talk it out
Wantin to work it out

Fuck that
I ain't ready
With each call I ignore I remind you
This was your choice
You said it was over
And I'm flowin with that

Use the time to catch up with my boyz
Maybe catch up with the Brother from the gym
Who's been workin my nerves
Trying to work on me

All I need is an excuse

Cause this break up to make up
Is tearin my black ass up

When enough is enough
When we torture long enough
To make you miss me
Make me want you
Here you go
Tims draggin up the sidewalk
Kissed with familiar steps
Heavy with the weight of your
Burdens

And there I go
Customary steps to invite you in
8 minutes of I'm sorry
5 minutes of I miss you
3 minutes of I love you
and it's squashed

You unpack your overnight bag
Replace your underwear
In the drawer
Shaving kit on the dresser
And slyly count the condoms in the nightstand
Where you lay your watch and chain
Your mind breathing a sigh of relief
To find them undisturbed

Undressing in dimness of candle light
In the medium of frankincense and myrrh
And it's off to the races

We make love
Obsession breathing with every exhale
And moan
Intensity flaring with the taste and
Movement of Blackness
Skin to skin
Flesh to flesh
This break up to make up
Shit is
Off the chain!!!!

Two days maybe a week
We get along
Then you piss me off with your
Attitude
Or I piss you off with my
Jealousy

Each time your silly ass
Or mine
Decide we can't take this
Shit
This homo shit
Or any other shit
This shit brings us to
We kirk out

Bounce on the walls
Yellin' at the top of our lungs
Fists throwin
Glass breakin
Police knockin
Removin you from my premises
Huffin and puffin from drama

And Here we go again

This break up to make up
Is tearin my Black ass up

2 Years 2 Months 2 Days

Every night you cry yourself to sleep
Wondering
If He loves you
Wondering
Where He is
Wondering
Who He's loving tonight

He ain't him, man
the man of your dreams
the Brother you've waiting for
He ain't him

2 years 2 months 2 days
Of love
Of lies He's told you
And you've told yourself
To compensate for your weakness
Against walking out the door
2 years 2 months 2 days ago

He ain't him

Loneliness keeps you still
Desperation keeps you quiet
Despair keeps you tied
Rejection keeps you miserable
His one Kiss keeps you guessing

I'm telling you
He ain't him

Strange voices on the line
Muffled conversations in the room
Vanishing acts in the night
Cold touches in the bed
No response to your love

The writing's on the wall
Brother
Take it from me
He just ain't him

Saga

She wants me home
        He wants me there
I want them both
        Neither will share

She knows nothing of him
        He knows but doesn't care
Lost from keeping secrets
        And found in his stare

She wants me closer
He wants me near
        What should be so easy
        Has never been clear

Been with her five years
        With him it's been three
With her I feel needed
        With him I feel free

She hints of marriage
        He wants to move in
My family adores her
        They think he's a friend

She's always on my mind
        But with him I'm obsessing
She tells me she loves me
        He keeps me guessing

I live for her softness
            Yet his hardness I crave
What should be all hers
            A part for him I save

To her I'm the one and only
            To him I'm his boo
She makes me feel like a man
            But then he does too

She kisses me softly
            His mustache tickles my face
She holds my arm
            He holds my waist

The feel of her against me
            Drives me wild
He celebrates my body
            She talks of a child

And when we make love
            I give it all I got
I make her moan
            He hits my spot

I do love her truly
            But my heart's just not there
My desires are for him
            And to her it's not fair

I don't want to hurt her
She deserves much more
            He's mentioned ultimatums
And I'm rocked to the core

Lived for everyone
Except for myself
        Happiness I've sacrificed
        For everything else

For expectations from family
And even those from me
        Masculinity and manhood
        And what a Black man's supposed to be

I'm stuck here in the middle
        Of two opposing lives
One promises sanction
        The other despised

This can't last forever
        And I know soon I must choose
But no matter where I go
        We might all just lose

With her I belong
        With him I want to stay
Until I know for certain
For this I pray:

        That no one will be hurt
        And from this we will all emerge whole
        No matter what comes

As this saga unfolds…

When Morning Comes...Come Daybreak

When Morning Comes…

It will find us here again
Sweating
Spent
Out of Breath
In complete silence
Lying here staring at the ceiling
Watching the fan above spin me
To calm

I pray silently for
Morning to come

He sleeps peacefully
Next to me
Now that we have completed
The ritual
The celebration of our love
The part of us that keeps us here
Black man to Black man

Breathlessness and exhaustion
Comes not from loving and holding
Onto each other
But from the agony of
Our pain and our Lacks

Our Fears

Imploding
Exploding
Manifesting
To Physical
Where we strike
Beating and kicking
Fists locked
Glasses thrown
Tables turned

This can't be right

Used to think our fights
Brought us closer together
Made us love more
Showed us how much we cared
For what we had
Proved his love for me

Now I don't know what to think
I don't think
I only pray

For
Morning to come

Bruises on my arm
Where he grabs me
Shows his protection of me
From the Brother
He thought I glanced at
Dark circle around my eye
Says he wants me to see
Only him

Clothes ripped from my body
Tells me he wants me to be
Sexy
To feel sexy
For him
Only him

Guarded lips
Swollen lips
For only his kisses to claim
To speak only love
And never "good-bye"
Drips my blood
On the pillow
From his black fist

My mind tells me to leave
My body won't listen

Where will I go
Who will have me
After he's
Staked his claim
On my skin
In my mind

This is comfortable
Familiar in my psyche
It is what I've known all my life

I saw my Father's love on my Mother's body
She stayed
I see my Brother's love for his wife on her body
She stays

And here we are
Two men
Black Men together
What more can I expect

Things are bound to get out of hand
Physical
When we are fighting for
Our love
Our sanity
To exist
Me and him against the world

Can't abandon him
Don't have a right to
Searched all our lives for us
Can't leave him now
Don't know how

When morning comes
It will all go away
I will shower
And wipe the tears from my eyes

I will change the sheets
And he will bring me juice from the kitchen
He will kiss these swollen lips
And say that he's sorry

He will hold me close
And cry a tear or two
And say that he loves me

We will make love
Passionate and Strong
To erase the scars

And this will all pass over
When morning comes…

                                    Come Daybreak…
                      He will think I'm sleeping
                                       I'm awake
                         Can't rest peacefully
                                  After this
                                  Our ritual

                      I listen to the rhythm
                         Of the fan above
                        Calming my breath
                  Soothing my exhaustion
           I can hear his low whispers
      His prayers for morning to come

                  I keep my back turned
                      Longing for daylight

                     Praying for daybreak

                 We fought again tonight
                          Over nothing
                      It's always nothing
                         We fight over
                      I don't know why
                            We do this
                        Don't know why
                              I hurt him

Don't mean to
Strike out
Strike him
With this rage

Pressure-cooks
Boils inside me
This oppression
This suppression
Brings about my
Obsession

Love this Brother
More than I love me
Don't knows if he sees that
Maybe that's the problem

Don't know why I stay
Don't know why he stays

Never ending Prayers
For daybreak

His gazes at another
Threatens what we have
I pull him to me close

His clothes
Provocative
Revealing gifts that belong
To me
Only to me
I tear them away

His lips
One day
Any day
Positioned to speak words
I never want to hear
"Good-bye"
I quiet them with my fist
Before he discards me

Somewhere in this confusion
And anger
In this love-hate
There is love

Don't know how else to show him
We need each other
We belong together

This is familiar to me
It's what I know
Fight for what's mine

I saw my father's love on my mother's skin
She stayed
I see my Brother's love for his wife on her skin
She stays

It has to be love
Because everything changes
I've seen it

Come daybreak

We need help
I need help
But nowhere to turn
This situation undefined
No help for Brothers loving Brothers

Two Black men
Struggling to keep each other
Warmed against lovelessness
And self-hatred

But it will all go away
In the daylight

Come daybreak
That is the time that he will awaken
And remove
My arms from his waist
I will feel him
Leave the bed
Leave the room

While he showers
I will slip out of bed
Surveying the damage
To my body
To our house
I will see his blood everywhere
Wipe the tears from my eyes
And regret

I will go to the kitchen
And pour Him some juice
He will change the sheets

I will bring it to him
And kiss his swollen lips
And tell him that I'm sorry
I will hold him close to me
And cry
And I'll tell him that I love him

We will make love
Passionate and Strong
To erase the scars
And this will all pass over

In the daylight hour

Come daybreak

Ooh Freedom/Side by Side

…And Before I'd Be A Slave, I'll Be Buried In My Grave, And Go Home To My Lord, And Be Free…

Oooh, Oooh, Freedom…Oooh, Oooh, Freedom…Oooh, Freedom, Over Me…

He lay down in a
Thicket of marsh to mask his scent
from the barking dogs,
And horses saddled with angry white men
hunting him
Runaway Slave
there to rob him of the freedom he sought
Frightened,
Hurting, and
Alone
He pushed forward

Before I'd Be A Slave, I'd Be Buried In My Grave, And Go Home To My Lord, And Be Free

Freedom calls His name
and guides his swollen bare feet
and malnourished frame
through the bayous of Louisiana
the muddy river banks of Mississippi
the mountains of Tennessee and the fields
of Kentucky

With the warm wind of
Freedom
On his face
and the wrath of angry bounty
hunters on his trail
the fate of his meaningful life in their hands
He runs

I will not be deterred
I will not turn around
Freedom is here
Just to the North of that there star
I can feel it
And it shall be Mine

Haunted by the memories
of his little Black babies
sold and separated to other plantations
His wife used by the massa for cleaning filth
and filthy desires
He cried and he prayed,
I will come for you
If death doesn't come for me first

> **Before I'd Be A Slave, I'd Be Buried In My Grave,**
> **And Go Home To My Lord, And Be Free**

Locked into the chains of
Slavery
from sun up to sun up
Working for free - given to eat what was discarded
from the main house

Beaten,
Humiliated
Robbed of Manhood
Stripped of Dignity
Denied Identity

You give me nothing to live for
So I shall take my chances
And die
> Running

Into the Brush
> Running

from the massa
I will die in the field
> Running

from the chains and the whips
I will die from exhaustion
> Running

into the sun

With freedom in my heart
and on my tongue
If I must die it will be on my terms
You will have to catch Me first

He wanted freedom or He wanted death

> **Before I'd Be A Slave, I'd Be Buried In My Grave,
> And Go Home To My Lord And Be Free**

He shuffled His feet when so called
Freedom
and wages came
Foot shufflin' nigger uncle tom

Cooking, chauffeuring, caring for their sick and their young,
Silent when insulted and scorned

But silence was his only salvation,
        Against the
hanging noose
        Against the
midnight riders
        Against the
burning crosses
        Against the
angry mobs,
        Against the
brutality

He shuffled, and shuffled, and shuffled some more
so he could go home
and send somebody to Howard
or to Morehouse or to Spellman

He had purpose in his shuffle
His shuffle a dance of fortitude
You may have me but not my children
No more demeaning
No more stolen humanity
No more

    Yes, before I'd Be A Slave, I'd Be Buried In My Grave,
        And Go Home To My Lord And Be Free

So there he sat at
white only - lunch counters
protesting injustices of his birth
with eggs, ketchup, insults, spit

obscenities hurled at him with vicious anger
and rage
Plates and broken glass and fists
smashed against his young, unwavering
Black body
Not moving, nor striking back
dragged, beaten, cut, cursed, and jailed

He stood his ground
with no protection
No signs welcoming him or his Black children

No relief
from the laws of jim crow
from the clubs of police brutality
or the vicious dogs biting at his flesh
or the water hoses desire to extinguish
Freedom's inferno in his heart

He stood his ground
never retreating
charged
riding Freedom busses from the North to the South
singing in harmony
meaning in melody and
proclaiming in praise,

Before I'd Be A Slave, I'd Be Buried In My Grave, And Go Home To My Lord And Be Free

nigger, nigger bitch, coon, boy, monkey, octoroon,
gorilla, dog, heathen
He heard them all but said,
defiantly and boldly,
My description cannot fit your tongue!

I sit here for my ancestors,
and for my children,
and for my children's children,
for my legacy and for my destiny
and I shall pray for you, my enemies,

Yes, before I'd Be A Slave, I'd Be Buried In My Grave, And Go Home To My Lord, And Be Free

He stood up for his community as a hungry
Angry panther
taking care of his own
discovering power and
beauty in self acceptance
Feeding his children and other hungry minds
truth and history to build self esteem and
Black Pride

He stood with his own in the lines of the
methadone clinics shaking off the chills of the heavy
snow storms that sought to divide and conquer a
solidified community

He stood up for his county in rice fields
in foreign lands
sacrificing his life for a country that never cared

Today, he stands robed
in front of the blind scales of justice
in front of the crack pipe
denying poverty
and behind the crack pipe
denying reality

Standing in soup lines
feeding a wanting soul
and in laboratories, searching and researching

In prison trapped by traps set for him by
racist laws designed to keep him impotent

In classrooms and campuses
teaching and being taught
Nurturing and developing new and
independent minds

On street corners
peddling his oils, his incense, his fabrics, his books and his
body to feed him and his

On Broadway, dancing the dance of freedom
and creating with the beauty of a new found
Pride

No longer a strange fruit
hanging and dangling from trees of
injustice
but a fruit of
Islam
Reconciling and Atoning

Recognizing
his ancestry and obligation

He breathes
Freedom
with every breath
and rejoices with every movement
and sings to ears listening and not…

Ooh, Freedom, Ooh Freedom, Ooh Freedom, Over Me,
And Before I'd Be A Slave, I'd Be Buried in My Grave
And Go Home To My Lord And Be Free

Free…

Side By Side

We Were There Together Brother - Side By Side
Laying In the Thicket of Marsh To Mask Our Scent
From Barking Dogs and Horses Saddled With Angry White Men
There To Rob Us Of the Freedom We Sought

We Were There Together Brother - Side By Side
When So Called Freedom and Wages Came
Shufflin' Feet - A Purposeful Dance
We Were There Together Brother - Side By Side

At White Only Lunch Counters Pulled and Beaten
Dogs Biting At Our Flesh
Protesting Injustices of Our Birth

We Were There Together Brother - Side By Side
Hungry Angry Panthers working for our Community
Dying In Rice Fields In Foreign Lands
Sacrificing Life For A Country That Never Cared

We Were There Together Brother - Side By Side
Learning, Teaching, Denying Reality, Denying Poverty
Through Epidemics of AIDS, Crack, Violence and Lock Downs
We Were There Together Brother – Side By Side
On Washington's Mall Reconciling and Atoning
We Were There Together Brother – Side By Side

And It Never Once Mattered Who I Loved

We Are Still Here Brother
Together
Side-By-Side

The Delta Elite

Release

                                                          ba-dum, ba-dum, ba-dum-tsh
                  I'm surprised to see your suitcase at the door....

Shit, I'm Not
..and I'm happy about it too
                  Remember the good times...Don't you want some more....

Not another minute!
                          It's not a perfect love....but I defend it....

No you don't and no you never did!
So Fuck you....
                                  It's not over.....over....over....

The Hell it Aint!!!
                     ba ba boomp boomp boomp boom....
                         so deep....so good....so deep....
                       so deep.....ohhhh so good....ohhhh....

In fact, Fuck you
Fuck it all
                   ba ba boomp boomp boomp boom....

Stupid ass...ain't even my boss
Who did he think he was talking to?!
                gotta have house....music....all night long....
                    ....move your body...rock your body....
                Gotta have house...music...can't go wrong....

That's right....move your body man
Shake it
Swirl those hip – Raise your arms
All up in the air
                Dunt...dunt...dunt...dunt...dunt...dunt...dunt....
                Dunt...dunt...dunt...dunt...dunt...dunt...dunt....

You are free
In this moment – in the space
This magnificent place
   I remember…when you would say….that you loved me in every way….
       You love me once….you loved me twice….
       But my boy hasn't been so niiiiiiiicccceeeeee….

Free from everything
The bills – the overdue bills
Shit, you'll pay them when you pay them
You ain't made of money!
     You used to love me….you usta feel me…you usta kiss me….
    You usta to touch me…you usta to please me….you usta squeeze me….
       You usta love me….you usta touch me….
        Ohhhhhhhh……ohhhhhhhhh….

Ahhh yessss….that's it
Groovee aby
Shake it off….
Let go…
Release…
       Baby….baby….I miss you so much….
      When you hold me with that lovin touch….
      You gotta know how you maaakkke me feel….
     For all those years….has it been fo' reeeeaaaaaall….

     Dunt…dunt…dunt…dunt…dunt…dunt…dunt…dunt….
     Dunt…dunt…dunt…dunt…dunt…dunt…dunt…dunt….

The pressure of the job
The pressure of your life
        I need a rhythm to put me in the mood….
        I need a rhyme to make my body move….

The pressure of expectations
The disappointments
The lies they told you
The lies you told

                          I need someone to play me a song....
      That'll make my body rock...body rock...all night longononongonong....
His lyin ass, his lyin ass, and his lyin ass
                      Bummm....bummm.bummmm...bummmm....
                   Please Mr. DJ get heavy on the bass....
                Gonna rock this party...gonna rock this place.....

The rent, the test, the overdraft fee
The test
Another sick friend

Take two step us, dip, turn around
Now grind on him...yea....work
Shake –

                      Do da...do da...bummm...da do...bummm....
    Don't you want....don't you want....don't....don't...don't you want some
                                                  more....
    Don't you want....don't you want....don't....don't...don't you want some
                                                  more....

This is it baby....right here on the dance floor
Leave it...
No worries right now...just the brothers in this club
Wrecking it

                        Dunt dunt dunt dunndada dunnnn....
                        Dunt dunt dunt dunndada dunnnn....
                We don't really need a crowd to have a party....
      Just a funky beat and for you to get it started and oooohhhhhh....
                              We're having big fun....
                And the partys just begun....yea...yea...yea....yea....
                                  Big fun....

Forget the suit
Forget the tie
The briefcase
That report you aint finished? Too Bad
                        Boomp…booomp…booomp…booomp….
                        Boomp…booomp…booomp…booomp….
                            Y'all want this party started right?....
                    Y'all want this party started quickly…right?....
             Set it off I suggest y'all….set it off I suggest y'all…..
                Set it off on the left…set it off on the right….
                                      Set it off….

Tonight it's about jeans
Tims and this tank top
You choose without accident
It shows too much
It shows enough
Just enough to attract and distract
Work it baby…work it
Work it out….work it off
And you know you're looking good
                Do be do…run…run…run…do be do…run…run…run….
                Do be do…run…run…run…do be do…run…run…run….

You see those fellas
On the floor
And on the walls
Checking you out
You got their attention now
So keep it
                                Uh…excuse me, Charles?....
                                  My name is on the list….
                                        What list?....
                                        The DJ's List….
        Ms. Thing, There is no Guest List Tonight…Tonight…Tonight….

You know you aint playin
With them tonight
No, no, no
Not tonight
They gets No play
Dip, Turn, Spin
Go to the floor now
Yea…shake that leg

                              Lonely people….lonely…..lonely people….lonely….
                                    Boom boomp boom boomp booom boomp….
                                        Da boomp….da booop….da booomp….
                          Aahhhhhh…ahhhhha………ahhhhha……..ahhhhhh….

Tonight it's not about one of them
It's about all of them
All of the brothers
This tribe of movement
Sound and soul
In a syncopated rhythm
Floor bouncing to us like a trampoline
It moves with us too

                              Tink tink tink tink tink tink tada tink tink….
                              Tink tink tink tink tink tink tada tink tink….
                                            Come on Let's work….
                                  Come on let's work it to the one….
                          Work it to the bone….bone….bone…bone…
                                                    Let's Work….
                                      To the bone…bone…bone….

Tonight we're all on a mission
Just came here to release
To let the beat move, move, lift
Far away from life
This life
The Life

                                    Is it all over my face…got me love dancin….
                                    Is it all over my face…got me love dancing….

This gathering is of soul
And familiarity
And understanding the pressure
The pain
Tension
Souls begging to be set free
In this moment
                        Oooooohhhhhhhhhhhhh….ohohoohho....yea yea….
                                        You got to show me looohoveee….
                        Heart breaks and promises….I've had more than my share….
                        I'm tired of giving my lovhove….and getting no where….

Do it all night
Set your spirit free
Let this bass stir your soul
Let it overwhelm and take control
Keep you head in the clouds to night
Ears ringing
                                Dant dant dant dant..tatata….dant a danta….
                                Dant dant dant dant..tatata….dant a danta….
                                                        Climb the wall….
                        I want to climb the wall….You make me climb the wall….
                                Dant dant dant dant..tatata….dant a danta….

Of sweat and funk

Just as the beats of the Congo
And drums – the African Diaspora
Sent many a tribe into a frenzied trance
      Oohhhhhhhhhhh ohhhhhhhhh yea….yea….
      Oohhhhhhhhhhh ohhhhhhhhh yea….yea….
 Do you know what I meaaan…..yea……….do you know what I meaaan….
                     yea…..

This is your natural
Your celebration of your roots
And the roots of your celebration
      Bada booompppp badda booomp baddda boooomp…..
      Bada booompppp badda booomp baddda boooomp….
        Treat me right….i'll be good to you….
          You treat me right….
        This aint no game….it's a love thang….
       Said it aint no game….it's a love thang….

This trip here tonight is celebrating
Remembering
Forgetting
Hoping
Laughing
Crying
Trying
Rejoicing
Mourning
Dying
Living

So Release….

Please Don't Tell My Mother

Shhhhhhhhhhhhhhhhh

Listen, please
I have a favor to ask of you
And nothing that would compromise your integrity
For That I'd never do

And I would never ask you to lie for me
Just to help me save my face
But a revelation of this kind, my friends
Might leave me in disgrace

See, my mom's been asking questions lately
And she just might ask of you
If you have any idea whatsoever
of what I may be up to

So I just have one simple request
Since you happen now to know the truth

Please don't tell my mother

Say I was celebrating lost veterans that Memorial Day weekend
When you saw me in D.C.
And not that I was there for Black Pride Parties
For Brothers loving Brothers like me

You can tell her you saw me eating one night
At a restaurant on Capitol Hill
Not standing in a line about a block and a half block long
To get into the Bachelor's Mill

And say that I was kissing a Brown-skinned Sister
Any Brother would be glad to taste
And not that it was Brother's tongue in my mouth
And arms around my waist

Now, you can tell my friend Andrew and I won't mind
Cause he was there with me too
Or my cousin Fred cause he's a crack head
And cares less 'bout what I do

But please don't tell my mother

Don't tell her you saw me dancing with a Brother
Late Friday night at the Edge
Cause if she knew we were grinding on the dance floor
It just might push her over the Ledge

Actually anything you tell her about what I've done
Might cause her to be upset
But especially if you say I was tipping naked boy dancers
Tuesday night at Club Wet

Tell her you gave me directions that time
And I was lost is your best guess
Just please don't say I was cruising boys
At that Bookstore over in Southwest

I don't mind if you tell my older Brother
He'd better not catch a spell
Cause though he doesn't think anyone knows
I found out he's on the DL

Just please don't tell my mother

Or maybe you can tell her you saw me one day
At the gym at 9th and N
And not as online as freakyblackman
Thirsty for some skin
You can tell her I was walking downtown that day
Or maybe riding my bike
And not on camera stroking myself
Butt naked on Skype

Say you saw me at worship service Sunday
With the spirit's glow over my face
Not walking around shirtless Sunday afternoon
For free drinks at the Fireplace

I don't care if you tell my Uncle
He certainly won't get mad or pout
Cause a couple of months ago at the family reunion
We'll, he kinda came out!

Just please don't tell my mother

And those times I ran into you on my travels
Across the USA
I wouldn't dare put words into your mouth
But maybe this is what you could say:

Say I was shopping the Underground in Atlanta
Or touring studios at CNN
Not at Bulldogs chillin with a dude in my lap
Sippin grapefruit juice and gin

Or say you saw me jogging after sundown
Or maybe just a little before dark
Not at two o'clock in the morning half naked
Cruising Brothers in Piedmont Park

Now you can tell my sister Charlotte
And I know that she won't tell
Cause she's been living with the same "roommate" for years
A butch girl named Michele
Just please don't tell my mother

Say you think it was a business trip or something
That must have brought me to LA
Not that I danced all night at Loretta's
Or at Ivan's First Friday's soiree

Don't tell her I was at the Fourth of July Beach Party at all
Cause that surely to cause a ripple
Especially since I had a red thong up my ass
And a newly pierced left nipple

And that time in New York when you saw me
Tell her I was taking in a Broadway show
Not at a Swerv Magazine party
That she doesn't need to know

Say I was at Junior's Restaurant in Brooklyn
Sipping wine and eating chocolate cheesecake
And not an underwear party at Langston's
That'd be an awful mistake

Now, you can tell my Aunt Laverne
And I'll tell her to go fly a kite
Cause for the past five years
She's been chapter President
For Seattle's dykes on bikes

Just please don't tell my mother

Say it was a frat convention in Texas
Or perhaps a reunion of my class
Not that I was strolling the beach half naked
Last May at Houston's Black Pride Splash

When you saw me collecting numbers in Detroit
Cause "*I*" was Hotter than July
Say I was there for the Detroit Jazz Festival
And that won't exactly be a lie

Now, you can tell my younger Brother, Derrick
And I won't hold my head in shame
Cause he's a performer in downtown Chicago
Krystal Klear's his drag name

Just please don't tell my mother

Shhhhhhhhhhhhhhhhh

I think I hear her coming
So if she asks, remember what you've heard
And I promise to do the same if you need
On that I give you my word

I'm asking you please 'cause I'm scared
And don't know what else to do
So if you keep this secret between us
I'll owe the world to you

Now remember,
Pleeeeeeeeeeeeeeeeease don't tell my mother

Shhhhhhhhhhhhhhhhhh here she comes

Hey Ma! I was just talking about you!

Journeys
The Art of Loss

Ounced

He came home
>   ***Announced***

To his parents
That he was loving another Brother

His Brothers and Father
>   ***Pounced***

On him to be beat the embarrassment
And vile shamefulness
From his already love starved soul

They
>   ***Denounced***

their love for him
saying not to
call
come
write
speak again

He
>   ***Renounced***

his love for them
closing the door quietly behind him
heartsick
heartbroken
And alone was he

They
        Pronounced
him dead at
3:15 a.m.

killed by
heartache
loneliness
and a single gunshot wound
to the chest
from a stranger
in the lateness of the hour
in the darkness of a park
where he thought he'd be loved

And He Was My Friend

Anthony's Journey
For my Best Friend Anthony Lamar Hopkins
September 20, 1965 - March 24, 1995

What Do You See, Nurse?
What Do You See?

Are You Thinking When You Look At Me
A Frail Young Man
Not Very Wise?
Uncertain Of Habit With Far Away Eyes?
Who Dribbles His Food And Makes No Reply
When You Say In A Loud Voice,
"I Do Wish You'd Try?"

Who Seems Not To Notice The Things That You Do
And Forever Is Losing A Sock Or A Shoe?
Who Resisting Or Not Let You Do As You Will
With Medicines And Tests The Long Day To Fill?

Is That What You're Thinking? Is That What You See?
Then Open Your Eyes, You're Not Seeing Me!

I'll Tell You Who I Am As I Sit Here So Still
As I Move At Your Bidding And Eat At Your Will

A Small Child Of 10, The Youngest Of Three
A Mother, A Father, A loving Family
A Young Man At 16 With Wings On His Feet
A Passion For Life, New Challenges To Meet

At 17 In College And Out On My Own
A Future Of Promise, It's Written In Stone
New Friends I Have Met, and the Time, It Moves Fast
But We Are Bound By The Ties We Know Will Always Last
Raising Each Other Through The Good And The Bad,
One Hundred Years Of Friendship Is What We think We Have

At 24, A Nephew Plays Happily Around My Knee
Lisa Has Made Me An Uncle, My Brother Darrel and Me
At 26, Another Nephew To Play With And To Hold
Overjoyed With Excitement To Watch Them Grow Old

I Have A Career Now Too, And Life Is Falling Into Place
I'm Moving Into Manhood With God's Loving Grace
I'm Living, Loving, Laughing, And Praising,
For The Blessings Have Been Truly Amazing

But Dark Days Are Upon Me, Is What The Doctors Have Said
I Look To The Future, I Shudder With Dread
For My Life Will Be Cut Short, So Young, I'm Barely Grown
I Think Of the Years And The Love That I've Known

My Loving Mother Mae, My Father John Lee
I'm Still Their Baby, So How Can This Be?
My Sister, My Brother, My Cousins, My Friends
This Can't Be Happening, I'm Not Ready To End
My Nephew Brian, My Nephew Shaman
My Friends, My Career, How Could It All Be Gone?

But I Kept My Faith, And Stopped Asking, Why?
I Asked Jehovah's Forgiveness, And Kept My Head Toward The Sky
For The Lives That I Have Touched, And For Those That Have Touched Mine
Have Made Life Worthwhile In This Short Passage Of Time

At 29, I Grow Weaker, This Disease Is So Cruel
It Make A Mockery Of A Life, Once Young, Vibrant, Nobody's Fool
The Body, It Crumbles, Grace And Vigor Depart
There Is A Stone In My Body Where I Once Had A Heart

But Inside Of This Old Carcass, A Young Man Still Dwells
And Now, Yet Again, My Bittered Heart Swells
I Remember The Joys, I Remember The Pain
At Peace With My Maker, And Living Life All Over Again

I Think Of The Years, All Too Few
Gone Too Fast
And Accept The Stark Reality
That Nothing Can Last

So Open Your Eyes, Nurse, Open And See
Not A Frail, Wasted Life,
Look Closer

See Me!

Max and Thomas

February 23, 2014

Dear Thomas,

I saw you out the other night. I have a feeling you saw me too - I could tell by the way Tony looked at me and rolled his eyes. He whispered something to you and the two of you left. I know he's your best friend but I can't stand his ass!

    Anyway, for whatever reason I couldn't bring myself to approach you or say anything to you. As much as I wanted to. Part of it is that I'm embarrassed over what I've done and the pain I caused you over the last couple of months. I wish there was a way to show you that I never meant to hurt you. I never did. I hope you can believe me.

    The other part is that I'm hurting now too. I don't know what else to say except I'm sorry and I want you back.

I love you still,
Max

February 25, 2014

What has been…can never be
It's what's best for you
And what's best for me…

Dear Max:

For two years, 2 months, and 2 days I gave you all I had to give. All of me. Everything that I am. Everything I thought you needed. And for 2 years,

2 months, and 2 days you took my love and my commitment to you for granted. My heart has been tested and tested, and now my disappointments are all that I have in memories of you. I hope one day that my love will show through all of this but for now my heart and my mind is on watch.

I been looking back lately. Trying to find the place where you stopped loving me. Looking for the place where you took your attention and love away. The place where you kept me satisfied with occasional calls and a dinner here and there all while you were entertaining the eyes and bodies of other Brothers. It's been hard trying to find that place and even harder finding the place where I left myself behind and let your part-time love become enough for me. This place - this situation - has been much too hard to deal with.

But now that I know the truth – the truth about me - I must let you go. Completely. This is what's best. I have to do what's best for me. I hope you'll understand.

Apology accepted.
Thomas

March 1, 2014

Dear Thomas,

I couldn't see it then. I couldn't see how much you love me. But now I do and I want to know it again.

I know I let everything and everybody come between us. I know I let other Brother's stares, glances, and offers make me disloyal to you. I don't know what I was thinking or if I was thinking at all. But you have to know that I never meant to hurt you. I didn't think you'd ever know about any of it and I tried to keep it from you. Somehow or another I believed that you would always be here and now that you're not I'm lost. I'm lost without you, man. And I don't know what to do.

I'm begging you to give me another chance. I want to make it up to you and show you what kind of man I really can be. I want to make it up to us. We had a real good thing going for us baby and I made a mistake. Please! Let's not make another one by giving up on us. I'm not afraid to love anymore. Please, baby, give us another chance.

I'm begging you…

Love Always,
Max

March 7, 2014

Dear Max:

I was patient. You were careless. I was loving. You were mean. I tried all I could to let you know that I loved you. You ignored me. I dedicated myself, my mind, my soul, and my body to you. You let others come between us and in your quest to keep it from me you made me feel like a fool.

 I dealt with your lies, your mistruths, half-truths, and your sneakiness. The way you left the room when your cell was blowing up and the way you'd minimize the screens on the computer when I'd walk into the room. I always knew somewhere in places I don't like to think about or want to think about that I wasn't the center or your attention. I wasn't the only one.

 I don't know what made me stay. But the more time that passes between us I understand more and more that it had nothing to do with you. This pain is my responsibility. The mistakes are mine to reconcile. I have some growing up of my own to do.

 And in my quest for understanding, Max, I've discovered or perhaps I'm just admitting to myself that you don't know the first thing about love. You toss the word around like it means nothing using it for your convenience - to get what you want. And I fell for it. You won me over. I believed you, man. I really did. I thought you did love me and cared about what happened. I wanted to believe it.

But now, after all we've been through I've come to know that love - in its truth - is outside the range of your understanding. I say that only because you had it right there in the palm of your hand and you didn't recognize it for what it was. You didn't honor it, Max. You simply let it go.

Max, I want you to go on with your life. I want to go on with mine. I want to be happy and I want the same for you. I'm finding myself again. Finding my way through the fog and fighting my way back to rational thinking. I've made some great strides in the last couple of months at capturing happiness again and I want you to do the same - only it's not what was once our relationship that's going to give it to you. There's nothing more I can do. You alone are responsible for that work.

Thomas

March 7, 2014

Baby, please!

You make it sound simple: "Just go on with your life, Max." But it's not that simple. I can't go on. I can't. I'm stopped in my tracks. I need you, Thomas. I need you back in my life. Nothing moves without you. My wounds are deep and I'm hurting more now because of the hurt I've caused you. You won't take my phone calls or answer the door when I come by. Do you know how much that hurts?

I've spent a lot of time reviewing the last two years in my head baby and as painful as it is for me to admit my own mistakes and give into the reality of what I've done I'm doing it. I know I got a lot of shit with me and I'm trying to work it all out. But I don't know where it comes from. Maybe it's because I don't really believe that I'm good enough to be loved by one person. Maybe it's because that kind of one-on-one love is too intense for me.

Maybe it's because I can't handle being responsible for somebody else. Maybe I'm just too selfish. My head is all fucked up about this but I'm trying to clean it up, Thomas. I'm trying to clean it up so that we can try it again - a fresh start without all the old baggage and drama. I'm doing this for us, man.

But I need you to tell me face-to-face, man-to-man that you forgive me. I need you to forgive me so we can try again. A new start. I need to know you still love me because I believe you do. I also believe you still care. Baby, don't do this to us. I know we're worth another try. Let me see you, please.

Loving and missing you bad,
Max

March 9, 2014

Max,

It's been over two years since our first glance; our first dance. I knew from the moment I saw you that you were the Brother I wanted to spend the rest of my life with. Part of me, my own insecurities, told me that I didn't stand a chance with such a beautiful man with what I thought at the time to be the world at your feet. Tall, handsome, intelligent, and confident. You had it all.

The other part of me, the part that believes in me, the one that never usually comes out in my personal life as much as it does in my professional life said to go for it! And so I did. I took the chance to ask you out and when you accepted, I know then I would love you for the rest of my life. Max, that will never change.

But the promises you made did change. Something in me knew that we wouldn't last long. Though you were captivating in every sense of the word there was still something about you that kept you from completely letting go; something that kept you from completely loving me. You mentioned some of these in your last letter and though I can't say for sure if it were one or all of those reasons I can say that I agree that it was something.

There was always something stopping you from giving me all of you completely. Still, I ignored it. I kept silent and kept hoping that together we'd be able to conquer all the mountains we were up against; manhood, masculinity, family, sexuality, fidelity, and love. All of them! But what I found instead was for each issue, argument, disagreement, or painful drama we overcame there would always be something else. The top of every mountain with you, Max, was always the bottom of another.

I ignored my feelings too. My feelings to flee after the first incident - after the first truth was revealed. That time when the cold that wouldn't go away was explained as I took you to the doctors weak and breathless. My heart bled for you when you told me you were HIV positive and that you knowingly contracted it because you were young and in love with him - your ex. And in your admission my soul listened and my compassion grew even stronger while my love for you in that moment intensified.

I thought to myself, '*I will love him and stand by him no matter what this illness brings*'. I know the story oh too well of friends and others who share the plight. I let you know then that I wasn't afraid. And I wasn't. There is no disease, circumstance, or situation that could erase my ability to love you and everything about you.

I ignored my feelings for the second time too. The feelings that begged me to run that same day when the nurse ran out after us in the parking lot to bring you the prescriptions you left on the counter; a prescription for a recently contracted sexually transmitted disease; an STD you contracted while we were in a relationship. In a relationship with me.

I saw the guilt and shame in your eyes. I heard your, "I'm sorry" as you rested your head on headrest of my car, eyes closed, lids heavy with embarrassment. For you know as I did that at that time of this revelation we had never had unprotected sex. This was of your doing with someone else.

And yet your desires for flesh outside of mine still couldn't weaken my desire to love you completely. It was because I saw so much good in you, Max. So much love, warmth, and innocence. I used to wonder what you saw in yourself. Even as we sat at dinner days later I expressed my desires to share my world all of my spiritual, mental, and emotional treasures with you.

I gave you a way out then - a time and place for to flee into the world of free sex and emotionless, loveless pleasures if that was what you really wanted. But with me, you said, was where you wanted to be and the past would be left there - in the past. I believed you and invited you into my heart, my life and into my head. But it didn't matter. It never mattered. You did what you wanted to do.

So now we are where we are. Both with regrets and both feeling the pain of this separation. You can go on, Max. I've had to. You will.

I can't be there as I once was. There is nothing more I have to give to you except my love - from a distance. I say again, go on with your life, Max.

Thomas

March 9, 2014

Dear Thomas,

I was a fool. I know I took all you gave for granted and now I feel like I'll never have anyone to love me like you loved me ever again. Do you know what that feels like? Do you know what's it's like to feel completely alone? To suddenly wake up after the party and after the afterglow to be alone and empty?

And I remember the day I told you I was HIV positive. You took it in stride - with love and calm. The truth is I thought I would lose you then. But you let me stay that night at your house on your sofa with my head in your lap and just let me rest. You eased the pain of my shame and without saying a word you told me it was all-good that we still could be.

But that frightened me even more I guess. I never in my life experienced that kind of unconditional love or that level of complete acceptance. You honored me by being in my life but I couldn't see it. I know that I violated your trust in many ways. I know it will take a lot to win it back but I'm convinced that there's still a spark - a hint of love still in you to give us a chance.

Or maybe it's that my HIV status bothers you more than you want to admit. Maybe this is a convenient way for you to exit away from the pain and memories of the friends and family you lost to AIDS. I can't blame you. I don't want to be reminded either. Maybe that's why I behave like I do. I don't know. But I just want the opportunity to talk it out with you. I need to hear this coming from you.

I love you so much,
Max

March 15, 2014

Dear Max,

I'm amazed that after all the time we spent together that you'd believe that your HIV status has anything to do with my decision not to get back with you. Your HIV status never mattered to me, Max. It never scared me. It was as natural to me as your beautiful eyes, your soft red lips, and the touch of your hand. It's not that I won't give you another chance because you're positive, Max. I won't give you another chance because you're *negative*!

Your HIV status was never a concern and deep down you know it. But what did matter to me was that you couldn't see the beautiful opportunity we had together; the love I had for you and the peace I was offering. I had for years before you maintained a single, celibate life in hopes that the next Brother would be the one I would spend the rest of my life with. I was hoping that Brother was you.

But you were clear in your admission. You said you'd rather have sex with strangers than to make love and a life with me. In that one moment I felt as though my heart had collapsed and I wondered aloud what the hell was I doing there?

I put aside my trust issues to give us a chance. With everything in me I defeated my fears. With all I know about myself and about love, who and what I am, I realized that I could reason as much as I wanted to about trusting another Brother. I could, talk about it, philosophize about it, and think about it all I wanted to but the only way I would be able to truly work through these issues would be to actively work on them. And to work on them meant that I would have to start by trusting myself. I did that, Max and in doing so I gave you my all and still found myself in the same old familiar dark pit.

But I don't blame you for all of this. I'd give you 98% for sure but the other 2% has to do with me. It has to do with me not responding to earlier warnings in my soul telling me to leave sooner. It's that 2% that I'm focusing on understanding. I need to know what made me stay despite all the signs. I want to know what it was in me that kept me there. I'm working that out. I learned a lot from us, Max, and I'm clear about one thing: I've learned to release you and to allow you to be who you are without it shaking my peace.

I've asked God to remove you from my heart in complete love and forgiveness. I've asked Him to let me love you as He does; nothing more, nothing less. I've released you and surrendered you in love, and I wish you only the very best that life can give you. But as for us, we're finished. We're through. We danced for 2 years, 2 months, and 2 days to separate rhythms, to different drums. I love you so much, Max, that I am letting you go.

May God bless you and keep you,
Thomas

Mirrors
(For My Father)

You Never Taught Me To Shave
The Nicks and Cuts
In My Heart
On this Face That Looks So Like Yours
Are Deep

Did You Use Disposable
Or Doubled Edged?
I Don't Remember
For When You Left
I hardly Had Hair On My Head

Do I use Clippers to Avoid
Razor Bumps?
Or Would Magic Shave Suffice
For My Skin
So like Yours?

I Look In The Mirror
And See Your Face
A Face I Sometimes Wish Not To See
Struggling to love nonetheless

This Replication
A Bitter Sweet Reminder
That You Never Taught Me To Shave

You Didn't Know

You didn't know what you were saying no to

How could you?

        You didn't know who you were saying no to
A love
A lover
    A friend

To stand by you in your hopes
    In front of you in your troubles
        Behind you in your triumphs
            Beside you in your trials

        You didn't know what you were saying no to

But you did

And now you want it back

Want me to love you and everything about you
And hold you in your stillness
As night and loneliness overwhelms you now

The night you left
I slept deep
In a dreamscape
A dream escape
Dreading the silence in the absence of you
And the perils I had to suffer
I was plunged into darkness
And strained by a noiseless wind

Slowly my memory curved
And when my eyes lifted
I returned here weary to gain strength

Buried the love I had for you
And surfaced the love I had for me

And now you want it back?

No, Baby
Not this time

What?
Did you think it was a game?

We'll, it wasn't
And so now
I've put you away
Where you belong
In a box labeled forgiveness
In my memories

And it's clear
As clear as mountain water clear
That there is warmth here
Even when the winds blow hard and cold

But not for you

Jason and Sarah

April 2, 2001

Jason,

I felt compelled to write you this letter to let you know how angry I am. I'm so angry, I don't know what to do! Yesterday, I buried my son. My only child. There's this hole in me now - an emptiness and a void that can never be filled again. I miss him so much, and I don't know if I can take it.

What I'm most angry about is how he died; a disease that he got from having sex with another man. With you, Jason. You corrupted him. I can't help but blame you for taking him away from me and for keeping his illness a secret from me and his father. How dare you be so cruel! How dare you take my son's life into your hands!

There's so much about my son's life that I didn't know, that I will never know. He's gone now and I'm trying so hard not to hate you, Jason, but nothing I try seems to work. Something in me wants you to feel the same pain that I'm feeling. That's why I didn't want you at the funeral. I didn't want to see you and I didn't want others to see you. I don't know what I would have done. It's bad enough that my son was gay but to have his boyfriend or whatever you call yourself at the funeral would have killed me too. I just want to erase this from my mind and try to get on with my life.

I will never forgive you, Jason, for what you've done. I want you to live with that!

Sarah Matthews

April 10, 2001

Dear Sarah,

    I know you're angry. I understand your pain. I feel it too. That void that you speak of is one that I now have as well. I don't know when the pain will subside but I do know that I cannot hang on to feelings of anger and resentment. These feelings only keeps me tied to the pain and I want to be able to go on from here. I have to. Marc would have wanted it that way.

    I was angry too, Sarah. Angry at AIDS for taking Marc away, angry at Marc for leaving me here alone and yes, Sarah, even angry at you and your husband for turning Marc away all those ago when you found out that he was gay. Six years ago when I met him, Sarah, he was lonely and very depressed. He was a broken man. That's why I always felt this need to shower him with as much love and affection as I could though nothing I could have ever done or said could have overshadowed his feelings of abandonment. That was something I don't think he ever recovered from.

    Marc loved you and his father, Sarah. He never had a harsh word to say against you. His only concern was that one day you both would come around to understand that he was not just a Black gay man, a homosexual or a "faggot" as his father referred to him but that he was your son. He tried as best he could to live up to your expectations and did to a large degree. He was an athlete for his father's sake, a scholar for your sake, and a positive, progressive Black man for all of our sake.

    In many ways Marc lived for everyone but himself. Funny thing is he was o.k. with that. Marc was content with making everyone around him happy. He always pointed out the beauty and the good that others couldn't or chose not to see. He wanted everyone around him to smile. He was bitter about nothing nor was he angry about anything. Marc maintained his capacity to love and forgive. Even when the doctors told him that he was HIV positive, the year before we even met, he was able to love and forgive. He said to me that it would do no good for him to be angry. He said that is was best to just let anger alone. He was amazing!

On the other hand, Sarah, I was very angry. Especially with you and his father. Each time the holidays would roll around and he didn't hear from you I was angry. Each time his calls weren't returned I was angry. Each time he would cry in the night about how much he missed being a part of your life I was angry. Each time there were no card from you or his father on his birthday I was angry. Each time I would see the disappointment in his eyes I was angry.

I used to think that a part of Marc died a long time ago and I blamed you and his father for killing that part of him. I was convinced that your caller ID killed him, that your pastor and your church killed him, that your stubbornness, your small-mindedness, and your inability to accept him as he was killed him. But I'm over that now and realize that it was simply his time to go.

Sarah, he didn't want to tell you and his father about his illness because he couldn't bear the rejection all over again. He couldn't bear to hear, "*I told you so!*", or "*You got what you deserved!*" pouring from your or your husband's lips. That would have taken him out long ago, Sarah. Mostly though he kept quiet to spare you and his father any pain and embarrassment knowing that he had AIDS would have caused. He wanted to keep it silent and I loved him enough to support him in doing so.

So, Sarah, I ask that you find a way to release your anger, your pain, and whatever guilt you or your husband may be carrying. Your son was loved. That should be all that matters to you and to those who loved him. I'm praying for you.

Respectfully,
Jason Beckman

April 17, 2001

Jason,

Don't you even try to turn this around as if it's my or my husband's fault! Marc knew where his father and I stood. We couldn't accept that he was gay and we never will! We prayed that he would be cured one day or that he would get some help. We would welcome him back with open arms. But he never was cured, and your influence didn't help him any! He chose to be this way!

And don't talk to me about disappointment! I'll tell you what disappointment is. Disappointment is finding out that your only son, a handsome, smart, Black man is gay. Disappointment is knowing that your son will never have a wife and that you will never have grandchildren.

Disappointment is knowing that your son is living a life of sin. Disappointment is knowing that your neighbors and friends know that your son is homosexual and look at you as if you did something to make him that way. Disappointment is know that your son is not in Heaven.

How am I supposed to live knowing that he's in Hell? You tell me, Mr. Smart Ass. How am I supposed to live with that?

Sarah

April 25, 2001

Sarah,

Marc was a hard worker, a dedicated friend, a faithful companion and a generous humanitarian - generous to a fault. In fact, Marc and I would argue about that all the time. I always thought people were taking advantage of his good nature but he would always say, *"The blessing is having the ability to do these things!*" It used to drive me crazy but you know something? He was absolutely right!

When you told me that you didn't want me or any of "our kind" at the funeral, Sarah, naturally people were hurt. Marc and I knew a lot of people and it was a blow to them to know that the family didn't want them anywhere around. I, on the other hand, wasn't hurt. In fact, I expected it. I was slightly disappointed but both Marc and I knew what your reaction would be. I understood.

You see, my conscious is clear. I said everything I needed to say to Marc before he made his transition and I was there when he finally let go. It wasn't necessary for me to see him in the coffin. I said my good-byes long ago.

But there were many of our friends from all over the country dare I say the world that didn't have that chance. So on the day that you scheduled his funeral there I planned a memorial service here. There had to be over three-hundred people who came, Sarah, and they came from everywhere: New York, Los Angeles, Chicago, and nearly every state in between. There were even friends who came as far as London, Paris, and Africa. The place was packed, standing room only, and the celebration of his life lasted for hours. I wished you could have been there to see what an influence your son had on so many people; Black, white, male, female, gay, straight, adults, children, and even the elderly. He touched so many.

There were tributes in song, dance, spoken word, and poetry. It was a definite celebration. The most amazing part of his memorial service were the personal testimonies from the people who knew Marc. They all had so much to say. But you know what, Sarah? Of all of the things that were said by the many who wanted to pay tribute to him not one and I mean not one, Sarah, said that Marc was a disappointment.

To the many people who knew and loved Marc he was no disappointment and nothing about his life was disappointing. He was the most kind, compassionate, and sincere man I ever knew and would do anything for anybody whether they asked or not. He loved completely.

I don't think God or anyone could condemn a person for loving. I don't think he condemned Marc for loving me and I don't think he will condemn me for loving Marc. Marc wasn't concerned about Heaven or

Hell, Sarah. He was too busy focusing on loving what lies in between: this world and everything and everyone in it.

I loved your son, Sarah, as did many other people. I only wish you really knew the person that he was. I cannot help but be saddened for you and your husband for missing out on such a beautiful experience. I'm praying for you.

Sincerely,
Jason

May 3, 2001

Jason,

To hear you tell me that you loved him sickens me. Love? What the hell do you know about love? It wasn't loved that killed my son. It was sex that did. It was AIDS that did! I still blame you, and I blame all the homosexuals spreading this disease.

Save your prayers, Jason, because I don't know who in the hell it is you're praying to but my God doesn't hear people like you. Please don't write me again.

Sarah Matthews

May 12, 2001

Dear Sarah,

There was no greater love than the love I had for your son. I did love him. More than anything else in the world. Oh, how I wish you could understand that.

You got it all wrong, Sara. Our relationship was not about sex. Our relationship was about love. It was about mutual support and respect. It was about the comfort zone; finding a place where you are free to love, want, desire, and feel safe doing so. This is the place that I and your son found, Sarah, and the place that kept him in love and in peace until he died.

I did love your son, Sarah, and did everything in my power to let him know that each and every day. So when he was cold I kept him warm, and when he was hot, I cooled him. When he was hungry I fed him, and when he was tired I rested him. When he was angry I calmed him, and when he was sick I nurtured him and made him well. When he cried it was on my shoulder and it was my hands that wiped the tears from his face. When he was happy I shared his joy, and when he was sad I felt his pain. I loved your son, Sarah.

I knew of his dreams, of his hopes, and of his desires, and I dedicated my life to helping him reach them, fulfill them, and experience them just as he had done for me. We danced like no one was watching, sang as though our lives depended on it, and lived each day as though it were the last one we had. We laughed - a lot -- and spent most of time giving each other whatever was needed or required. Yes, Sarah, I loved your son.

When Marc became ill it was I who made sure that he was comfortable. When he was in pain I held him until it subsided. When he broke out in cold sweats I wiped the sweat from his brow. He was never alone at the doctor's office or during his long stays in the hospital. I'd sit there by his bed side, night after night, day after day, feeding him, rubbing him where he ached, brushing his teeth, cleaning him, shaving him, talking to him, or sitting with him in silence while he slept. And during the times when he was most frightened he would ask me if I thought if you and his father still loved him. I'd reassure him that you both still did and I would tell him that you always did and that you always will. Oh, how I loved your son.

On the night that he passed away I held his hand. I held his hand all that day and all that night, and when I saw in his eyes that he was ready to transition from this world I encouraged him to let go. I told him that it was o.k. to leave That he could go and rest. I reassured him that you and his father loved him. And I loved him. More importantly, God loved him. I held back my tears because I didn't want him to see me cry. I didn't want him to see me feel bad. I just wanted him to go peacefully and with all of the joy of knowing that what we had was wonderful and that he forever changed my life. I wanted him to know that his life meant something. I wanted him to know that love was right there with him and I wanted him to feel love as his last experience on this earth. Yes, Sarah, I loved your son.

He looked at me just before he took his last breath and smiled. It was a smile that I will never forget – warm, kind, and forgiving. There was no fear. After that he closed his eyes and went away. It was the most beautiful and spiritual moment of my life. I kissed him gently on his lips and thanked him for all that he'd given me. I said goodbye and let go of his hand.

I loved your son, Sarah, and to tell you the truth it really doesn't matter whether you believe me or not. God knows it, Sarah, and your son knew it. That's all that matters to me.

Sincerely,
Jason

p.s. I don't know who you pray to but my God listens to us all. My prayers are still with you.

May 19, 2001

Jason,

The only thing I ever wanted was for my son to be happy. His father and I worked very hard, scratched, scraped, and went without to see to it that he had. We wanted to make sure that he was educated so that he could one day be a help rather than a hindrance to society. We raised him to be an independent thinker, a hard worker, to be prosperous, and to work for the good of the community.

We raised him to believe in and love himself and to be honest and to be compassionate. We raised him to be a man's man! We did the best we could.

Sincerely,
Sarah

p.s. Three hundred people is a lot of people.

May 29, 2001

Dear Sarah,

You did an amazing job!

Sincerely,
Jason

p.s. The memorial service was recorded. I would be happy to send you a copy of the video if you'd like to see it.

June 5, 2001

Dear Jason,

I would very much like that. Please do.

Sincerely,
Sarah

p.s. Thank you for taking such good care of my son.

June 15, 2001

Dear Sarah,

No thanks are necessary. It was my pleasure to take care of your son. It was my honor. Enjoy Marc's service.

Sincerely,
Jason

June 30, 2001

Dear Jason,

I watched the video a couple of days ago. You were right. Many people had good things to say about Marc. I had no idea he was so loved. Thank you for opening my eyes.

    I can't stop crying now, Jason. I feel so foolish. I realize now that I was never angry at you or at Marc. I'm angry with myself. Angry with myself for turning my son away, for denying him access to my heart and to my home. I loved him so much, Jason. You must believe that. If I could only turn back the hands of time to tell him that I loved him. If I could only have one more chance to show him how much I loved him and to tell him that I never stopped. If I could only have one more chance to ask him to forgive me. Dear God, I would do anything to see him to hear his voice and to hold him just once more.

    I was so stupid, Jason. I can't believe that I did this to my only child. I can't believe that I let his sexuality prevent me from talking to him from seeing him, from holding him, from kissing him, from telling him how much I loved him, and how much I missed him in our lives. I will never be able to forgive myself for this. I will never be able to think of him or look at another picture of him without realizing what pain I caused him and how broken hearted he must have been. It's killing me, Jason. It's worse than burying him and I don't know how I'm going to live with the guilt. This burden is too much to bear. I miss him so much.

You are right, Jason. You have always been right. The only thing that should matter is love and I'm grateful to you for giving him that when his father and I were unable to. Jason, thank you for loving my son. Thank you for making sure that he was taken care of and for making sure he was not alone when he died. I was so wrong. I know that now. I'm asking God to forgive me. I was wrong. So, so wrong.

Sincerely,
Sarah

p.s. Jason, do you really think he knew how much his father and I loved him? Do you really think he forgave us?

July 1, 2001

Dear Sarah,

There's no need for guilt or regrets. Marc knew well into the depths of his soul that you and his father loved him.

And yes, he had asked God long ago to soften his heart so that he would be able to forgive you. Sarah, he did forgive you. He forgave you both long ago. You must find peace with that. Now you must find a way to forgive yourself.

If there's ever anything I can do for you please let me know.

Sincerely,
Jason

July 9, 2001

Dear Jason,

Thank you for putting my mind at ease. It will take some time but I'm working very hard at forgiving myself. My husband is too. He visits Marc's grave just about every day and cries well into the night. I think it is healthy for the both of us that we acknowledge our mistakes so that we can move on from here.

A couple of weeks ago I was talking to a woman I met in line at the fabric store in town. She was buying this beautiful piece of fabric and I asked her what she was going to use it for. She smiled at me as she began to tell me that she had lost her son. She told me that he had died of AIDS. What struck me most about what she said was the manner in which she said it. There was no remorse in her eyes. No embarrassment. No guilt. Only love and compassion could you see as she told me that he was her only son and that he was gay.

She said that her daughter suggested that she go to a group counseling session for parents who had lost their sons to AIDS and it was there that she found out about the AIDS quilt project. I burst out in tears, Jason. I couldn't control myself. When she asked me if I were o.k., I told her about Marc. It was the first time that I had admitted to anyone that Marc had died of AIDS. It was such a big relief for me and she was so compassionate as she listened to me - a woman on the verge of collapse - at the register of the fabric store. She held me until I calmed down and told me she knew how I felt. She was so comforting.

Afterwards she invited me to go with her to a counseling session. Naturally, I had reservations about going but she was so kind to me that I couldn't say no. Besides that, she said that it helped her a great deal and I was willing to try anything. So I went, Jason, and I've been going ever since. I can't tell you what it has done to help me deal with all of this. I'm starting to feel much better about everything. What's strange, Jason, is that I never saw that woman again. She never came to the session she invited me to nor did anyone know who she was when I asked about her. Isn't that strange? Jason, do you believe in Angels? We'll, I do!

Marc's father and I have decided to make a panel for the AIDS quilt project. We're in the process of sorting through the things that you sent us of Marc's to use on it and were wondering if there was anything you would like to include. Please let us know. We also heard that the entire quit will be on display in Washington, D.C. this October, and we're planning to take the trip. We were wondering if you would like to join us since you were Marc's special friend. If you don't, Jason, we will understand. But we really wish that you could. We really want to meet you. We really do.

Let us know if you can make it. And please invite the friends that you and Marc had. I would love to meet them too.

Please promise to stay in touch.

With Love,
Sarah and John

July 18, 2001

Dear Sarah,

I wouldn't miss it for the world! Thank you and John for the invitation. I'll call you at the end of the week so we can discuss meeting in Washington. Our friends would love to come too. We're all anxious to meet you and Mr. Matthews.

Please expect a package from me this week. There are a couple of things I'd like for you to include on the panel for the quilt if you don't mind.

Thank you, Sarah. Thank you!

Love Always,
Jason

Missing
For Leonard Brice and Charlie Harrison

I Know Your Hearts Are Aching Now
And I Do So Understand Your Pain
The Loss You Feel, This Terrible Anguish
Is Like An Endless April Rain

It's Difficult To Accept Those Things In Life
That Have Now Since Been Denied
To Miss Something on Which You've Come To depend
On The Things You've Come To Rely

I Know You'll Miss Him

He Was Your Brother, Cousin, Friend
And Your One And Only Son
And The Depth Of The Love You Have For Him
Can Never Be Undone

I Know You'll Miss Him

But He Loved All Of You, Each And Every One of you
In His Own Special Way
So Hold This Truth In Your Hearts Forever
For Eternity And One Day

I Know I'll Miss Him

He Was A Very Special Friend
And We Created Many Experiences Along The Way
To Which We Saw No End

Perhaps We Were Foolish To Think We'd Live Forever
Or Perhaps We Were Just Naïve
But I Want You To Know, Right Here Today,
You're Not Alone When You Grieve

I Took A Walk Along The Mississippi The Other Day
Just After Receiving The News
And Off In The Distance, From Beale Street In Memphis
I Could Hear The Faint Sound Of The Blues

So I Sat Down To Reflect On The River's Bank
And Gathered Some Stones From The Sand
Tossing Each One Into The Water Below
From Out of The Center Of My Hand

And As I watched The Stones Pierce The Water
It Suddenly Became Clear To Me
That His Life Like The Stone To The Water
Extended Well Beyond His Family

You See,
When A Rock Is Tossed Into An Undisturbed Pond
The Ripples Extend Far and Wide
So Had His Life Extended To Me
Where He Stood With Me, Side By Side

And Though Our Friendship Was Cut Short of its Existence,
Far Too Soon and Oh, So Brief
I Want You To Know, Right Here Today

You're Not Alone In Your Grief

> He Was My Brother, Too

In Good Times And Bad, Through Thick And Thin
In Seasons From Summer To Winter
And Like Spokes On The Wheels Passing By Me That Day
We Radiated From The Same Center

But Nothing In Life Is Ever Constant
As Necessary and Strong As It May Seem
For Even A Hole In A Rock Can Be Opened
By The Water Of A Steady Stream

Still, My Life Is Richer Now
Unselfishly You Let Him Share His Light
And It Shines Through Me In The Mornings And Evenings
And Comforts Me Into The Night

I'm An Extension Of His Light, Life, and Love
And Therefore an Extension Of You
So When You Find Yourself Longing For His Company
Here's What I Want You To Do

When You Feel The Need To Touch Him
Gently Place You Hand On My Face
And If You Need To ever Hold Him
Simply Fall Into My Embrace

And Should You Feel the Need To Kiss Him
Just Plant A Kiss Right Here
And when You Need To Talk With Him
I'll Offer The Listening Ear

And When You Need To Remember Him
I'll Fill In The Missing Part
For His Love For You, His Gratitude
Remains Forever In My Heart

And If You Ever Need To See Him Again
Look No Further Than My Own Eyes
And I Promise You'll Find Him Waiting For You There
To Silence Your Soulful Cries

He Was My Brother, Too…

Never Far Away

My Dear, Dear Family
What Is It That I Could Say
To Comfort You When Your Need It Most
Now That I've Gone Away?

I Could Start by Saying
I Love Each Of You
But That You Already knew
I Could Say That I Know You'll Miss Me
And This We Know To Be True

But Mommy,
We Know Nothing Last Forever
And We Knew This Day Would Come
When We Would Have To Say
Goodbye
Daddy
I know This Is Hard For Some

But My Faith Has Always Carried Me,
And God's Word Has Always Been
My Own
For He Promised Me Everlasting Life
But This Body
Is Just A Loan

My Brother,
We Were All Created
From The Flesh of His Flesh
And Sprang
From The Bone Of His Bone
But It Is
The Spirit
That Lives Forever In Us
For This Body
Is Just a Loan

So What You See Before You Now
My Sister,
Is Merely and Empty Shell
It Is The Space That I Once Occupied
In A Time You Knew So Well

And As This Body Grew Weaker
My Family,
My Faith Grew Ever Strong
I Looked Toward The day
There Would Be No Pain
And He Would Come
To Take Me Home

My Friends,
We Were Blessed To Have The Time We Had
To Love As Much As We Could
But This Imperfect Flesh Grew Tired
And We All Knew That It Would

So What I Want You All To Remember
As I Take This Long Journey Home
Is That
We Were Blessed For The Many Years We had Together
But This Body
Was Just A Loan

I know You'll Miss These Loving Arms
And Wish Them To Hold You Just Once More
To Comfort, Love, and Guide You
And Hold You As Before

But Remember
It Was My Spirit That Filled Your
Hearts and Minds
And Nurtured With Love You've Known
From Time I was A Baby At Your Feet
Until I Was Out on My Own

So When You Find Yourself Missing Me
Hold On Tight To Your Faith
And Feel My Spirit Surrounding You
Filled With God's Merciful Grace

Just Close Your Eyes
Feel The Warmth Of My Love
Surrounding You Every Day
And Remember
I'm Alive In Each Of You
So I'm Never Far Away…

Samuel and Jeremiah

April 6, 1996
Dear Jeremiah,

I hope this letter finds you well. I've been thinking very hard about you over the past couple of weeks and the days since the funeral. I really wish you would have let me stay a few more days to help you get things back in order. But, I understand you need your space and you need time to start putting this behind you now that Kenny's gone. I hope you're finding your way.

You know I think back on our friendship, the friendship I shared with you and him and each time I do I can't help but smile. Your relationship with Kenny was one built for the ages. You were so happy together. One thing I know for sure is that Kenny loved you, Jeremiah. He really loved you with all he had. And I believe that the love continues. It continues way past this world out of our understanding. It carries us through even until our own last breath. Always remember that. Always.

Take it with you wherever you go - as you move on through life - a new life with new beginnings and possibilities for love. Remember only the good and know that in time the sorrow will subside. Though you will always miss him you'll find a sacred place to store this in your heart.

I love you, my friend, and I'm here if you need me.

Love always,
Samuel

April 12, 1996
Dear Sam,

I was happy to get your letter. It means a lot to know that I'm in your thoughts. This is a difficult time for me, very difficult but little by little I'm finding strength. Everybody's been so kind and I don't know how I'll be able to thank them. All. And you.

Your being here meant everything to me and I really appreciate your wanting to stay longer but I've got to make some movement of my own. Besides, you have a life you need to live. You can't just sit here and help me lick my wounds. I'm fine. Really, I am.

But I miss him, Sam. I miss him so, so much and sometimes I don't know if I can take this. I'm a wreck – terribly sad and terribly depressed. He was my world man – my everything - and I watch my world disintegrate and crumble to pieces. I watched him go from a Brother full of life to someone I hardly could recognize. He wasn't even a fraction of his former himself.

Thinking about the last five years makes me so sad. How could this have happen to him? To us? I wonder all the time and I want to know why. We fought so hard for us - to love and preserve us - and now it means nothing. He's gone and it's just so permanent. Now I'm left to face this alone. I don't know how I'm going to do this. I don't know how I'm going to go on.

I don't know how it's going to be possible to find meaning again. It's like the world has stopped and I'm frozen in time. Eight years is a long time – eight years of loving one person, one lover, my soul mate – all the love and all the passion we once knew. How do I put that away? Where do I put it?

We were happy, Sam, genuinely happy. And In love. We had our ups and downs no doubt but more ups than anything. He loved me without condition and without compromise he loved me, and I loved him just the same. It's not fair it had to end so soon; so young.

And I can't help but wonder where God in all of this was. Where was He? Was He looking? Did He care? You know somebody said to me at the funeral that God needed him more than I did. I don't believe that. I can't believe that. I need him here with me. Why would they say such a thing? And if it's true why would God do such a thing?

Anyway, there are a million unanswered questions that I'll probably never have answers to so I'm trying to find a way to cope. I'm taking steps, although small, because I can't get my body and mind to agree to get up and move.

I'm trying today because as you said before you left life goes on and I've got some things to do today as a matter of getting on with life. I'll close here. I'll write back soon. Thanks for your love and friendship.

Your friend,
Jeremiah

April 30, 1996
Dear Jeremiah,

I know this is hard for you and though my compassion and empathy is always with you I can't pretend to understand what you're going through. Eight years is a long time to love someone and have to let them go. But you have to now, Jeremiah. You have no choice and besides, Kenny would have wanted you to. You know that.

He would want you to move on with your life, heal from this, and find new love. He would want you to still experience the goodness and sweetness of life, to be happy, though he can't share in it anymore. That Brother loved you, man. I could see it in the way he looked at you - the way he always looked out for you. There's no question in my mind that he would want you to do great things from here. So do it.

It's been nearly two months now and you've got to find strength to get out of this depression. It's not healthy for you. Why don't you take a couple of weeks and come see me. I'll take some time off and we'll do something - anything you want to do. Think about it and let me know.

In the meantime, Jeremiah, you have to pray for a lifting of this burden of pain. God is with you and there is where you'll find the strength. I'm praying for you, man. Now you pray for yourself.

Always your friend,
Love,
Samuel

May 6, 1996
Dear Samuel,

Thanks for the offer to come. I'll think about it and let you know. Some time away may do me some good. To be honest I've been thinking about some permanent time away from here. This place, this city, this apartment, this town. It's feels like it's closing in on me.

Everything reminds me of him and when it surrounds me, when the grief takes over, it's like the air is being sucked from my lungs. And there are times, many times, that I wish it would. Sometimes I believe that death would be easier than the pain and emptiness – and the unknown tomorrow. Seems like it would be easier than God's judgment and abandonment. He doesn't hear me. I've stopped believing that he ever did.

I don't pray anymore, Sam. I stopped praying over a year ago when despite my prayers that the treatment, drugs, and therapies would work nothing made Kenny better. I stopped praying because nothing was ever answered. It wasn't like I was praying for a miracle. I wasn't in denial about his illness. I just wanted a little more time with him. Just a little more time. But, oh well, it would have never been enough.

You know, I used to think that death and dying were a natural part of life; a part of being human. These days, I have my doubts. I've dealt with death before, my grandparents and my parents. It's not a new experience to me. But now this is different.

See, they were older and had seen things, done things, experienced life - the goodness and bitterness of it - but they experienced it. They lived to old age. But here I am at 30 and I've buried more friends in three years than they did in their lifetime. And now the love of my life, my friend and lover is gone. This isn't fair. It just isn't right. I shouldn't be doing this. I shouldn't have to go through this.

What is this thing that overwhelms us? What is it all about? What sense does it make to have everything; life, happiness, and love, and have it all snatched away so painfully? So cruelly? What kind of trick is God playing with us?

Where is the good in this? Life and death and that's all? I don't know, man. It just doesn't make sense and with each question I have answers don't come. Maybe in time it will. I'll just have to wait and see. I'll let you know what I find.

Love you, my friend!
Jeremiah

May 18, 1996
Dear Jeremiah,

My heart goes out to you. I can hear the pain and confusion in every line and I cry with you. I wish I could do something to help you remove the pain and clear the clouds. And it's not that I wouldn't want to it's just that I can't. The reasoning of your pain is something you have to work out with God. Only he can offer you the peace that nothing in this world can.

I know that it's difficult for you to have faith and believe now especially after what you've gone through and since the pain is so new. I know that it's shaken the very roots of your faith in God but you have to find a way back. He's with you every step of the way. You have to step back from the pain long enough to notice it. You do this by turning to God for the answers. He never left you, Jeremiah. He's there with you now.

No matter how much time you would have had with Kenny it would have never been enough. Kenny was tired. He wanted to rest. He needed to rest. His poor body had been through enough.

It was the same way when my father died. I felt much the same way. Like I was robbed of time. But I know deep in my heart my father was tired of disease. He was tired of cancer and was ready to let go of this world. I just wasn't ready to let him go.

And I had the same questions. I asked for the reasons too. Good reasons why he left so young with so much unresolved between us; so many things left unsaid and so many things left undone.

Nothing gave me comfort. And then I kept hearing the same things you've been hearing, "It was his time", *God called him home*", and "*God needed him more than I did*". God needed him more than I did? To do what?

I just couldn't believe that, man. How could God need my dad more than I did? I was only 16 at the time and my dad was my everything; my hero, my strength, and up until the day he died I hadn't done too much living or experiencing without him. I loved my dad man more than anything I've ever loved then or since. But God needed him?

Every time somebody said that to me I just wanted to punch them in the mouth. I know they meant well but they couldn't understand what that meant to a 16 year old boy lost without his father - without his best friend.

Then one day this preacher stops in to check on my mother. So I asked him exactly what that meant – that *"God needed him more than I did"*. He started to spew out some gibberish about my father being in Heaven, home with the Lord, and all that stuff but he still didn't answer my question. So I asked him what the Biblical passage, *"He even put eternity into their minds"* meant. He looked surprised when I asked him that.

See, I had been doing a little Bible research of my own to get some answers to my questions and there in black and white was this passage that said, *"He even put eternity into their minds"*. He said it meant exactly what I thought it did. It meant that God instilled in us a desire to live forever. So then I asked him, how could a God that instilled the desire for us to live forever turn around and want us to die? Why would God want to call us home? And what would he want us to do? I mean, after all, isn't life for the living?

I asked him all these questions, Jeremiah, and do you know what? He couldn't answer them. But I really didn't expect him too. It just seemed so hypocritical. I told him that it would be horrible game - vicious even - for God to do that to us. And when I told him I thought it was hypocritical my mom sent me up to my room. But oh, well. I never got a good answer although for years I tried. So I was left to find my own understanding.

Now you know I'm not big on religion. I guess I'm more spiritual than anything but from my limited understanding and experience with death, I truly don't believe that death and dying was ever God's will. I couldn't believe that because had I believed it I would have been just as angry and disappointed with God as you are.

Knowing that it must be something else involved perhaps evil forces or the devil himself who's responsible helped me. Getting angry at God isn't the way, Brother. This is the best time, the most opportune time, to get closer Him. He never abandoned you. How could He when He lives in you?

I don't know what it all means either man; death and dying, sickness, and all the rest. I don't know why we experience so much grief over and over with our friends but I do know this, Jeremiah, I'll worry about Heaven (or hell as the case may be) once it's all said and done here on earth. In the meantime, I'm living and I'm living with no rage or anger in my heart.

We're alive and breathing and though we can't get back the past and Kenny will never be there with you again think only of the love that you shared with him. You loved him and he loved you in a space and time that has no space and time. That was Heaven. That is Heaven

The memories are Heaven; the love you feel now is Heaven. The pain, the sorrow, the grief, and the pain you're feeling is hell. You've got to let it go.

You know something I noticed over the years - something I noticed from all the friends we lost? I noticed that not one of them, not one single one of them, started living until they knew they were dying? Isn't that something?

They wasted no more time in delaying vacations or in trying to work on broken or poisonous relationships, or in jobs they hated. They finally realized that a search for love, happiness, joy, or personal fulfillment outside of themselves was a fruitless waste of time.

As for AIDS, I don't think we'll ever understand it. I don't know why it came but I do know that it probably doesn't want to be here anymore than we want it here. The world hates AIDS, Jeremiah. Would you want to stay any place where you're hated? I wouldn't.

I think it's here with us because we keep it here. We invite it to stay each time we have unprotected sex or share needles or do other risky things out of lovelessness and self-hatred. Each time we lose sight of our own love and self-worth we demand it to stay. So the problem isn't AIDS Jeremiah. The problem is us.

I know it's caused so much pain for us, so much grief with all it's taken away but if we only look at the bad it's all we'll ever see and we'll forever be depressed and broken.

As hard as it is to believe AIDS has done some good. We have to look at how it's softened many hardened people and made us all more compassionate and understanding, more tolerant and kind. And it's brought a lot of us down on our knees in collective prayer asking God for help. For healing.

I truly believe that once enough of us are on our knees as soon as we all learn to submit to God's plan for us we'll see the day when AIDS and other illness are no more. We'll witness miracles and we'll all be healed. When we see this then it will all make sense.

So again I say to you, Brother, pray. Pray long and hard and keep praying. Eventually you'll be released and able to look at these experiences with Kenny as a divine gift in a moment that in reality had no ending because it had no beginning. It was. It is. Amen.

I love you, Brother. Please come for a visit. Sit for a while with me and we'll work it out. We can do some soul work and I guarantee that you'll feel better and start seeing things differently. Please say you'll come.

Always your friend,
Samuel

p.s. Remember, its o.k. if you don't believe in God. He still believes in you!

May 23, 1996
Dear Samuel,

You're right and I know you're right. Thanks for snapping me back into reality. I know there has to be more to life than just death and I know that God isn't angry with us or with me. I loved Kenny. God and I are working this out. I'm praying that He'll help. Of course I still need some time to make sense of this but I am feeling better. With each prayer I'm finding it easier to let Kenny go. I miss him still. I guess I always will. But I still feel him. I really do.

I've decided to hold off making any major decisions about moving or leaving for a while. Everyone tells me that I should wait at least a year or so before making any big decisions. I guess it takes that much time to get used to the idea of death and separation. I think I can wait.

So my friend, I'll be coming to see you in a couple of weeks for a couple of weeks. After that I'm off for a week or so to see Mike and A.B. You're welcomed to tag along if you can. It'll be nice to have everyone together. I'll ring you up in a couple of days with the details. Thanks again, my friend. You always know the right things to say. I love you for that.

Your friend,
Jeremiah

My Warmest Dream
For Every Mother Who Has Lost A Son

There is the Hope
I Keep Like a Chest
In My Chest
In My Heart
That I will See You Again

My Warmest Dream
My Moon
My Light
My Morning
My Sun

Shining in the Widows
Of My Hope

My Son

I Close My Eyes and Feel
You Move in My Womb
And We Talk
Of my Hopes for you
My Dreams for you
My Love for you

My Son

I Feel You In My Arms
Rocking You Slow
Feeding You Mother's Milk
To Make You Become
Protecting You
Guarding
Against All
That Has Ill Will For You

My Son

You Restored Me
Made Me Whole
Gave Me Purpose
And Direction

Watching You Grow
With the Wind at Your Back
The Sun on Your Face
Wings on Your Life

My Son

You Showed Me
The Way
Taught Me To Laugh Again
Love Again
Trust Again
Even In Death
You Teach
You Teach And You Heal

When I Think About the Now
Why You Are No Longer Here
Answers Don't Come Easy
Slowly I Creep Into Fear

You Come to Calm Me
Moving Away My Tears
Hushing With Your Gentleness
You Whisper
"Hold On, Mama...Take Your Time"
And I Feel You Move Right Through Me
I Smile

I'll Be Fine,
My Son
I'm Keeping My Faith
I'm Holding onto Hope
Like a Chest
In My Chest

For I Know that I Will See You Again
My Moon
My Sun
My Warmest Dream
He Has Promised This To Me

And On That Day
When Paradise Is Restored
When the Blind Ones See Again
When the Deaf Hear His Call
When those Silenced Speak
Of His Greatness

On the day when Desserts Blossom
As Does the Rose
And From Barren Ground
Fresh Waters flows

It Will Be On That Day
That I Will See You
My Son
I Will Hear You Call Out To Me
"Mama"
And I Will Run To You and Fall
Into Your Arms

I Will Hold You and I Will
Tell You As You Have Heard
Before
I Love You, My Son,
And I Have Missed You

The Committee

Date: The Here and Now

To: Same Gender Loving men Of Color
 Men of Color who have Sex with Men
 Brothers in the Life
 Brothers on the DL - Whatever that means
 Same Sex Attracted Black Men
 Bisexual Brothers
 Black Gay Men

From: The Committee of Brother's Since Passed
Subject: Getting It Right With Yourselves

Our Dear Brothers:

The **Committee of Brothers Since Passed** is an organization of Black men that you knew and once loved. We are from all parts of the world and represent all walks of life. We are same gender loving Men of Color and same sex attracted Brothers or however you wish to call us; gay, straight, bisexual, transgender, transsexual, curious, and the many other labels ascribed to us. We were your former friends, your former lovers, your cousins, uncles, fathers, and Brothers.

Let me first say that on behalf of the entire **Committee of Brothers Since Passed**, including the Board of Directors, Executive Leadership and it's membership of thousands, we would like to take this opportunity to let you all know that we love you and we miss you and wish so badly that we were there with you. Having said that we would like to get to the heart of the matter.

We formulated this committee here for a number of reasons. The first was out of the growing need to address the issues you still seem to be attached to that we never confronted when we had the opportunity. Secondly, we formulated this committee because of the recent conditions we've become aware of from those who keep us informed of your progress or lack of progress as the case may be.

We have toiled and toiled over this memo for days and days struggling and grappling over its presentation. Now, don't misunderstand. This is not to say that we argued in anyway or that anyone got an attitude, walked out, or sectioned themselves off into clicks talking about everyone else. No one became envious or jealous of the Brothers who planned the strategy or those who were chosen to lead this effort. We have learned to put our petty differences behind us in the name of Brotherhood and love.

In fact, one recent member of the freshman class (The Newcomers Committee) having just arrived last week put it best when he said that he, "...*Never knew such love and peace existed in any community of Brothers*". Sadly, based on his experiences and our own experiences prior to coming here he was right. And this is exactly the purpose of this communique'.

The Issue At Hand
Some of our Newcomers (meaning Brothers with one year or less time in service) have given us quite a few astonishing details about the goings on in the community. We have heard some amazing stories that quiet naturally concern us deeply.

Among the things we were hearing is that there is still a great deal of disunity within the ranks of Brothers and an even wider gap between the Brothers and our same gender loving Sisters. We hear that many Brothers as still hanging onto unhealthy relationships and that physical and emotional abuse continue to run rampant among you.

We heard that alcoholism is increasing in the community and that drugs and the abuse of them thereof, is now the norm. It has also been said that there is now a growing market of Black sexual exploitation with an influx of internet use and videos featuring the Brothers posting their own sexual escapades often with several partners and often using no protection.

Most disturbingly, however, is that we've heard of an absolute sexual revolution occurring with the Brothers. We've been told of the numerous orgies both public and private that more and more of you are attending and of this blatant disrespect you seem to hold for the Spirit - your Spirit and the Spirit of your Brothers. We've heard about the raw sex – unprotected sex. Yes, we've heard about a terrible unspoken, unresolved pain which we believe – we know is the gateway to such behaviors.

We first took note of the status in the community nearly two Earth years ago when Brother Darryl upon his arrival here gave his Earthly Confession Report at the Newcomer's Seminar. As Brother Darryl began to cleanse himself through his confessions and describe some of his activities and some of the actions of the Brothers there a hush went over the room. We were stunned.

Of course, we didn't want to believe that these things could be going on. We found it very hard to believe. In fact, we thought it impossible! Especially after all we went through over the last thirty years. But since denial is forbidden here unlike where you are we had to face these confessions as truth. What a bitter pill for us to swallow!

I guess the main reason why we were so shocked and appalled was that we took for granted that things would change as a result of everything you watched us go through. We took for granted that you would take those painful but no less valuable lessons we thought you'd learn from our earthly experiences, and we hoped that you would take these lessons and apply them in your own lives. We thought you'd use what you knew to avoid the same pit falls and save yourselves and each other.

Obviously, we were wrong for being passive and believing that watching us die in agony, in pain, and sometimes alone would make you want to see things differently; to try a new approach to living. The Committee of Brothers Since Passed apologizes profusely and will take ownership of that faux pas.

Understand that there are reasons that we didn't act immediately. Our primary reason was because Brother Darryl was from the East Coast and we assumed that his report was an isolated occurrence. However, since that time more and more Newcomers representing all parts of the country (and some international Brothers as well) have been joining us and bringing forth the same reports, sometimes worse! This caused a panic among the Us here. In fact it caused near hysteria among us all.

So the Brothers immediately called for an emergency session of The Committee of Brothers Since Passed to form a plan of action to address these concerns. I've highlighted that Action Plan below so that you can understand just how serious we consider this matter.

Action Plan
We formed a Blue Ribbon Panel lead by the Sub-committee of Brothers of Corporations. When these Brothers were on Earth with you they were the movers and shakers of major companies, corporations, and government agencies.

We drew on their leadership skills and organizational capabilities to conduct a study, an audit if you will, and come up with the Program Charter, and to develop the goals and objective of the teams and finally to develop a Strategic Plan. We were looking to adopt new resolutions and operating procedures in order that we might once again attempt to reach you and point you in a different direction.

These Brothers immediately went to work meeting and organizing themselves, setting up information systems, databases, preparing surveys and polls, and reviewing statistics. They did a miraculous job conducting this study dedicating countless hours and giving up most of their RIP (Rest-In-Peace) time to accomplish this mission. But never once did they complain.

They realized that this was a great task before them and took the mission quite seriously. They did so hoping that they could still help you turn your lives around and see the things that they were once unable to see. They believed they could help even though they aren't physically there with you any longer.

The first course of action the Blue Ribbon Panel put before the membership was to get approval and funding to conduct a more detailed study - an onsite visit - in each of your areas. This was a necessary next step they believed to prove or disprove the allegations. The referendum passed unanimously.

So to assure we had the kind of coverage necessary to ensure the studies weren't bias, we commissioned The Sub-Committee of Older Brothers to select from among their members two representatives from each city and township to journey back and conduct independent evaluations.

The Sub-Committee of Older Brothers seemed like the most logical choice as these Brothers know their towns well and remember the places (parks, bathhouses, bookstores, cruise spots, etc.) where you would or wouldn't be. We also figured that they would be best able to recognize the same behaviors (depression, guilt, fear, anxiety, and alcohol, drug and sex addiction) that aided in their qualification and subsequent membership into the Committee of Brothers Since Passed.

The Sub-Committee of Older Brothers, therefore, was also assigned to work with other delegates from various other subcommittees to aid in the study. We wanted to ensure that all sub-cultures and ages that exist in the Same Gender Loving Men of Color community were adequately represented. We sent with this group representatives from the following areas:

> The Sub-Committee of Brothers Who Identified as gay (BIG)The Sub-Committee of Brothers Who Were Bisexual (BBI)
> The Sub-Committee of Same Gender Loving Men of Color (SGLMOC)
> The Sub-Committee of Brothers On the So Called, DL (DL)The Sub-Committee of Brothers Who Creeped and Tipped (BCT)

The Sub-Committee of Brothers Young (BY 15-24)
The Sub-Committee of Brothers Who Refused To Be Named (BRTBN)

Rounding out this Sub-Committee was representatives of the Sub-Committee of the Queen and Her Court (DIVAS). This Sub-committee consists of the Transgender community, both post-operative and pre-operative Transsexuals.

The Journey

So all the Brothers got to packing and preparing for this lengthy trip. Everyone was excited about seeing old friends, former partner, and family even though they couldn't be seen or communicate with them. More than that they were anxious to come back to the full membership board and report that there were perhaps a few isolated incidences to report on, minimal at best and that overall the reports have been over exaggerated.

Each one of them left here with the hope and belief that you would all be vindicated and that we could focus our collective attention to healing the wounds of a few Brothers there that we know are still struggling.

Our primary objective, however, was to focus our resources on the younger Brothers who will never know of us and what we suffered emotionally, physically, financially, socially, politically, and otherwise. We are working through a few of the conscious Brothers we left there with you to give these Brothers a new way of thinking and looking at themselves.

The Brothers finally got situated and left for their assignments after a short delay. Apparently, the Sub-Committee of the Queen and Her Court (DIVAS) was so indecisive about what to wear and what to pack that it took them some time to get it together. But that's another story entirely.

Nevertheless, they went off on their trip to visit you and were back as quickly as they left. Since the measurement of your time and our time differs so and the concept is so unimaginably different it will be difficult to explain in Earthly terms how long they were there but suffice it to say that it became painfully obvious to the teams that journeyed to you that they didn't need to spend as much time as was originally anticipated. In fact, they couldn't wait to get back.

We were told that the voyage back was spent in complete silence. Most of the Brothers seemed to be in some sort of shock when they returned. In fact, more than the majority of Brothers came back completely heart broken. They were so dejected. Tears were shed here for many days. I don't ever recall such grief. It would take several of your Earth days before we could call the body of Brothers together in a General Session to hear the results of the study.

When we were finally called together, the Chairman of the Committee of Brothers Since Passed read from the lengthy report. Not a sound could be heard uttering from the vast membership after he relayed detail after detail of the study. After the report was read all you could hear was whimpering, crying, and of Why? Please don't! And, "What are you doing yourselves? I have never seen the Brothers in such condition. Not here.

It was quite an experience. This again went on for several of your Earth days. Finally, the Chairman of the Committee of Brothers Since Passed decided we should adjourn. The body unanimously agreed to a motion by a member to have a Moment of Grieving and Prayer on your behalf.

The Results
There were many disturbing points surfaced about what's going on with you now but there were some encouraging advancements as well. For instance, it was reported that there are now many Same Gender Loving Men of Color who are healing their lives, maintaining healthy relationships, forming support groups of all kind, organizing politically to bring about change in the community, marrying and even raising children.

We read one committee report that details the number of Brothers who own businesses and an insurgence of Same Gender Loving Men of Color who are writing about our experiences, producing documentaries, and movies that is giving credence, purpose, and importance to our lives and our struggles. Indeed there is much for us to rejoice in.

Yet, in as much as there is much to rejoice in we have found that there is so much that you Brothers have missed, forgotten, ignored, or never learned. The general conclusion that we all have come to is, to put it bluntly, that some of you have lost your ever-loving minds!

In retrospect we should have recognized something was wrong and acted sooner. The number of Newcomers has been on the constant increase and they seem to be younger and younger than before we left. But like you we fed into misinformation that indicated that the number of AIDS cases was on the decline. What this information failed to outline was that these decreases didn't include Men of Color. Had we only paid more attention! Had we only looked more carefully at the rolls!

Then again, we all agreed that The Committee of Brothers Since Passed couldn't take full responsibility for this. As previously stated we thought you would have learned well from our lives and if not our lives then perhaps from our deaths. Those of you who survived the HIV and AIDS epidemic in the community know the details of our journey. You remember the many illnesses, the bouts with pneumonia, and with side effects of medication. You remember us being ostracized by our families, by our communities and even by some of you. You remember our denial and how we refused to be tested for HIV yet continued to have unprotected sex.

This very topic was discussed at the most recent strategy meeting of the Sub-Committee of Brothers Who Knew But Did Not Tell (BWK). These members realize what a mistake they made by having unprotected sex with some of you and infecting you with the virus. Even so, they concluded, part of that responsibility still belongs to some of you. The full body of the Committee of Brothers Since Passed wholeheartedly agrees.

Now some of you may be thinking that the Committee of Brothers Since Passed is being judgmental. Perhaps we are. But we can afford to be simply because it took us to find membership here to figure to get to the root of our own issues. It took us a life's journey and our subsequent deaths for us to find peace, fellowship and love. We didn't know at the time and we didn't have enough strength (or the resolve) to find out who we were then. We had no awareness of the power of love and neither did we have the information, the medication, counseling, and prevention mechanisms both in messaging and in medications that you now have. If we did, we wouldn't be here today.

Report Briefs

It is evident to us that the Black community as a whole bears the greatest burden and carries the greatest weight of the HIV AIDS epidemic as has been witnessed by some of the Earth studies gathered. What we found startled us. The Blue Ribbon Panel has discovered that AIDS is the leading cause of death for Brothers between the ages of 25-44. It was the same over 25 years ago.

Here is a briefing of what some of the Sub-Committee representatives found. We warn you that some of these reports are very depressing to read:

- **The Committee of Older Brothers found that Men of Color now comprise 52% of all AIDS cases among gay and bisexual men. Young African American gay and bisexual men (aged 13 to 24) experienced an 87% increase in diagnoses. This number has increased an amazing 31% more than a decade ago.**

As a large majority of **The Sub-Committee of Older Brothers** were with you 10 years ago, this is particularly disappointing for them. They have been inconsolable since their return.

- **The Sub-Committees of Brothers Who Refuse To Be Named and Brothers Who Were Bisexual all brought back reports** that 24% of African-American men and 15% of Latino men infected with HIV and AIDS through same sex contact identified themselves as being heterosexual.

The Sub-Committees of Brothers Who Refused To Be Named and **Brothers Who Were Bisexual** recognizes the stigma associated in society with identifying as "gay but have come to embrace the concept that it's not in a label or name. It's in the behaviors and actions. They are deeply disturbed by this continuing trend.

- **The Sub-Committee of Brothers Who Creeped and Tipped** reported that the Sisters still represent that fastest rising racial/ethnic group infected with HIV and AIDS.

The Sub-Committee of Brothers Who Creeped and Tipped were overwhelmed with grief as they discovered that Sisters represent 56% of new AIDS cases. Imagine their horror to also discover that our beautiful Black children, the innocent children represent 58% of pediatric AIDS cases. We don't think these Brothers will ever be the same.

- **The Sub-Committee of Brothers Young** found that of young men between the ages of 15 and 24 who have sex with men, 16% of Brothers and 13% of Latino Brothers were diagnosed with HIV infection. Young people were the most likely to be unaware of their infection. Among people aged 13-24, an estimated 51% of those living with HIV didn't know.
- **The Sub-Committee of Brothers Young** were sadden by the familiar naiveté lack of self-love, the lack of self-esteem as well as the feeling of invincibility that allowed them to place themselves in harm's way by having unprotected sex. They remember, too, how some older Brothers who they thought would love and protect them only used them sexually and discarded them. They are positively heartsick.

- A post review of the reports by **The Subcommittee of Brothers in Medicine and Psychology** concluded that many of you believe that because new treatments are available to prolong life that the risks are not as great. This committee is equally concerned these new drugs and treatments may not be available to you noting that these treatments are very expensive they wondered if you would be able to afford them, if your insurance would cover it, or if you have insurance.

Additionally, they have discovered that Medicaid, of which People of Color are disproportionately dependent, does not provide access to the program for low-income people until they have developed full-blown AIDS. At this stage treatment is less effective and more expensive. Even so, they concluded, would anyone really want to spend the rest of their lives taking medications?

If

Oh how we wish that we could be in your shoes! We talk about that here all the time. It is what is on everyone's tongue. Because we know for a fact that given the chance to do it all over again we would do it so much different.

If we could change places with you right now and have a second opportunity to live we would take this time to deepen our relationships with God. It is in Him that you find everything you will ever need. We know this now for a fact!

We would take that time and the love within ourselves and nurture the precious gift of life. We would take nothing for granted and count every single breath we take. We would take better care of ourselves and our Brothers and Sisters and make certain that we create a culture that we could be proud of and relish in. We would love so much deeper than we did before. We would love so much more.

We are only concerned that it will get worse before it gets better and more Brothers will join us. Though we welcome each Newcomer with open arms and introduce some of them for the first time to love in its purest and most spiritual form it is important for us to say this: We don't want you here! We don't need you here! Not like that!

We Remain
The Committee of Brothers Since Passed has unanimously agreed that your lives are worth saving even if you don't think so. We have been searching for methods and tactics to help you understand what a beautiful opportunity you have not only to love and heal your life but what an opportunity you have to heal each other.

In light of this, we will not let you discard us. We will remain in the hearts and minds of those who chose to remember. We cannot allow you to let our lives, our precious lives, be a distant memory; something you can just turn your back on and dismiss.

Conversely, we can't allow you to let your lives, your precious lives, fade into shadow of darkness, shame, and disgrace. You must see the opportunities you have to love and heal by seeing the significance in us. You will recognize the importance in our lives and in our deaths. Can't you see? Don't you get it? Everything we went through was so that you wouldn't have to.

We are the Martyrs of an era that still exists. Our lives represented all the good and wonderful blessings we were created to enjoy. Our deaths represent all the good and wonderful blessings you still have the opportunity to enjoy. Unfortunately, most of the Committee of Brothers Since Passed didn't start living until we knew we were dying. The number of Newcomers still entering is staggering.

Conclusion

We gathered together today in a general assembly of The Committee of Brothers Since Passed, the many thousands of us, and we collectively prayed that from this day forward you will think about the things we've said in this memo. We've asked that you will stop for a moment and research the things in your life, the pain and the unhealed wounds that cause you to act irresponsibly with your bodies, your minds, and your hearts. We've asked that you will all question your motivations. We've asked God that He help you to find your love.

The Committee of Brothers Since Passed recognizes that among all else this is a love issue. This is why the epidemic continues to spread and more of you continue to join us. None of the prevention and education will reach your mind or your heart if you don't find your love – surface your self-worth. It will never apply in your life or in the lives of those with whom you share your body if you don't love yourself.

We've asked God to guide you back to that path of love, peace, and understanding. Now we ask you to listen to Him. Pray to Him. Believe me, Brothers, He is everything you have thought Him to be. He is Love.

So know this, Brothers, we will always remain in your conscious no matter how you try to deny. We are watching, we are hoping, and we are praying that you will take your lives more seriously. No matter how you try to drown out your personal pain and sorrows in liquor, drugs or sex we will insert ourselves in.

You will think about our journey and us, and you will see our faces and you will know that we are counting on you to do the right thing. We are counting on you to save the world by saving yourselves. We love you Brothers and believe it or not we still need you too. We are depending on you.

Turn this around and get right with yourselves. It's not too late. Really, it's not.

With Our Undying Love,
The Committee of Brothers Since Passed

What Price

I asked myself last week
What Price?

What Price, Baby,
Do I pay to be with you?
To be your Man
        Your Bae
                Your Boo?

How much does it cost?
Must it cost?

A couple of days ago
    I thought about it
Stepped back
        Evaluated
You know
Divorced myself from the game

You know
The one you pretend you don't know you play

All of your
      Hurts,
             Pain,
                      Disappointments,
    Fears
           Guilt
Perfectly packaged in a sexy frame
With looks I was looking for

But all your beautiful lips gave were
                Cold kisses
Offered on a
        Bed of lies from a
                Silver tongue

My flame against your extinguisher

What Price?

        Yea, man, you won
For a little while
                I craved your flesh
Melting
        From the warmth of your touch

Did everything you asked me to
Compromising
    Self
        Integrity
        Morality even
To let you know
Here is where you belonged

But at What Price?

No other commands my attention
Like others do yours

Disappearing acts
        Strange voices on the phone
                Asking for you with intimate familiarity

I can hear it in the tone of his voice
He ain't your cousin,
              Coworker,
                            Straight friend from the gym
He knows you
He knows you like I know you
              And he wants to know more
Don't know if I can go on like this

Yesterday
            A new day
                      I woke up with this on my mind
And asked myself

What Price?

Recalling I've dealt with worse pain before
I've buried family
            Buried friends
                  Buried myself

Been rejected in the name of love
            By family
                By friends
                      And even by me
So truthfully,
This ain't shit

Am I mad?
Naw, Baby…Never That
You gave me more than you will ever realize

Couldn't hate you for that
        Couldn't hate you for not giving me
                What you couldn't give yourself

All the hate you showed me
        Taught me how to love myself more

So I thought about it this morning
And asked myself

What Price?

Then it came to me
        You ain't the problem
           I am
Sat here and let you charcoal
        Your issues onto my canvas
Thinking if I gave you what you wanted
        You'd give me what I needed

Not So

So I thought about it this evening
What Price?

And as I sit here packing your shit
        It's clearer to me now than ever before

I simply can't afford you

        Peace!

Fifteen Funerals

Fifteen funerals
This year alone
How many more?

I'm dying inside
A friend has died
I've lost another piece of me
A Peace in me
                                        My existence
My love
My spirit

I'm angry
Confused
Conflicted

No one knows my pain
Seeming not to care
My Brothers are dying
Often
        Slowly
                Painfully
                      Alone
Compassion is lacking
Only talk
Judgments casting
Matter of fact like on their tongue

I scream against the pain
Seething
Boiling from my toes
To my throat
Defending against all I hear

He was a sinner
                                      No, He was my friend.

He was a homo
                                      A Dayum Good Friend!

He was a faggot
                                      Good to everybody he met.

He was a punk
                                      Kindest Brother you would ever know.

He was a sissy
                                      I loved him like a Brother!

He got what he deserved

                          God Loves Us All…

A Child Shall Lead Them All

One late evening in January 2000, I lay in bed watching a PBS special on Children with AIDS. The program profiled an 8-year-old boy named Travis Jefferies who was infected with HIV at birth from his drug-addicted mother. The program detailed the struggle of this young Brother being raised by his Grandmother to live with full-blown AIDS.

Travis was a beautiful little man-child with a contagious smile and glowing personality, yet he was in so much pain. Throughout the program all Travis wanted to do was to play with his cousins and his friends. He just wanted to be a child and do as his contemporaries did. In one part of the documentary Travis sat crying in his Grandmother's arms because she wouldn't let him play in the snow. Through his tears Travis said, "I hate being little!" I don't think I cried as much as I did that night than I had in years.

I was struck by the determination of Travis to be normal, yet I was more in awe of his wonderful innocence and wisdom beyond his years. Travis was so forgiving. During one interview the producer asked Travis was he angry with his mother [for passing the virus onto him]. Travis responded almost angry and insulted at such a question, "Why should I be angry with my mother? It's not her fault!" He said that twice and with such conviction. It seemed to me that Travis was much more aware of the conditions in this society that causes a climate that make people turn to drugs and to other behaviors to forget. Travis was able to see past blame and past anger. Travis only wanted to play.

At the end of the program Travis' treatment included Protease Inhibitors that had initially worked but were now not as effective. It appeared that the infection had found a way to beat Travis' treatment and was recreating itself inside of him. Although the documentary indicated that the producer of the film has passed away, no other information was given about Travis.

The very next morning I called PBS headquarters and made attempts to contact those associated with the production of the film to find out where Travis was and if he was all right. I wanted to embrace this little Brother and offer him and his family some encouragement and financial support. I wanted to tell Travis how loved he is and how much his little wisdom has a far-reaching effect than he would ever fully understand. Unfortunately, numerous attempts to locate Travis and his Grandmother were unsuccessful. I don't know if Travis is still with us.

Travis, I wrote this piece for you and for the millions of children worldwide who have lost their innocence. I love you Travis. We all do. I hope one day in this world or in the next that I will find my way to you.

All of these years I have still carried you with me. Wherever you are, my thoughts and prayers are there with you, Little Brother, and I send all my loving energy to you.

Love,
Always and Always,

Sundiata

Travis

His eyes tell the whole story
Lips trembling through his
Tears
He hates being little

So much pain
So much love
Too much understanding
Knowing things
Seeing things
Feeling things
A child just ain't supposed to

Travis
Battles with the monster
He calls it
Growing
Inside his weakening
Stunted body
Channeled through the birth canal
From a drug addicted mother
Too harsh being
Little
Too unfair being

It's the only life he's ever known
When you cry
Travis
I taste your tears

A little man
With a Giant's wisdom
His old soul
Monumental with Spirit
Embraced by
Grandma's hands
Enfolding
Comforting
Reassuring

The power of Grandma's hands
The power of Grandma's prayers
Feeding his hopes
From God to his Soul
Feeding him food
Through tubes in his stomach
Feeding him Breath
From the humming machine
Next to his weak and fading shadow
He sleeps painfully, peacefully
But he only wants to play

Why should I be angry with my mother?
He turns to the camera
Why should I be angry with my mother?
He Protests
It's not her fault!
Convinced beyond reasonable doubts

His compassion
His Forgiveness
His Soul Strength
Speaks to my Reason
And I let go of my own anger

Against mother
Against society
Against evil's lurking
And the unconsciousness
That keeps pain with us
Travis melts it away
Until It Subsides

I wish I could be so brave

AIDS is killing Him
Taking everything away from
His precious beginning
Still He teaches
Of Love
Of Forgiveness
Of Release
From feelings unreal
That can only do more harm than good
To his Innocence

I heard you
Travis
Loud and clear
What you were telling me
What you were telling us

I wanted to jump into the screen
Into your Grandma's living room
To hold you and tell you
That it's not your fault either
Travis
That you are little

I wanted to wrap these arms
Around you
Little Brother
And wipe the tears from your face
To calm you and tell you
That you are loved
In ways too many to mention

I don't know where you are
Travis
Frozen in my mind
As the Little boy
Who hates being little
Who only wants to play

I searched for you

I wanted to tell you that everything
Would Be fine
That You are watched
That You are in God's mind
And in His Good Care
And you will not have to worry
Ever again
The pain and memory of this world
Will one day be no more
You will sail away on wings of time
To reawaken from your slumber

And You will play again
I just know you will
Fully restored and

Fully renewed
Resurrected
To run freely among the
Animals
And the breeze
You will be back

Your mother will be there
With you
And Grandma's eyes
Will watch you both
And her ears will
Hear you heart
Sing of Laughter and of smiles
That you now long for

Let this world and its
Painful disappointments
Leave you
Let it pass you by
There are rich rewards awaiting you
Travis
It won't be long
Little Brother
Before you forget all about this

You will
Play again
Dance again
Love again
And never know again
The Pain
in being little

I love you, Travis
God loves you
And He is Watching

Bless you
Travis
Bless you

My Blue Heaven

He was mine for a time
6 months maybe seven
At least for three or four
It felt somethin' like Heaven

Something like Heaven is what I said
'Cause he took advantage of insecurities in my head
Didn't think I would ever be loved much to my own dread
So instead of seeing him for who he was
I made him someone else instead

He did everything right
Knew exactly what to say
Called me three, four, five
Sometimes six times a day

Wined and dined me out on dates
I fell hard and strong and sealed my fate
Served my heart and soul to him on a plate
Cause I found My Blue Heaven… And Heaven can't wait!

Chillin' on my couch watchin' DVDs
Sittin' by the ocean takin' in the breeze
We had it all, I'd do anything to please
His hand in mine strollin' Avenue Ease

Time stood still when he touched my hand
Had me pantin' like a dog moanin', "*Oooh Gottdayum!!!*"
Strung out like a whale beached on California sand
Kickin' like a drum major in a Black college band

The friction of his body close to mine
Feelin' so high I was loosin' my mind
Like I smoked three rocks and popped ecstasy with wine
I wouldda sold my house just tell me where to sign!

And when we made love the universe collided
The shit was so on it got me inspired
Couldn't get enough, I never got tired
Just thinkin' bout that shit is gettin' me excited!

The scent of our passion was thick in the air
Inhibitions lost and I didn't care
Had me reachin' for shit that wasn't even there
Like he studied the tale of the tortoise and the hare…

See, he wasn't concerned about lightenin' pace
He knew slow and steady was sure to win the race
I was loosin' my breath like I just got maced
Then started hummin' bars of Amazing Grace

Amaaaaaaaaaaaaaaaazzzzzzzzzzzzin' Graaaaaaaaaaaaaaaaaaaace
How Swwwwwwwwwweeeeeeett Theeeeeeeeee Soooooooouuuunnnnnd

How Sweet, How Sweet, How Sweet the Sound
Lovin' like that should be sold by the pound!
I'd describe it to you but there's no adjective or noun
I can only stretch out my hands and kiss the ground!

I was there in love and what it all means
Plannin' a life with this Brutha and what it all brings
I'm talkin' a wedding ceremony complete with the rings
'Cause now I know Why the Caged Bird Sings!!!

Now this went on for quite some time
I was convinced beyond reason that the Brutha was mine
Clingin' like a grape on a vineyard vine
But even a blind man could see I was wastin' my time

Why I say that?
Well, at first it was the sneaky late night calls
Then cancelled dates that had me climbin' the walls
Then his cell blowin' up from some dude named Paul
Some Brutha he said sold him shoes at the mall

Hmmmmmmm??

The hickey on his neck was enough alone
And so was the smell of another Brother's cologne
And whenever I'd go to touched him he was as cold as a stone
But had a bigass grin when Paul was on the phone

Then one solid week I didn't hear from him had all
Took seven whole days before he returned my call
This was I think around the beginning of fall
I shouldda left his ass then – don't know why I stalled!

Of course when I asked him he firmly denied it
And couldn't understand why I got so excited
Told me he loved me and we'd always be united
My Blue Heaven loved me and I was delighted!

But I'm not that dumb, I knew it was a line
There had to be another Brutha beatin' my time
And if he wanted him he could go, no reason, no rhyme,
I could find another Blue Heaven, shit, I know I'm a dime!!!

So late one night when he crept out of bed
I got this idea to follow in my head
Didn't take my car - rode my bike instead
I know that sounds desperate but –
Fuck it - I was!!!

So he walked up to this place on Avenue Krauss
I jumped off the bike as quite as a mouse
This dude opens the door and lets him in the house
And he kissed him on the lips...Yup, right on the mouth!

The name on the mailbox said, Mr. Paul Lee
So I moved in closer to see what I could see
And gather all the evidence I'd need to be free
Of that sorry mutha fukka for tryin' to play me

I peeped in the window they were butt ass naked
On the dining room table like they were tryin' to break it
Cut like a knife - didn't think I could take it
I was mad as hell - I ain't even gonna fake it!

Got back to the house poured a glass of Grey Goose
Grabbed a thick white cord and started tyin' a noose
Now don't get me wrong - I ain't into abuse

But I was gonna hang his sorry ass!!!

I was up when he came in much to his surprise
Said I was finished with him and all his lies
And that I saw him tonight between another kat's thighs
He could only say sorry between sobbin' and cries

When sorry didn't work he got mean, even salty
Said he never loved me - and that it was my faulty
Next thing you know I was charged with assautly

'Cause I Whooped His Ass up!

All's well that ends well is all I can say
I just paid my fine and walked away
From My Blue Heaven that fateful day
Never saw him again; I think it's best that way

I learned so much about myself from that brief love affair
To love myself first – and do it beyond compare
To let someone else do it for me I won't ever dare
'Cause if I don't find it in me I won't find it anywhere

And now I understand like I knew from the gate
But for a life lesson learned it's never too late
I don't want "Somethin' like Heaven" - I want a full plate
And that means all of Heaven…

So Heaven *Can* Wait!

Storytelling
The Art of the Griot

Author's note: Please forgive me. I was in a silly mood....

Adventures

Well, now I've been here down south all my life. Don't know no place else. Truth is never even thought bout goin no place else...cept here lately. Don't know why either but it's like I'm feelin like my life needs some excitement. Some adventure. Down here it's quiet. Almost too quiet at times and I'm kinda getting tired of the same 'ole same 'ole.

I gots me a few friends livin up north, well, up north on the east coast north. They be tellin me all the time bout the things they do and places they go to and see. And it's a lot! They used to live here but when they lives called fo adventure they took it! Ain't never looked back either. I envy that. Takes a brave man to leave all that's familiar to grab a hold of adventure. Been wishin here lately that I could see some of it cause I'm bored wit my life and all these things around me. Yes, sir! I want some adventure.

Now don't get me wrong things here ain't all that bad. We got us a nice house Jr. and me. Jr., well that's my friend you know. We built us a house here on a heap of land - 2 whole acres - round bout five years ago. And we happy... well kind of. Ain't got a whole lot of money. We ain't rich or nothin like that but we live well. Jr. from here too. Been here all his life just like me cept he content wit his life, happy being round here in the country wit all the trees and the grass and the rollin hills and the slow pace. He don't care none fo no adventure. Don't never wanna go nowhere new or different. He happy just being here in our house lovin me. But that's just the kind of person he is. But see me? Naw, not me! I wanna do things. Experience things. I know there's life outside of this here yard. And I'm wantin to see it.

See here this city, this town, this house, yard and Junior is all I know. We been together now right round ten years. Ten years! That a long time! We was just in our twenties when we found each other, twenty-one to be exact, though I'm bout 4 months older than he is. I mean I'd been knowin him from round the area where we growed up but I ain't never really know nothin bout him. But we got this one place round bout twenty-five or so miles away from here where fellas like us go and that's where we found each other. He was just as surprised to see me there as I was to see him! Anyways we got together soon after that and been together ever since.

He's a good man. I mean a real good man and we put a lot into what we got. He taught me a lot too bout everything - bout love, bout life, money, education, and stuff like that. See, Jr. went to college. Got a real good education cause he smart. I mean smart as a whip! Got a good job payin a lot of money. More than me but you would never know that. He don't flaunt it or use that against me or make me feel less than a man. No, sir! He says that all we got is *ours*. Don't matter who bought it. That the kind of man he is!

Me on the other hand I wasn't really all into studyin and books and school and stuff like that. I like to work wit my hands. Been a mechanic fo as long as I can remember. Worked on em wit my daddy since I was round bout knee high but ain't never had made no real money from it. So after we got together he helped me get into school to get a certificate to work on cars. Made all the difference in the world. Made me feel good bout myself, proud like, that I did it and folks started payin me fo what I was worth! See, he good like that! Always takin care of folks and makin sure they do the best they can. You can't help but love him fo that!

I mean I love him fo other reasons too. He's good to me. Real good. Cooks, cleans, looks after me. Always doin somethin nice fo me to show how much he loves me. And he does. He loves me like nobody ever did. Now don't get me wrong he ain't soft or nothin like that. Not at all. He's a real man and if he ain't tell you he was lovin me you would never know. Ever! Tall and black as coal. He a real good looking man too. But he gentle. Kind. Loves simple things. Things I used to love too but getting sick and tired of.

All the girls here was lined up to marry Jr. when he got back from college and some of em still lined up - the ones that don't know no better or don't care he lovin me. And 'b'lieve me there's a lot of em out there like that! Most folks round here know we lovin each other but won't openly say so. They just act like it ain't nothin and so do we. Our business is our business. That what me and Jr. always say. Now I ain't foolish to b'lieve they ain't sayin stuff behind our backs but long as they don't say nothin directly we o.k.! He say all the time, "*love conquers all*", and I used to b'lieve that until here lately.

Cause here lately I been feelin like the world is revolvin but I'm standin still! I want some adventure. I'm bored wit doin the same things all the time - work, home, church, and home again. We don't ever go nowhere cause Jr. don't like goin to that place we met all them years back or any other places like that. We go on occasion but hardly ever! And we don't have many friends, I mean not like us that we get together wit. There ain't many like us here least we don't know em. I mean there are other fellas round here that's like us but mostly the kind that real lady-like. Now I ain't sayin nothin wrong wit that but them kind of fellas I don't like bein round. So er'body like us pretty much keep to themselves. We all gotta kinda keep quiet bout it in our own way. Folks can't stand folks like us throwing it in their face. I hear its different up north, east coast north, where folks got stuff to distract em so they ain't all worried bout other folks business. Whew! I wish I knew what that was like!

So really it's just me and him and this house and them trees, and the grass, and the rollin hills behind us. No excitement. No adventure. The only thing that keeps me from losin my head is the yard work. I love workin in the yard. Like I said I like workin wit my hands and when I ain't workin on cars, cuttin grass, trimmin hedges, doin stuff in the yard satisfies. Yes, sir! Every weekend Saturday mornin just like clockwork I get up real early to tend to the yard. I love a good clean yard and a well-kept one.

A lot of folks don't know this and I suspects you don't either but how you keep your lawn says somethin bout the type of folks you are. Sho do! Let me tell you how. Fo instance if you got long grass in your yard that ain't been cut and bushy hedges that ain't been trimmed it means you got trouble goin on in your house - fightin and cussin and stuff like that. Now, if your hedges been trimmed but your grass ain't means one of you ain't right bout something. Somebody sneakin round. Got grass growin round they feet cause they tryin to cover they tracks. See what I mean? Now if your grass ain't cut in the front or the back and your hedges ain't trimmed, well that means that you just plain lazy! Yes, sir! I can always tell what's goin on inside somebodys house just by passin by and lookin at they lawn.

Now our lawn well it looks good! Always does. That's my job round here to keep our business off our lawn! He cares fo most everything else out here though. But the truth is ain't really much else to do after the grass is cut and the hedges trimmed or rakin leaves come the fall season. We got a few flowers growing round but mostly the kind that don't need much tendin to. Got a lot of trees though. Lots of em! Make fo nice shade in the summer cause summer can sho be hot here! And when the trees come together and they all touchin at the top and coverin the yard it like we under a blanket. It sho can be pretty.

Jr. like it out there. Spends a lot of time, too much time I think, specially on summer mornings walkin barefoot in the grass mongst the trees though he there most of any time of year. Yep! Rain or shine he there readin or just relaxin listenin to the wind or the birds. Say it his thinkin place. He talks to them too - to the trees - say it keeps em healthy - the trees that is. Now I b'lieve that cause my grandmamma usta talk to her trees and they the tallest you ever seen! She been gone bout ten years now. Rest her soul.

Anyway, he say they talk back to him too. Tell him things. I b'lieve that too! My grandmamma usta know everything! Said the trees told her secrets and I b'lieved her cause you couldn't sneak or hide doin nothin! No, sir! You couldn't fool her bout a thing! Yes, sir! Them trees and her had a special relationship, just like Jr. do I suppose. But me? Once I finish wit the yard I'm finished wit the yard! I go inside fo a cold drink and sit down and watch a game or eat somethin Jr. cooks. He's a good cook. Always somethin good to eat round here hot, good food too! Not like me. Can't boil a egg!

Anyway I like to work in the yard but when it's done so am I! I admit I do tend to get bored sometimes wit all the trees and hedges, and flowers, and stuff. Truth is tho I won't say it to him or not nobody else I'm gettin kinda bored wit him. He tries but it just ain't enough no more. I suppose I'm lucky to have him and all what we got. At least that what I used to think. I'm not so sure these days. I needs me some excitement. Some adventure is what I need. Yes, sir! I needs some adventure. Been thinkin bout it hard too! A lil voice in my head keep tellin me that and I'm listenin more and more.

Part II

I b'lieve when things is callin to you in your head you can't ignore em too long. I mean you can try but somehow it finds its way too you! That just what happened a couple weeks ago. See, me and Jr. went to a party in that same town what I told you bout - the one bout twenty-five miles away. Like I said he don't like to hardly go nowhere but this was special. He got a friend he went to college wit who lives up north, east coast north, Washington, D.C. or thereabouts. He from here but when he left he never came back. See, that's what I mean! A lot of folks from here did that - went lookin fo adventure, found it and stayed wit it! Anyway, another friend he went to college wit (who obviously don't want no adventure and still live here) threw a party fo him - Jr.'s friend from school that is - so we went. I was excited too! Hadn't been out nowhere in a long while and I was just happy to get away from the house and the yard and the trees.

Well, we get there and turns out his friend brought some friends of his own from where he lives up north - east coast north. Real nice lookin fellas, handsome and tall, like Jr. And they was nice. Real nice! Ain't try to make fun of our simple life and simple ways. Lot of folks do that you know. Make fun of folks from the south b'lievin they all sophisticated and better than us. I can't stand when folks do that like its somethin wrong wit us cause the truth is we all one generation, maybe two, from southern roots. Some folk seem to forgets that!

Anyway, there was this one fella there - one that was real, real nice lookin - so nice lookin he stood out from the rest. I couldn't take my eyes off him! Jr. ain't notice cause he was too busy talkin to his old friend. Cides, I wasn't doin nothin wrong, right? I was just looking. Ain't nothin wrong wit that! And Jr. ain't the jealous type no way. Then again I ain't never gave him no reason to be.

So all night long I'm just a lookin and lookin at him thinkin bout what his life must be like up north - east coast north - and all the adventures he must be havin wit the parties and travelin, and meeting new folk and having new experiences. A part of me wished I was him bein in the middle of all that excitement and adventure. Another part of me was also wishin that I was sharin them experiences wit him. Now to tell you the truth I ain't never in my whole entire life thought bout bein wit nobody else cept Jr. But this fella, well, he just looked excitin and full of adventure! Look like he could open me up to a whole world of things I always dreamed bout doin.

Anyway, I was all lost in my thoughts - so lost in em that I ain't notice he had came over near where I was standin to fix a drink. Whew! I got nervous! I mean real nervous specially when he looked at me and smiled. I wanted to say somethin but I ain't quite know what to say. Can you b'lieve that? Here I was wit adventure starin me straight in the eye and I couldn't say not nothin! I guess he musta noticed cause he extended his had fo me to shake it and introduced himself. Sean was his name and man was he nice! He told me he had been watchin me the whole time I was there and thought I was nice lookin. Can you b'lieve that? He thought I was nice lookin! Well, I thanked him fo the complement tryin not to sound too dumb or nothin although I gotta admit my tongue was all twisted up in my mouth.

He talked most of the time so I ain't have much to say. He asked me had I ever been to Washington, D.C., and I was almost too embarrassed to say no but I did anyway cause I ain't want him to ask me some question bout it that I couldn't answer, and besides my mama ain't raise a liar! Anyway, he looked at me real sly like ya know and winked at me and said I should come fo a visit. All I could think bout was adventure.

We talked fo a while there by the bar. I don't know where Jr. was but I really ain't care. Not to sound cruel or nothin but I was standing at the gates of adventure and it was openin up fo me! He scused himself to go to the bathroom I think and when he came back he handed me his number, well, two numbers - the one at the hotel where he was stayin in town and the one up north - real sly like again so nobody could see. He said he was goin to be in town fo two more days and I should call him and get together maybe show him around. Can you b'lieve that? Now, not only was adventure starring me in my face but now it was in the palm of my hand!

I told him that I ain't know if I could and I was being honest! I ain't know if I could. Cides, I told him I was there wit my friend (Jr. calls me his "partner" - sometime he say "lover" but I just can't get used to that. I just say "Friend" cause that what we is. I mean we other things too I s'pose but we friends too. Anyway, I figured he would know what I meant but you know what? It ain't seem to bother him at all. Not none in the least! He kept right on talkin like I never said a thing and made me promise to call him the next day. The only thing that made me know he heard me say I had a friend was when he turned to me fo he walked off and asked me, "*Are you happy?*" referin to Jr.

Well, since this was the first time and I mean the first time anybody had asked me that I had to think bout that fo a second but only a second cause if I was happy, I mean really happy, do you think I'd be thinkin bout adventure strong as I do? Anyway, b'fo I had a chance to really think bout it, I said, *"No. I'm not! I need some adventure!"* He looked at me and said real sly like, *"So you really need to call me tomorrow!"* And you know what? I did.

I called him the next day and went over to the hotel where he was stayin. Now I ain't never in my whole life cheated on Jr. and I wasn't tendin to that day either but I parked my truck way round back anyway cause I ain't want nobody seein me goin in that hotel. You know how folks can talk and I was just protectin Jr. Well, I got up there in that hotel room and whew! We had some good adventure! Up north fellas - east coast north fellas - sho know how to show you adventure! Afterwards, we just laid there and talked. He was telling me bout things to do and see in Washington, D.C., and how much fun it is up there and man I was wishin I could just go to Washington, D.C. right then!

He told me I could come up there and visit wit him if I wanted to and he would show me round and made sure I had a good time. He said he liked me too. I mean like he really liked me like "love" like me. Well, I ain't think that was possible 'cause we had just met and all but I was feelin like I like him too, like "love" like! He even told me that if I liked it up there I could stay. Can you b'lieve that? Stay in D.C.? Well, I made up my mind right then and there that if I liked it I was leavin that house and them trees and them hedges and that lawn fo good! Now let the trees go and tell Jr. that!

Anyways, we had a couple more adventures fo I had to leave. He kissed me good-bye, a real strong kiss, and told me one more again that he wanted me to come to D.C. soon. And he really meant it too. Know how I know? Cause I could see it in his eyes starin at me all puppy-dog like. He gave me that kind a look that made me feel like he really wanted me (the kind of look JR. usta give me and still sometimes do only I don't feel it like I used to). Well, that done it! I ain't know'd how I was gonna do it but I was goin up north - east coast north - to get the excitement and adventure my life was callin fo. I mean what else was I gonna do wit adventure speakin directly to me?

From that day forward on not a cotton pickin thing round here was the same to me! Not the house, not the yard, the trees, the grass, the hedges, nothin! Not even him - Jr. that is! All I could think bout was Sean and all the adventure I was missin out on waitin fo me in D.C. Even right now it's all I can think bout. I been in so much thought bout it that after I trimmed the hedges and Jr. leaves to run some errands I run inside the house to call him. Every time we talk we talk fo a long time, two-three hours bout how he misses me and how he loves me and how he wants me to come see him.

I get so caught up in thoughts of being wit him and all that adventure waitin on me that I loose track of time. Not that it matters to me cause adventure is now only a phone call away. But fo the past two weeks we been talkin so long and so much that I been forgetin to cut the grass. Its round bout ankle high now. Jr. said something bout it today. Said he ain't understand why I ain't cut the grass yet. I'm sho glad he don't know what I know bout lawns. He'd know something was goin on fo sure!

Could be he already spect somethin goin on the way he been talkin to them trees lately. If they tellin him secrets they must surely be tellin him bout my conversations! And we ain't gettin along lately. Been arguin a lot bout nothin and ain't made love in weeks - not since we went to that party and I grabbed a whole of adventure. Makin love just ain't excitin to me no more - not like it was wit Sean. I'm missin him. I really am. The last time we talked I told him I was commin. I done delayed adventure long enough! Even set the date and all!

So I told Jr. I was going to special mechanic training school in Washington, D.C. fo four whole days. Told him it was fo a new car the dealership I work at is startin to carry. Now I know I said my mama ain't raise no liar but what was I s'posed to do? Tell him I was goin on adventures wit somebody else? I ain't that cruel. No, sir! I ain't cruel enough to hurt him on purpose. Cides, what he don't know won't hurt him much anyway! He ain't said much after I told him I was goin to Washington, D.C. He just went out and sat out wit the trees. And I don't care! I don't! I don't care what them trees mumblin to him. I'm gettin on wit my adventure and I ain't letting nothin stop me - not him, not the trees, not the grass, not the yard, not the hedges, or them rollin hills. Nothin!

Part III

I ain't never been one fo a lot of travel. Ain't really had no place to travel to but even when I do I drive. I like to be in control of where I'm goin and what's gettin me there so the only thing I was hesitatin bout was gettin on that plane. But I was determined not to let nothin, no trees, no hedges, no grass, no yard and no Jr. keep me from doin what it was I was gonna do and I wasn't bout to let a plane ride do it either! I brought my flask, what look like a small jar, wit me and commence to drinkin from it the second I got on the plane! It ain't make me drunk in the head or nothin but it sure helped me to relax while that thing bounced around in the air! It wasn't as bad as I thought it was gonna be. Cides, I kept my mind on what was waitin fo me on the other side of the ride; Sean and my adventures. I couldn't wait to see him.

Soon as we landed I jumped up off that plane and grabbed my carry bag out of the bin cause I ain't check no luggage (wasn't no need to cause he told me I wouldn't need much clothes - that what Sean say) and all but ran off that plane! He was standin there in the inside airport buildin looking all good and smellin all good and just a smilin. See that the kind of welcome I need - somebody happy to see me when I come in from somewhere! Not like Jr. He don't seem happy to see me like he usta anymore specially here lately. Says I'm d'stracted. Well, I don't know what he mean by that but if it mean what I think it mean he right! I am d'stracted. But what else could you s'pect when I been askin fo adventure and it slap me plumb in the face? My mama ain't raise no liar and she ain't raise no fool either!

Anyways, we got in his car. A real fancy one - the kind I imagine somebody excitin like him to drive - and headed over to his house. On the ride from the airport all I could see was all these buildings - the kind that you know a lot of interestin adventures happen in. I mean there were tall ones, short ones, big ones, little ones, all kinds. It's quite a site to see! And you know what? There ain't hardly no grass nowhere! And the trees. Them poor trees. Look like somebody just propped them in the middle of all that concrete just fo show! No other use fo them I suppose. But then again who would want all that here wit all that's goin on? Who needs grass to cut or hedges to trim, or trees tellin all your secrets or lawns showin all your business fo the world to see? Not me! Not no more!

We drove up to his house and there it was. He called it a row house. I guess they call it that cause they all lined up in a row right next to each other lookin exactly the same. I mean really right next to each other all attached! Can you b'lieve that? They all attached and ain't got no drive way. I mean you have to park your car on the street and walk to your house! And man are they small. I mean really small! You can put his whole house in my living room and still have room fo two maybe three more. I kid you not. They that small! Got a lil piece of dirt on the outside what supposed to be a lawn I guess but ain't no room to cook out in or have your family over. He pay a whole lot of money fo it too! A whole lot more than what Jr. and me pay fo ours but I guess that's what it takes to live in the middle of adventure. Hell, if this is what adventure calls fo then so be it! I could get used to it.

After I got all settled in we sat on the couch and kissed a while and hugged, and told each other how glad we were to see each other and all kinds of romantic stuff. He was sitting there lookin good and temptin while he was rollin a cigar - a blunt I think is what he called it. Now my granddaddy usta roll his own cigars but two things was different: one, granddaddy ain't neva called them no blunt and two, they ain't look like the one Sean had! Granddaddy's tobacco was brown - doo doo brown - not to be nasty or nothin - but Sean's tobacco was green and still had seeds in it. Can you b'lieve that? What kind of tobacco store would gone sell you tobacco leaves wit seeds in it?! And man did it smell funny! Smelled funny and tasted funny! I mean I'm not no smoker or nothin but he offered it to me and I ain't wanna be rude. Cides, ain't this what I came here fo anyway? Some excitement? Some new adventures? Yes sir, that's what I'm all bout!

We finished smokin the cigar - well, some of it anyway - and was just kissin all over each other and I swear to you his kisses were makin me dizzy. Makin my head spin. I was gettin hot too. Not in a sweaty kind of way like I get when I cut the grass on Sat'day mornings but hot in the other way. And he was too so he led me upstairs - almost had to hold me up cause I was still dizzy from his kisses - and we made love three maybe four times cause he loves doin it. And all of a sudden so do I! After while we woke up although I don't remember falling asleep but I have to tell you my head was still all foggy from his kisses.

We took a shower, got dressed, and went downstairs to the kitchen. I was hungry. I mean real, real hungry. So we ate a couple of sandwiches, some left over chicken, a couple of bag of potato chips, some Doritos, and a half dozen day old donuts. I wanted some more to eat but his cabinets and refrigerator was empty. Can you b'lieve that? I ain't never in my whole entire life seen a refrigerator so empty! But I'm sure there's way too many adventures going on to cook stuff. Take too much time outta your schedule.

Back home where I'm from cookin is part of the schedule. Round here tho there's all kinds of eatin places on every block and they stay open just bout all night long! He said we'd grab somethin later and that was alright wit me. He was takin me to a club - like the one back home twenty-five or so miles away where fellas like us go - only this one ain't that far from where he lives. In fact, he got a whole lot of clubs near to where he live. I ain't ever knew there were so many clubs like that in the whole entire world let alone one city!

And man, whew! You walk into them and they packed. I mean it must have been hundreds — looked like thousands — of black fellas all crammed up into this club! I ain't never seen nothin like that in my whole life! All shapes, sizes, skin colors, hairstyles, and everything! I mean some look real tough too like you would never imagine them bein in a place like this. But they are. Soon as we walked in Sean saw folks he knew I suppose and went over to talk to em. I just wandered off in the corner takin in the sites.

A few fellas there was nice enough to come talk to me asking me how I was doin and where I was from, if I was wit somebody, and stuff like that. They was awful nice. Makin sure I was havin a good time and had somebody to show me around. And you talk bout accomodatin! Man, whew! A lot of them invited me to come home to sleep at they house. Can you b'lieve that? Offering me a place to sleep and they don't know me! Ain't that somethin?!

Well, I thank them just the same but told them I had a place to stay but maybe the next time I come I would sleep at they house. Some preciated that and even gave me their numbers to make sure I would and other ones well they just left me standin there - ain't gave me no number or nothin. They just went on invitin other folks to come sleep at they house. I guess they must be part of some welcomin committee or somethin. I suspect when they know you o.k.

ain't no need to keep invitin you. But a couple of them did and even said I could bring Sean too! Can you b'lieve that? Invitin me and Sean to come sleep at they house! I tell you what, the south is known fo bein hospitable but these kinda gestures put folk back home to shame!

Anyway I just stood there waitin fo Sean while folks kept commin up to me welcomin' me to sleep at they house and complimentin me like I ain't never been complimented fo or since! They kept sayin how nice lookin I was and what a nice body I have. Now I will admit that my body is strong. I mean I don't lift weights or nothin but when you grow up on a farm like I did and do as much work wit your hands in the yard as I do your body can't help but be strong! Anyways, they gave me all kinds of invitations fo a party by somebody named D.L. I don't know who D.L. is but he sure is popular! He got a whole heap of parties going on round here at different places. Some of them at the same times. I don't know how he manage that!

Anyway, we left there bout two in the mornin and I thought we were headed home but turns out we were headed to another club. Can you b'lieve that? Another club at two in the morning? I ain't never knowed a club to be open so late. The one we sometimes go to - the one twenty-five or so miles from where we live - close at twelve sharp! But this is my adventure. So we got in the car and Sean pulls out what was left of that cigar and me, him, and this other fella named Rodney that Sean said was a friend he met in the club all smoked on it.

We got to the other club and it was just as many fellas all dancing and having a good time. By this time my head was spinnin from the drink I had and the cigar we smoked. I felt like I need to dance it off. I always liked to dance and I keep up with the latest one by watchin them videos what they play on BET. Jr. like to dance too but not like me. So we go to the dance floor, all three of us, and we dancing and dancing havin a good time. My head's still spinnin and I'm feelin hands all over me. I don't know whose hands they belong to but I ain't stop em. No, sir! I was enjoyin it the whole time thinkin this is what adventure is all bout!

We left there, all three of us, but I don't know what time and went back to Sean's house. I guess the other fella didn't want to go home at this late hour and disturb nobody comin in or maybe he was woozy in the head like me so we all sat on the couch and Sean rolled up another cigar. I ain't wanna smoke no more cause I was tired. I mean at this time of the mornin - when the sun start to come up - I'm usually gettin up wit it to leave the house not come in to it! But I wanted adventure and here it was fo me to have.

I smoked some of the cigar anyway cause I ain't wanna be rude and Sean smoked some and Rodney the other fella smoked some. Sean put on some music, nice and slow music, like the romantic kind and dimmed the lights. He came over to where I was sittin' on the couch and started kissin on me. Now I know I was still woozy from all that had happened but I was thinking, "*Just how is he gonna be romantic wit me and this other fella is in the room?*" Plus, the other fella was just a lookin and starin at us like it was alright fo him to be there. I mean, some folks don't know when it's time to leave! Well, I musta been the only one thinkin that cause it sho ain't seem to bother nary one of them none!

Next thing I know the other fella, Rodney, come over and start ta kissin on me too. I mean he was kissin me and then he was kissin Sean and kissin me again! Can you b'lieve that? Kissin two fellas at the same time? I ain't know what was goin on and I think Rodney musta knowed it cause he raised up from kissin Sean and came over kissin on me again and said, "*Relax. Ain't nothin wrong wit lovin two people at the same time!*" Well, I ain't never heard that b'fo but because I was so woozy and I admit I was feelin good being in the middle of this adventure I did just what he told me to. I relaxed.

By the time I woke up it was two in the afternoon. Two in the afternoon! Can you b'lieve that? I ain't never in my whole entire life got out of bed at two in the afternoon (cept this one time when I was sick wit the flu and that's only because Jr. wouldn't let me get up!). I looked over and Sean and Rodney was there too still sleeping and we was all butt naked! I couldn't remember nothin. I mean not nothin! - Only I could tell we musta made love cause my body felt like we had. Man, whew! I ain't never done nothin like that b'fo, ever! (I only wish I had known what I had done so I couldda took note of it as one of my adventures!) Anyways, I took a shower and went downstairs hungry like a grizzly bear but wasn't nothin to eat. So I fell asleep on the couch hungry watchin T.V.

By the time I woke up this time it was almost eight o'clock in the evenin. That's right. Eight o'clock in the evenin! Can you b'lieve that? Now normally that's the time things start to quiet down back home and me and Jr. preparin to go to bed. But oh well, its adventure. Sean was up and had picked up some food. Good thing cause I was nearly starvin to death! But the other fella the one what was name Rodney was nowhere in site. I ain't ask Sean bout him either. I just ate my food while he rolled another cigar and told me we were going to a party. Adventure…

We smoked a little of the cigar cause I gotta admit it sure makes my adventures more excitin! Somethin bout that cigar that help you to slow down and take everything in that's happenin round you if you don't have too much and wit all these adventures goin on at once you need a lil somethin to slow you down or at least make you think bout slowin down. Thing is tho it make you do things and like things you normally wouldn't think bout likin but it make you forget bout em just as soon as you do it! Anyway, after we finished smokin the cigar we went upstairs, made love two times - cause he really like doin it - took a shower and got dressed fo the party.

We got there round bout 12 o'clock I'd say or a lil after. Can you b'lieve that?! Goin to a party after the midnight done crept up? Well, where I come from ain't no self-respectin person showin up at nobody house at that time of the night, party or not! But I s'posed it was o.k. wit the person what owned the house cause we wasn't the last one to get there. And there was a lot of folks there too. Some I remember seein from the night b'fo and some new ones. Sean stayed close to me this time not like in the club. I guess he was scared I would feel uncomfortable around all those new folks or somethin. But fo whatever reason he did and I was glad he did. I like bein close to him.

Anyway, we was have a good time drinkin and stuff and eatin some of the finger food, what they call horder-somethin, that was all laid out when I saw Rodney walk in the door. I waived at him but I don't think he saw me although I swear he looked at me dead square in the eye. He was wit this other fella and seemed to me Rodney looked real nervous specially when I walked over to him. Well, I was only tryin to be nice and do the neighborly thing by speakin. Afta all me, him, and Sean had shared a big adventure that very mornin and I just wanted to let him know that I had a good time (although I don't remember if I did or not but it wouldn't be polite to say I didn't!). He looked at me all scared and all but I ain't understand why. Seein folks I know always makes me feel at ease!

So I walked over and introduced myself to the fella he was wit and reached out to shake Rodney's hand like a gentleman is s'possed to do. I told him I was sorry I missed him b'fo he left that mornin but I had a real nice time makin love wit him and Sean. Well, you wouldda thought I told him his house burned down and somebody shot the dog! I mean he got all pale in the face like he was gonna have a spell and fall dead! And that ain't the worst of it. All of a sudden the fella standin near to him - the one he walked in the door wit - well he commence to callin me all kinds of cuss words like trick, hoe and dirty bitch. Can you b'lieve that?! Well, I know I ain't the most saintliest man on the planet. I done wrong things just like er'body else has-but I ain't never pulled a trick on nobody a day in my life!

Everybody in the party stopped what they was doin lookin over at him carryin on cussin and swearin and pushin and slappin on Rodney tellin him it was all over between em. I ain't know what to say so I ain't say a word! Then he, the fella was wit Rodney, commence to look at me again sayin he was gonna kick my ass! (actually he said he was gonna F-me up!) Can you b'lieve that? Kick my ass? I ain't understand what was goin on and why he was so mad and I told him so. Sho did! I told him that Rodney was the one who told me straight out of his own mouth that there wasn't nothin wrong wit lovin two folks at the same time! Well, that set him off somethin awful! Next thing I know I felt somethin hit me up side my head and the sound of glass breakin! Everything went black after that.

Part IV

When I woke up again I was back in Sean's bed and man whew! My head was just a hurtin and a spinnin. I stumbled downstairs to look fo Sean but he was nowhere to be found. I looked up at the clock. It was 4:00 in the mornin and I was feelin real bad. I went back upstairs and found some aspirins in the medicine cabinet and took three of em. I laid down fo a while but I couldn't sleep a wink cause my head was hurtin so bad. So I went back downstairs and grabbed a half of cigar-what Sean left in the ashtray. I figured the cigar could at least help me sleep some and take a load off the pressure in my head. It did. I slept til bout 2 in the afternoon.

When I woke up (again for the second time in the same day if you wanna b'lieve that!) Sean was sittin' in the livin room rollin another cigar. He asked me if I was o.k. I told him I was tho it wasn't the truth. The truth is I was feelin bad, mighty bad, and I was hungry to boot! Felt like I could eat anything! But I ain't want him to know that I was startin to feel like this adventure I wanted so bad was startin to kill me! I had only been there fo two days and already I was tired. And not the kind of tired you get when you done worked all day on cars or in the yard but tired - like tired in your spirit. Seem like to me adventure take way too much outta you. But it's what I had asked fo and I was right smack in the middle of it!

Anyway, he told me that I got knocked out the night b'fo at the party cause of what I said. Cause of what I said! Can you b'lieve that? Cause of what I said?!? Well, I ain't ever been the type to say nothin to hurt nobody on purpose. I ain't know I said nothin wrong and I told him so. Well, he told me I shouldda never said what I said to Rodney's friend bout lovin two folks at the same time. Turns out Rodney's friend is Rodney's *friend*. I mean like in the sense me and Jr. is *friends*. Well, you tell me just how was I supposed to know that? I mean Jr. is my friend but I ain't never cheated on him (cept fo now but only cause I'm in need of adventure). Cides that even though I'm doin what I'm doin I would never do nothing what like I did with Rodney and Sean with him and nobody else! I apologized anyway but Sean say "D*on't sweat it.*", and just kept right along rollin that cigar talkin bout the plans fo later on that night. Another party. Another party?! Adventure…

To tell you the truth I'm a lil partied out. I ain't never done so much partyin in one weekend in my whole entire life! But this is what I came here for. Escape from the old. Cides, it would be rude not to go. Only this time I promised myself that I was gonna keep my big mouth shut. Yup! I'm gonna shut my mouth and keep it shut! So we did our usual; smoked a cigar, made love two times took a shower and got dressed.

And that's another thing. I ain't never made this much love in my whole entire life! Only we don't exactly make love. We have sex. Makin love is when you really love somebody, like I love Jr., and you make love wit passion, wit tenderness, soft like but strong - wit feelin. And when it's all over, when both folks satisfied, you kiss, you caress, and hold each other, and talk bout things - all things - nothin in particular but usually things that bind two folks who love each other together. Me and Sean don't do that. No tenderness or passion or kissin, or holdin or sweet talkin or caressin when you done. No nothin!

He just wants to smoke a cigar and have sex, ruff and hard, like he's punishin himself fo somethin he did wrong and in all kinds of strange ways. Kinda make me feel bad too, guilty-like, like I'm hurtin somebody I'm s'posed to be lovin on. And he ain't one fo sweet-talkin either. No, sir! Nothin sweet bout the talkin he like me to do! He likes me to call him names - bad names - names I would never in a hundred, billion years call Jr. And when it's all over he gets up wit a coldness like he don't know nothin bout you and don't want to!

And when he walk away from me after we done wit no huggin, caressin, or sweet-talkin make me feel like he don't care nothin bout me - about who I am. Like he ain't concerned wit me at all! It ain't like that when I'm wit Jr. He make me feel happy, feel loved, special-like. Like he really care bout what goin on wit me. But wit Sean it's different. I feel all empty-like you know? The feelin like you get when somebody done stole somethin from you. Adventure wit no love sho is a strange thing!

I guess how they do up here though. And I understand how that can happen. Here, they got way too many things goin on always someplace to go or somewhere to get to. No time to slow down and enjoy the rhythm. Now I can deal wit a lot of things along these adventures but that I don't know bout. Don't know if that's somethin I can use to. Can't imagine anybody gettin used to that - love wit no feelin.

Anyway, we get in the car and he lights up another cigar. I pass this time cause my head is still swoonin from the last one and I gotta admit my body is tired like I don't know what! There ain't been no time to rest in this adventure, not good rest, like the kind I get back home. This kinda rest is *recovery* rest. The kind you try to get when you need to make up fo some you already done loss. But I don't know how it's possible to get back what you done let go pass you or even if it's possible at all!

So tonight he say's we headed to D.L.'s party. I remember just the party he was talkin bout too! The party from the flyer the other night - the one what

D.L. gives at different places and at different times. I have to admit I'm excited to go, too! I wanna see how he does it - throw so many parties on the same day at the same time. I'm hopin he's gonna be there cause I sho plan on askin him! I'mma ask him what his initials stand fo too! Round where I come from you don't call nobody by they initials unless you either know em that well or they tell you to!

We commence to drivin up to this place what kinda looks like a house – like somebody lives there kind of house but not on a street that look like other folks live on. Kind of commercial lookin like they got businesses that run up in there durin the day. The first thing I notice bout the house is that fo a party it sho is dark. I mean no light commin from nowhere and the windows were all blacked out like somebody painted over them on purpose! We park the car round the corner round bout five blocks away cause here ain't no driveways to pull your car into. And the parkin lots well you have to pay to put your car in to if you can b'lieve that! But they all full anyway so it don't matter. I can tell a whole lot of folks already at this party tonight!

We start headin fo the door and there's a line bout as long as I ever seen one all wrapped around the corner. Well, we don't get in line at all but just walk right on pass the folks in line right up to the front door. Can you b'lieve that? Right to the front door! I'm thinkin that Sean and D.L. must really be good friends. Don't nobody just walk up to the front door of nobody house like that unless they real good friends! I start to feel kinda bad fo them poor folks standin in line. God only know how long they been standin there or how long it's gonna take them to get in. But the place looks big enough on the outside to hold everybody so nobody got to worry bout being turned around at the door. That's got to make them feel o.k. bout standin there so long.

I was right that Sean and D.L. was real good friends Had to be cause even though they was chargin 20 dollars to get inside (which is a whole lot of money fo anybody's party - least I think it is) we ain't have to pay a single solitary thing! In fact the fella at the door said to me that he should pay me to come in. I was thinkin that he must be D.L. cause only a person wit a whole lotta money or a person who is the host would make a offer like that jokin or not! But I ain't ask if he was D.L. cause if he was I s'pose he wouldda introduced himself to me.

Round where I come from you don't invite strangers into your house wit out introducin yourself. Well, that's just plain rude! Cides, Sean was movin fast tryin to get in like he was in a hurry or somethin and I was tryin to keep up so there was no time fo introductions.

Well, we get inside all good pass the front door where you pay your money and turned the corner and run smack dab into another line. I mean er'where you go here, not just here tonight but all over, there's another line fo you to stand into. I don't know what this one's fo, maybe drinks or somethin, so I just stand there next to Sean waitin fo him to ask me what I wanted to drink. I was gonna tell him I ain't want a single solitary thing! I've had my fill of liquor. Yes sir, I have!

I ain't really had not time to say so cause just like we always do we walked straight to the front of the line and he commence to talkin to the fella behind the counter. I was thinkin that maybe that fella was D.L. but I really don't think so to tell you the truth cause him and Sean ain't really talk long like you would s'pect good friends to talk. Anyway the fella hands Sean two black bags, like garbage bags - the kind you use fo linin' your outside garbage cans wit or the kind you put your leaves into once you rake the lawn - less you burnin em. I was wonderin what that could be fo?

Well, we keep walkin and the further we walk to the back where I s'pose the party is the darker it's gettin. I'm really tryin to keep up wit Sean now specially in the middle of all this darkness. We finally slow down - almost to a halt - outside this door leadin to another room and the only thing is see is a blue light up in the corner - you know the kind you have in your basement or the ones you see in the juke joints where I'm from. Off in the corner right under the light are these benches and what I see next I don't b'lieve I see although I'm starin straight at it!

First thing I see is another line (but I suspect you already figured that one out) but the next thing I'm seein is all these fellas takin off their clothes cept their underwear and socks, and stuffin them in these plastic bags. Can you b'lieve that? They stuff they clothes in a plastic bag like they fixin to do laundry or somethin! Well, they take them bags and hand em over to another person behind the counter. The man behind the counter, the one collectin the clothes, gave em a ticket in return fo the bag. Well, first thought what come into my mind was I know that he - the fella behind the counter collectin them bags - can't be D.L. I say that cause why would a man as popular as D.L. check trash bags (or lawn bags - I'm not sho which ones they is) at his own party? The second thought what came to my mind, which really wasn't a thought at all but more like a question, was just what on God's green earth is goin on?!

So I think bout this fo a minute. Thinkin bout why folks had to check they clothes to come up in a party and then it becomes as clear as the nose on my face! They make folks check their clothes in here because that way they can't hide no weapons you know, guns or knives, or nothin like that to break up D.L.'s party or maybe even hurt D.L. himself. That got to be it cause when we came to this party they didn't pat me down or make me walk through a metal detector like they did when we went to the other clubs the night b'fo and the night b'fo that.

No, sir! D.L. was smart! He made sure folks couldn't come up in there wit no weapons like guns and knives and such cause wit out no clothes on ain't no place where you can hide em (cept maybe in your socks but who ain't gonna see a big ole' gun or knife stuck down in your socks?). Cides that it gotta cost less to have folks check in they clothes than to hire security guards or buyin them long sticks they used on me at the airport to see if I had somethin on me I wasn't s'posed to. And cides that who would wanna buy one of those to keep in they house anyways? Don't make no sense if you ask me!

Now while I'm thinkin bout all this and tryin figure all this here stuff out I done fell way behind. Sean is all but undressed cept his drawer and his socks, and I'm standin there lookin like a country bumpkin all fully dressed and all! I ain't wanna look like a fool so I commence to disrobin and throwin all my stuff in the other plastic bag. I handed it to the fella behind the counter collectin clothes and took my ticket. I stuffed it in my socks (bein as though I ain't got no pockets and ain't wanna lose it) and run to catch up wit Sean.

I catch up wit him and follow him through this long hallway and I mean it's almost pitch black cept fo this tiny little red light (the basement or juke joint kind like I saw earlier but instead of bein blue this one is red) way up in the corner. I keep followin him til I can't see him no mo and then I try to grab a hold of his hand but I was too late. He let my hand go and quick as a whip had disappeared. I was walkin round fo a lil bit tryin to see if I could find him but when I say tell you it was dark I mean it was dark! I was so busy tryin to find him I ain't really notice what was goin on in D.L.'s party that is until I felt somebody – or two or more somebodys – rubbin and tuggin at my private parts. Quick as a flash I tuned in to what was happenin!

Part V

When I looked around and got as much focus as I could all I could see was naked bodies sprung out all over the place makin love – well not makin love, havin sex - cause wasn't no love nowhere up in there! I mean nowhere! Can you b'lieve that? All those fellas up in there all over each other havin sex in all that dark? I mean who you supposed to know who you makin love…I mean having sex wit? Now I remember what Rodney had told me the day b'fo yesterday when the three of us was makin love - I mean havin sex - bout nothin being wrong wit lovin two folks at the same time and cept fo the fact that smokin on that cigar made me think strange I wasn't too right bout that neither! But all this? Well, I'm not no educated man not in the book sense like Jr. but I tell you what had to be somethin wrong wit what I was seein. Any fool can tell you that!

When my ears caught up wit my eyes all I could hear was moaning and groanin, and all kinds of instructions being givin to folks tellin other folks what to do to them in the most awful soundin language! Things I surely cant repeat! Well, right then and there I made up my mind. I had had enough of adventure! Yup! I was done wit it and didn't care if I ever had it again! Ever! I don't know quite what I had in mind when I left home in search of adventure but I tell you what, this wasn't it! No, Sir! This surely wasn't it! Now all I needed to do was to find Sean and tell him I had enough so he could take me outta there bein that he had driven and all. But man, whew! I looked fo I know what musta been a good hour or more fo Sean but I couldn't find him nowheres.

I s'pected he musta been lookin fo me too once he found out the kind of party D.L. gives and was waitin fo me by the car! So I found my way back to the front - back to where they had took my clothes in the plastic bag. Don't ask me how neither cause I really don't know. Look like my feet just took over. Anyways, I reached fo the ticket the fella behind the counter gave me what I had put in my socks, got my bag and put on my clothes as fast as I could. I shot outta there like a bolt of lightnin! And that ain't no lie neither!

The fella we first saw when we walked in (the one what told me he shouldda paid me fo commin to the party-although no amount of money in the world he could offer me could get me to go back to a place like that!) caught me at the door and asked me if er'thing was alright. I guess he could tell somethin was wrong by the way I was runnin so fast - determine like - to get outta D.L.'s party. Well, I told him like I'm tellin you right now that I ain't never been to such a party in my whole entire life! I told him that round where I come from D.L. and every single fella in there would be in a whole heap of trouble if the law ever found out about the kinds of parties he had! Well, he kinda looked at me real strange, like I had lost my mind or somethin or like I was tellin a lie about what the law would do to D.L. and every fella caught up in there. And I wasn't! I was tellin him the straight honest truth!

Afta while, his expression changed when he saw I was serious bout what I had said. He kinda grinned at me and said fo me to come closer cause he had somethin to explain to me. So I did and well you ain't gonna b'lieve this but come to find out, D.L. ain't even a person at all! Can you b'lieve that? D.L. ain't a person? All this time I'm thinkin D.L. is somebody and turns out he ain't. Well, hang on to your hat cause not only ain't D.L. no person. D.L. is a s'pression. Now what it means - least what the fella at the door told me it means - is way too complicated to be understood or s'plained by a average thinkin man like me! All you got to know fo this purpose is that he ain't no man and that's that!

Well, anyways Sean wasn't nowhere to be found. I figured he was probably still tryin to find his way out that dark place so I walked all them blocks to where we had parked the car and sat on the curb nearest to it cause I ain't have the key to sit in it. I sat there and sat there and sat there and was startin to b'lieve that Sean couldn't find his way out and maybe stuck in there til mornin time (not that sunlight would be able to pierce through all that black paint on them window but maybe some light would help him find that hallway wit the counter where they take your clothes in the plastic bag).

In betweenst hopin Sean would find his way to the door and worried about the fact that I had to pee real bad I gots ta thinkin bout all my adventures over the past three days and how much all this excitement and adventure wasn't really as excitin and adventurous as I thought it would be! Seem to me it was more dangerous than anything. More like chaos, the kind you see on the TV or like Sodom and Gomorra like what grandmamma used to read us about in the Word!

I started thinkin bout home and bout Jr. and bout the yard and that grass, them hedges, them trees, and them rollin hills - all peaceful to be where they are. I was wonderin what Jr. might be doin on a night like tonight, clear wit the stars all bright and close - like you could snatch em right outta the sky. It was really the first time in all my adventure (cause there ain't really been no time otherwise when I think about it) that I had thought bout him and sleepin next to him feelin him near me and feelin his love all over me.

Yes, sir! It was the first time I thought bout our house and them crickets chirpin and the hustle of the leaves in the trees bendin backwards and forwards and makin all kinds of calmin sounds. Sounds I ain't heard since I been here. I closed my eyes and imagined that I was right there next to him and we had just made love and had fallen off to sleep - a deep peaceful lovin sleep - after we had done satisfied each other and kissed and caressed. I was thinkin bout our sweet-talkin and holdin on to each other like somebody was gone steal us away and separate us if we didn't.

Yes, sir! I was memberin all of it and missin it. Missin Jr. mostly when all of a sudden I felt somethin cold and hard up against my head, right at the temple - the left side - directly adjournin my ear. I opened my eyes scared as I could be to see these two fellas, one in the front of me and one on the left side, holdin a gun. I was so scared I ain't no what to do cept pee my pants which I ain't really intend to do but I s'pose when you scared outta your wits your body has a mind of its own!

Anyways, I was as still as I could be cause I was too scared to move fo fear the one holdin the gun would get scared from me being scared and accidentally pull the trigger and blow my head clean off! The other one, the one what was standin in front of me, started feelin all over my pockets but he was careful not to touch the places where I had done peed all over myself but could you blame him? I mean it's different when little children pee they pants and you touch it cause you gotta change em or somethin but a grown man?

Anyways, they was both just a hollerin and screamin at me to give em my money which I gladly did thank you very much cause I wasn't tryin to be no hero - and like I said my mama ain't raise no fool! I reached down into my jean trousers and handed them the twenty dollars I had (and that's all I had cause that's what it was gonna cost me to get into the party and like I say we ain't had to pay to get in). But I suppose that just wasn't enough fo him and his friend to do what they needed to do cause when I gave it to him he got fightin mad and said, "*That all you got, niggah?!*" Next thing I know b'fo I had the chance to answer the young man's question he hauled off and slap me dead side the head wit that gun he had! Everything went black. Again!

Part VI

When I came to I was in the emergency room at a hospital (and I was sho hopin it was the "mercy" kind cause I ain't think to bring my insurance card on my adventure) all stretched out on a stretcher. My head felt like somebody took a vice to it - the kind like my granddaddy usta use to hold horseshoes wit- and tightened it as hard as they could. I ain't never felt that kind of pain b'fo never! The doctor had already stitched me up and bandaged up my head. The nurse told me that as soon as I felt like I could stand up I could leave. Well, I ain't feel like I could stand up so I laid there. I got up afta while to get my mind right to make my feet move and you not gone b'lieve this but my shoes was gone! I asked the nurse nearest me where my shoes was and she said I ain't come from the ambulance wearin none. Can you b'lieve that? They took my money and my shoes!

The nurse said I should call somebody to come get me and tell em to bring me some shoes. I told her they was the only pair I had brought wit me on my adventure and I ain't had no money, not a single solitary penny to my name to make a phone call. Well, she took pity on me thank goodness and let me use the phone to call Sean which I did but either he ain't made it home or had fell fast asleep waitin on me in which case I was really in trouble. It was only 9:00 in the mornin and God knows he sleeps sound til bout 3 or 4! I don't know where he was or what he was doin but the point is he ain't answered the phone.

I told the nurse I couldn't get a hold of nobody and she took pity on me again and gave me a piece of paper they give to folks who can't afford a ride home to get a ride home. She called me a cab and I walked slowly to it barefoot and all! I gave him the address and the piece of paper what the nurse gave me and sat back and watched all the concrete and the buildings – big ones, small ones, tall ones and short ones – and the trees that look like they was put there fo show pass right on by me. I felt sick to my stomach.

We pulled up to Sean's door and I stumbled out of the cab. I knew he was home cause I saw his car parked right there on the street. I pulled myself up the side rails of the stairs to his front door and knocked as loud as I could cause I knowed he was sound asleep. I knock and I knock, and knock but there was no answer. I kept on a knockin till round bout five minutes later this fella, some fella I ain't never seen a day in my life, came to the door and asked me what I wanted. I imagine he musta thought I was a bum or somethin beggin fo food or money lookin the way I was lookin all bandaged up wit no shoes. Heck, it's what I wouldda thought if somebody I ain't know come walkin up my driveway knockin on the door early in the mornin!

I told him that I was a friend of Sean's and that I had been stayin there fo the weekend. Well, I don't know what bothered him so much bout what I said but he opened that door up just as kind as he please like he was gonna let me in, drew back his fist, and punched me dead square in the eye! I fell backwards off the steps straight onto the sidewalk backside first! Bout a second later I hear all this yellin, and hollin, and arguin between Sean and the other fella, the one what had punched me dead square in the eye. He was yellin at Sean about havin a man in his house (his house bein the one what had punched me square in the eye) and cheatin on him while he was out of town.

Well, I couldn't b'lieve my ears (partly because they was still ringin from getting slapped upside the head with the gun that fella hit me with)! Can you b'lieve that? Turns out Sean had a *friend* too! And not only that but it wasn't even Sean's house! Well, I'm sittin there takin all this in and the next thing I know here comes my bag (the one what I stored in the bin on the plane cause Sean said I ain't need to bring much clothes) hauled straight out the second floor window right square on the top of my head! I ain't never knowed such pain!

So there I was tired, barefooted, bleeding, and hurt - spirit and all - on the sidewalk in the middle of a city I hardly knew. I was feelin bad, mighty, mighty bad! I mean my body felt bad don't get me wrong and everything on me was hurtin. But when I say I felt bad, I mean my heart and soul felt bad! It felt bad fo a whole lot of things too but mostly fo what I had done to Jr. I felt bad fo what I had taken him through over the months leadin to my adventure and what I had done to us - our relationship - and all we had built together in the name of excitement and adventure. I was sorry. Deeply sorry.

In the middle of feelin all that sorrow and badness the only thing I could think of was that house, that yard, them trees, and that grass. Yes, sir! All I kept thinkin bout sittin on that cold concrete was the feelin of grass wet and freshed up from the mornin dew under my feet when I walk on the lawn to get the paper. And in the middle of smelling exhaust fumes from all the cars passin by wonderin what I was doin sittin in the middle of the sidewalk I was longin to smell fresh cut grass ticklin my nose. I never missed anything or anybody as much as much as I did right there!

I picked myself up off the ground, dusted off, grabbed my bag, and started walkin up the street. My plane wasn't leavin until the next mornin but you know what? I had all the adventure I could take! I had some extra money stashed away in my overnight bag, enough to get me a pair of flip-flops from a store on the corner where er'thing cost a dollar (sometime more than that but the sign don't say so!) and enough for a city bus ride to the Greyhound bus station. I bought a one-way ticket headed back home and wit the rest I 'bought a couple of candy bars and a Yoo-hoo. I climbed on that bus black eye, bruised head and all, ate my candy bars and tried to forget all bout that adventure.

I got home that next mornin right bout 5:00 a.m. Just bout the time we normally get up, Jr. and me, to slow down each other and love on each other and what we got b'fo we go out to face the world. As I walked up the driveway toward our house I was just as grateful as any man could be! I looked around the yard at them trees, and them hedges and that grass, and them rollin hills, and it all looked so pretty. So brand new to me. Quiet and so safe. I'm man enough to tell you that I cried to see it all - all of what we had built together - and I cried fo what I was bout to trade away in the name of adventure.

And then I cried to see him. Jr., my partner. Yup, I said it. My partner. The love of my life. Standin like he always do in the early mornin hours mongst the trees. Talkin to them and listenin to them while they tell him secrets. He turned around and saw me there all battered and bruised and dirty, and came runnin to me just as quick as he could. He told me that he was spectin me right at that moment at that exact time. Said the trees told him so and I b'lieve it! He kissed me and say that he loved me and that he missed me. Then he just held onto me. And I held onto him too like somebody was gonna separate us from each other if we didn't. I told him that I loved him cause I did love him. I do love him. In that particular point in time I loved him and missed him more than he could ever know.

Epilogue

Been round bout a year ago or so now since I got all them fool thoughts bout excitement and adventure and stuff like that outta my head. I done come to find out that all that adventure ain't healthy fo you. Ain't healthy fo nobody! It don't mean nobody not nary a soul! When it comes right down to it ain't really adventure after all. It's escape! Yup, that's exactly what it is. Escape! Only what you find out is that what you really tryin to escape from is yourself and that the worst problem of all cause no matter where you go you're always gonna be exactly where you are! Can't escape yourself is what it mounts to. Ain't never met nobody livin or dead was able to do that and come out alright!

Wasn't nothin wrong wit my life and the things what was in it. Wasn't nothin wrong wit Jr. or the life we have together. Wasn't nothing wrong at all! It was just me. I was looking to see m'self different through the eyes of new experiences and new folks that ain't meant me nary bit of good! What troublin is I ain't give one single solitary thought to tryin to findin excitement and adventure wit what I got wit Jr. Never crossed my mind to romance him or to share in adventures in other places-together-or create new excitement of our own!

Can you b'lieve that? I never thought of anything so simple as to make some new sparks wit the man who love me and who I love. Some folks never ever get to experience the kind of love Jr. got for me and I'm talkin male or female no matter who you lovin! I'm just blessed I guess. Blessed that he still loves me and got a forgivin heart. I'm blessed enough to have a lovin man that let me make a plumb fool of m'self and still find enough in me to love despite my wayward ways.

Well, all those fool ideas bout excitement and adventure have been laid to rest. These days we spend more time in the yard amongst the grass, and the hedges, and under the blanket of the trees lookin out at them rollin hills and lovin and holdin onto each other - like somebody gonna separate us if we don't. We talk and make plans and you know what? Everything is excitin to me now. Everything done took on new meanin and new importance in my life even them trees what tell your secrets. I done learned to preciate what they do fo Jr. and what they done fo us.

Sometimes, and I know you gone find this hard to b'lieve but when Jr.'s out runnin' errands or doin things away from our house - I even talks to em. And you know what? They do talk back! Can you b'lieve that? They really do talk back! And you wanna know what they say? Well, I tell you what they say. They say that adventure is where you make it and they say that you can't make real adventure wit out real love. I sho do b'lieve em! Sho do!

These days we got the finest yard you ever did see. Won blue ribbons, Jr. and me, from the Blue Creek County Horticulture Society this year. I got to admit tho it is the most beautiful lawn in the state. The hedges is trimmed, Fthem trees keep right on swayin offerin shade so welcomin, and look like the flowers when they bloom got minds of they own.

And our grass. Well, lets just say that if anybody passing by know what I know bout lawns and how they tell all yo bidness they'd know fo sho that ain't nothing goin on here but love. Just love. True, plain, simple, and strong!

Made in the USA
Middletown, DE
08 October 2018